Dear Reader,

You know the saying. Old soldiers never die, they just fade away. Or in my case, they turn to a life of murder and mayhem—purely fictional, of course.

I'm thrilled to return to my military roots with this novel in the Cleo North series. As a squadron, base and wing commander, I saw firsthand the expertise air force special agents brought to their always demanding, often gruesome investigations. As an author, I want to portray their dedication and gritty determination to safeguard air force people and property.

I hope you enjoy this glimpse into the world of undercover agents, past and present!

All my best,

Merline Lovelace

MERLINE LOVELACE

THE LAST BULLET

MIRA

ISBN 0-7783-2181-9

THE LAST BULLET

Copyright © 2005 by Merline Lovelace.

www.MIRABooks.com

Printed in U.S.A.

This book was written with joyous memories of my father, MSgt Merlin Thoma, USAF (Ret). Dad served as loadmaster aboard C-47s during World War II and never ran out of stories about the planes, the crews and their hairy missions. My favorite is the time when he jettisoned a cargo of gold bullion over the Med by mistake. Then there's the one about airlifting supplies and mules to Yugoslavian resistance fighters, but that's another book....

ACKNOWLEDGMENTS

With special thanks to:

Lieutenant Colonel Eddie Howard, USAF, who kept me straight on all things OSI. Thanks for the terrific input, Colonel.

John Liddiard, whose brilliant photographs of wrecks captured my imagination and started the wheels turning. His willingness to talk technical diving with someone who has yet to master a snorkel was *most* appreciated.

Stella Cameron, a lovely lady and author of the delightful 7 Mayfair Square series, for sharing her memories of Weymouth.

Linda Fildew of Harlequin Mills and Boon and Ewa Högberg of Harlequin Sweden. Thanks for showing me your beautiful cities and for your so gracious hospitality during my visit.

And most especially my agent, Pam Hopkins, who had almost as much fun watching Cleo come to life as I did.

Prologue

He'd had to kill him.

He'd had no choice.

The assassin stood at the window, his gaze on the bare stalks of the rosebushes he tended with such love, his mind as cold and desolate as an ice-bound fjord.

It wasn't his first kill. He'd eliminated many others. That was what he'd been trained to do. What he'd excelled at. He'd never taken joy in the act, though. Never felt a thrill at bringing down a target. Even this target...

His lip curled. Such a greedy, venal man. A disgrace to his uniform.

There would be more to follow that one, though. Less greedy. Better skilled. He knew it.

The sense of inevitability seeped into his bones, making them ache. He was too old for the hunt, too tired for the chase. Yet there was no escape. He'd chosen this life. Chosen this twisted, dangerous path.

Sighing, he turned away from the roses.

1

Former USAF special agent turned private security consultant Cleo North crouched behind a dripping rhododendron bush and blinked the chilly, early May rain out of her eyes. Chewing on the inside of her lip, she worked a hair-thin wire through the cable box of a neat, single-story Denver bungalow.

The high-powered executive who'd hired her to beef up his security staff was inside the bungalow. He was either: (a) being held hostage by the thugs he'd gotten crosswise of in a not-so-shrewd business deal; (b) hiding from said thugs; or (c) sneaking in a little afternoon delight with his mistress of the moment.

Whatever the situation, he'd voluntarily or otherwise deactivated the sophisticated security systems Cleo had installed in his office. He'd waited until

Cleo had gone down to the cafeteria for lunch to exit Worldwide Systems' high-rise corporate headquarters by the back stairs, then disabled the GPS tracking device she'd installed in his car.

Cleo had tracked him via the device she'd concealed in the heel of his shoe after the last time he slipped off to conduct a little "personal business." She'd been tempted to walk away from the job altogether at that point, but the exec's wife had received a phone call advising her that her husband was a dead man if he didn't withdraw his bid on a multi-million-dollar contract to construct a new shopping mall. The very real threat—and the outrageous fees this bozo was paying—had outweighed her growing disgust with the man.

If she found him with his pants around his ankles, though, she was outta here! North Security and Investigations, Inc., didn't need his hefty retainer. Cleo has as much business as she and her part-time staff could handle. Particularly since the air force had tapped her to work some *very* interesting cases lately. With *very* sexy OSI agent Jack Donovan, who was, at this very moment, in D.C. unraveling the tangled threads from their last adventure.

Hunching her shoulders against the rain, Cleo fed the wire in another few inches, just enough for its ultrasensitive fibers to pick up sounds inside the bungalow. Her client had given her permission to install whatever devices she deemed appropriate to his safety. His authority didn't specify this location, but Cleo wasn't too concerned about that minor technicality at the moment.

Shoving her wet hair out of her eyes, she activated the receiver and tugged on a headset. She heard a thud, magnified to ear-pounding proportions, then an agonized scream.

"No!"

The screeching, megawatt decibels sent Cleo staggering back into the rhododendrons. She hit the ground butt-first, sputtering as the leafy petals shook and gave her another drenching.

"Oh, God, no! Noooo!"

That *could* be the scream of a woman at the peak of a mind-blowing orgasm, but Cleo's instincts said otherwise. Her client hadn't struck her as the type who would take the time to bring a woman to that kind of shattering release.

Tearing off the headset, she scrambled to her feet and reached under her jacket for the 10 mm Glock holstered at the small of her back. No time to call for backup. She'd have to use the element of surprise to best advantage.

She raced around to the rear of the bungalow, jerked up her knee and had her boot heel aimed at the back door when it was suddenly wrenched open.

Her client froze just inside the portal. He was naked, wild-eyed with terror and bleeding like a stuck pig from the pulpy mass that used to be his nose.

"Cleo! Thank God! Get me out of here."

The first rule of protective services was to hustle the protectee away from danger. Cleo would have done just that if another agonized scream hadn't ripped from the front of the house.

"Who's that?"

"Never mind her." Panting, the bare-assed exec tried to bulldoze past her. "I'm the one who's paying you."

"Wait, dammit! Tell me how many are inside."

"Two hired bruisers and Janie. Let's get *out* of here!"

The thud of pounding footsteps added frenzy to his efforts. He shoved Cleo aside and plunged into the rain.

She let him go. No way she was leaving a woman to be brutalized by two hired sleazoids. She was ready when a beefy thug barreled into the kitchen, a .45 clutched in a fist that showed bloody, skinned knuckles. He did a double take when he spotted Cleo, which gave her more than sufficient time to fire. She shot the .45 out of his fist, making sure she took a good portion of appendage with it.

He doubled over, howling and clutching his arm to his chest. Cleo dropped him with a swift chop to the neck and kicked his weapon out of reach under the stove.

As she anticipated, the ruckus brought the second thug running. He pumped out two wild shots before she took him down with one to the kneecap. He fell forward, just happening to make contact with Cleo's knee on the way. His jaw cracked. His head snapped back. His eyes rolled.

Satisfied he was out cold, she scooped up his weapon and continued down the hall to find a naked, sobbing Janie huddled in a tight ball on the bedroom floor. Her face, too, was a pulpy mass, making Cleo wish to hell she'd aimed for more vital areas than hands and knees.

She helped the woman up, holding her awkwardly with one arm. With the other, she reached for the cell phone clipped to her waist.

"It's okay," Cleo murmured. "You'll be okay. I'm calling 911."

The Denver police arrived on the scene first, the EMTs mere minutes later. Cleo was in the middle of giving her statement when her cell phone vibrated against her waist. A glance at the number flashing on the digital display made her pulse jump.

"'Scuse me a moment. I have to take this call."

Three hours later, she'd hunted down her client, assured him that the police were hauling in the man who'd hired the thugs and collected the remainder of her fee.

By then it was too late to check out of her hotel, so she made reservations for an early-morning flight to D.C., with a short layover in Dallas en route to pick up a few essentials. Like her passport and several pairs of the sexy, lace-trimmed hipsters she'd recently discovered at a new boutique.

She breezed into the north Dallas condo that doubled as her home and office just after ten the next morning.

"I've got to jump a plane to D.C. in a few hours," she announced to her staff of two, "then I'm off to London. The air force wants me to work a murder case."

Mae, her part-time office manager, looked up from the latest issue of *Golf Digest* and gave an absent smile. "That's nice, dear. What happened to the Denver gig?"

"It's done. Fini. Completo."

The miniature schnauzer draped across Mae's lap was more appreciative of Cleo's sudden reappearance. Baby lifted his head, wagged his stubby tail and emitted several shrill yips.

Doreen, Cleo's stepcousin-in-law, made instant shushing motions. She was on the Natuzzi leather sofa, one plump, dimpled knee hooked over the other. Her entire being was concentrated on the flatscreen, high-definition TV mounted on the wall.

"Hold it down a sec, cuz. This is the bit where Bart stuffs toilet paper down Lisa's sax."

Cleo swallowed a sigh. She'd hired the laid-off electronics whiz at the request of her stepmother. Just until the girl could find more permanent employment, Wanda had begged.

The "girl" had recently turned thirty, was addicted

to the Bart Simpson cartoon series and now considered herself permanently employed at North Security and Investigations.

"Here it comes." Doreen gave a gleeful cackle. "I *love* this part!"

Cleo and Mae locked glances. At full volume, Doreen's whinnying laugh could shatter glass. Even at half volume, her high-pitched brays rattled teeth.

With an agile grace that belied her sixty-plus years, Mae propelled herself and Baby out of her chair. "Your passport is in the safe. I'll go get it."

"And I'll pack."

Cleo scuttled in the opposite direction. As an air force undercover operative, she had infiltrated drug rings, exposed white slavers and busted a procurement fraud case that involved a former secretary of defense. Since leaving the air force to go into business for herself, she'd taken down stalkers, kidnappers and murderers. Highly trained in all forms of combat, Cleo could defend herself with her bare hands or any number of the world's most sophisticated weapons.

There was no defense against Doreen's bone-jarring laugh, though. It followed her through the kitchen, battering at her eardrums. Wincing, she closed the bedroom door behind her and forced herself to focus on the case she'd just been handed.

The call had come from her old boss, General Sam Barnes, commander of the USAF Office of Special

Investigations. Cleo and the OSI chief had parted on somewhat less-than-amicable terms six years ago. Barnes had accepted her resignation with grudging words of praise for her ability to bust cases. He'd then tacked on rather scathing—and, Cleo had thought, completely unnecessary—comments about her hardheaded independence and tendency to bend the rules.

Her relationship with the Old Man hadn't improved over time. And matters had taken a definite turn for the worse when the ship hijacking that Cleo had recently helped foil had ended in an explosion that destroyed tons of air force munitions.

Like it was her fault the bullet she'd put into one of the hijackers had spun him around at the precise moment he'd decided to launch a shoulder-held missile? At least she'd saved the Navy Seahawk helicopter the bastard had been aiming at, along with its crew…and the British operative who'd just climbed out of the chopper.

Now that operative wanted Cleo to investigate the murder of an American officer stationed in England.

Cleo *and* Special Agent Jack Donovan.

Shivers danced down her spine, one part professional, two parts pure sex. She and Jack had worked together briefly while Cleo was still air force. On one memorable mission they'd dodged bullets and bad guys while plunging through the Honduran jungle. That was the first time they'd jumped each other's bones, a definite no-no where the air force was concerned.

Cleo was a civilian now, though, no longer subject to air force rules against fraternization. She and Jack jumped whenever the opportunity presented itself. Unfortunately, the opportunity didn't present itself often enough to satisfy either of them. But now she was off to London.

To work a murder.

With Jack.

Humming, she tossed her things into her leather carryall. She pretty much lived in jeans these days. She usually paired them with silky tops, short- or long-sleeved as the weather dictated, and hand-tailored jackets. Pendleton wool for winter, linen blends for summer.

London in early May could require either. She'd wear the linen on the plane over. A red wool went into the carryall, along with a calf-length sheath in slinky black that could be dressed up or down, stacked sandals that only added two inches to her five-eight frame, her favorite Dallas Cowboys sleep shirt and the sexy new hipster briefs. She'd modeled lingerie part-time in college and still had a weakness for satin and lace.

Her Glock, extra magazines, ankle holster and shoulder harness went in on top of the hipsters. She'd have to complete reams of paperwork to get the weapon through Security, but the Glock had been

specially balanced for her hand and was worth the
hassle. She'd also take the T-26 scanner, she decided
as she hefted the carryall and started for her office.
And the ultracompact personnel ID kit. And…

She skidded to a halt in the kitchen. Doreen had
levitated from the sofa to her favorite perch at the
marble-topped kitchen counter. She had her tool kit
open and was screwing the back onto a small, flat
case. Cleo knew better than to touch the gizmo without getting the facts about it first. She'd learned the
hard way.

"What's that?"

"I call it a moon-spinner."

Doreen had a brilliant, diabolical mind when it
came to electronic gadgetry. Her last device—a high-
intensity forever light—had almost blinded Cleo. It
had also saved her life.

This little case looked innocuous enough. Still,
Cleo approached with extreme caution. "Okay, I'll
bite. What's a moon-spinner?"

Doreen swung around on a bar stool that creaked
ominously under her weight. "Ever hear of the U.S.
Army Soldiers' Systems lab at Natick, Massachusetts?"

"Sure. The lab designs uniforms and personal gear
for the troops."

"Correctamundo. All ergonomically engineered
using the latest scientific advancements. Recently
they've been experimenting with light-refracting
microfilaments."

"Experimenting, huh?"

"The lab is looking at ways to spin the microfilaments into uniforms and bodysuits. By refracting light, the garments would make the wearer practically invisible to the naked eye and redefine the whole concept of camouflage. Hold out your arm."

"Uh, I really don't have time…"

"Come on, cuz. I tested it on myself earlier. It didn't hurt. Much."

On that less-than-reassuring note, Cleo stretched out a cautious arm.

Doreen thumbed the flat button embedded in the case. There was a small hiss. Something shot through the air. What felt like hair-thin fishing line wrapped around Cleo's sleeve. Three seconds later, her arm from wrist to elbow disappeared.

"Holy shit!"

Jaw sagging, she gaped at the disembodied hand that now hovered in midair, clutching her leather carryall.

"I've packed hundreds of yards of filament into this case," Doreen said with a proprietary smirk. "Enough to wrap the Superdome twice around."

Cleo bent her arm. Straightened it. Bent it again. The leather carryall arced through the air without any visible means of support. Only when she stepped away from the pot lights above the kitchen counter did a skeletal shadow appear.

"This stuff is incredible!"

It was also starting to constrict her blood flow. The tingling sensation in her fingers was dancing up her arm to her elbow.

"How do you keep the threads from twisting so tight?"

The smirk slid off her technical adviser's face. "Natick hasn't figured that out yet. Neither have I."

Cleo's arm had progressed from tingling to numb. "Doreen…"

"Hold on, I'll cut the line." Plucking a kitchen knife from the drawer, she slid the tip under the line. "The good news is that this stuff is almost indestructible. The bad news is…"

"It's almost indestructible," Cleo ground out as Doreen sawed at the invisible fiber with tongue-in-teeth determination.

"I've almost got it. There!"

The strands parted. Blood pulsed through Cleo's wrist. Her fingertips regained their normal hue. She flexed her hand a few times while Doreen clipped the moon-spinner onto Cleo's key ring. It snuggled against the forever light as if it had found its soul mate.

"I don't think I'll need that."

"Take it with you," Doreen insisted. "You never know *what* might come in handy in your line of work."

Cleo couldn't argue with that.

Dumping her carryall in the passenger seat of her MG, she backed the battle-scarred vehicle out of the garage. She had her passport tucked in her purse, reservations on an eleven-fifteen flight out of Dallas-Ft. Worth International, and an important chore to take care of before she left town for an unspecified period of time.

Thrusting the gearshift into Drive, she restrained herself until she hit the North Dallas Tollway. Cleo had learned to drive in Thailand, where her father had been working on an irrigation project for the U.S. Agency for International Development. She could dodge *benjo* ditches and water buffalo with equal skill. The insanity that passed for Dallas traffic was something else again.

Resisting the urge to lean on the horn and barrel down the center median in the best Thai tradition, she threaded the lanes like a second-string fullback determined to make starter. Horns honked. Angry scowls arrowed in her direction. The occasional finger flipped, but she made it to her father's two-bedroom patio home without adding to the MG's collection of dents. Wheeling into the drive, she killed the engine and dragged in a deep, bracing breath.

She could do this, she lectured herself. She'd had almost six months to get to know the woman her father had met and married in a whirlwind courtship after twenty-plus years as a widower. She could smile and nod and hide all signs of how Wishy-Washy Wanda made her back teeth ache. With that resolve firmly in mind, she poked the doorbell.

Patrick North answered and drew his daughter into a bear hug. "Hey, kiddo!"

"Hiya, Pop."

Cleo returned his hug with a wave of unqualified, unrestrained love. Her father had been her sole parent for most of her life. She retained only vague memories of her mother. A dabbler in classical poetry, Claire North had died just a few years after giving birth to her daughter at the Aswan dam site in Egypt. She'd named her in honor of that country's legendary queen. Unfortunately, she'd also tacked on the name of her favorite Greek goddess. Few people ever called Cleo by her full name—Cleopatra Aphrodite North—and lived to brag about it.

"What's up?" her father asked, releasing her.

"I came to tell you I'm off to D.C. and possibly London to work a case. Don't know how long I'll... Good grief!" Eyes rounding, Cleo surveyed the wreckage that used to be the dining room. "What happened here?"

"We're knocking out a wall to open the dining area to the kitchen." Hope sprang into her father's face. "You wouldn't have time to go shopping for light fixtures with Wanda before you take off, would you?"

Cleo repressed a shudder. Her stepmom made shopping an Olympic event. The petite blonde had the stamina of a marathon runner, but invariably came home with only a sackful of maybes.

"Sorry, Pop. I don't. Besides," she added with a

wry grin, "Wanda's a little nervous about going anywhere with me these days. She hasn't quite recovered from being used as bait by those bastards who wanted to get to me."

Her big, bluff father grimaced. "I haven't quite recovered from that particular incident, either. What kind of case are you working this time?"

"Someone pumped two bullets into an American air force pilot stationed in England. The OSI wants me to consult on the case."

"The OSI, or Jack Donovan?"

"They're one and the same."

And therein lay the problem. Donovan was career air force. Blue to his bones. In for the long haul. Cleo was North Security and Investigations. Their separate careers took them to opposite ends of the globe.

Usually.

She and Donovan had worked two cases together in the past four months, though. Maybe, just maybe, the third would be the charm.

"I'll have my cell phone with me," she told her father. "Keep me posted on the great light-fixture adventure."

They both knew her real concern wasn't light fixtures, but the angina that attacked him periodically. Patrick acknowledged her unspoken concern with a gentle fist to the chin.

"Will do. Have fun hunting down your murderer."

"Will do," she echoed, grinning. "*Tachi-dao*, Pop."

He returned the grin and the farewell that was part Japanese, part Chinese, and uniquely theirs. "*Tachi-dao*, kiddo."

Cleo's flight landed at Reagan National just past 3:00 p.m. General Barnes had sent a staff car and driver for her. The unexpected luxury raised her brows until the driver mentioned he had orders to stand by during her meeting with the OSI commander, then whisk her straight to the flight line at Andrews Air Force Base.

So she and Donovan were traveling by military air. That made transporting her weapon easier, although getting it through Customs at the other end would still require detailed paperwork. Having a man with a shield at her side might help in that respect, though.

A quick call to Mae ensured the cancellation of the commercial reservations she'd made after the call from Barnes. It also elicited the information that Goose, the former Special Forces type who served as Cleo's personal trainer, had called to reschedule their next session.

"He's still in San Diego," Mae announced with an irritated snap. "Says he won't be back for another week, if then."

Cleo wasn't surprised. Her sixty-something officer manager had recently developed a severe case of the hots for Goose, which terrified the six-six hunk of solid muscle.

"He said to give him a jingle if you need him," Mae added on an annoyed huff. "*I* said what he needed wasn't a jingle, but a good, solid workout between the sheets with a real woman instead of those tie-dyed bimbos he picks up at biker bars all the time."

Cleo wasn't going to *touch* that one. With a hasty promise to check in after her arrival in England, she flipped the phone shut and settled back to enjoy the view while the driver headed across the Fourteenth Street Bridge.

Washington, D.C., was decked out in its best spring finery. The cherry trees surrounding the tidal basin had shed their blossoms but still wore the feathery green leaves of May. The white marble columns of Jefferson Memorial sparkled in the sun, as did the clean lines of the federal buildings in L'Enfant Plaza. Construction around the plaza slowed things to a crawl until the exit for the Capitol Street Bridge. Crossing the Potomac once more, they cruised along the Suitland Parkway.

Security was supertight at Andrews. Understandable, as the base was home to the 89th Airlift Wing, which flew Air Force One and other VIP support aircraft. The driver did a careful zigzag around strategically placed concrete barriers. At the sandbagged gate Cleo was asked to provide two pieces of identification. Even with a military driver, she had to wait while the security force specialist called OSI visitor control to verify her appointment.

Once cleared, the driver angled right and followed the perimeter road to the boulevard of flags leading to the 89th Wing headquarters. The semicircular building also housed a number of tenant units, including Headquarters, United States Air Force Office of Special Investigations.

Charged with providing professional investigative services to air force commanders, the OSI conducted criminal investigations and counterintelligence operations around the globe. To accomplish that mission, it fielded more than eighteen hundred federally credentialed special agents.

Cleo had once been one of them. Recruited right out of college, she'd figured all those years living abroad with her dad and her fluency in several foreign languages would make her a really cool spy. That was before she learned OSI agents did a whole lot more than sip martinis and zip around the globe in the finest James Bond tradition.

Along with recruits from other agencies, she'd attended the Federal Law Enforcement Academy. There she'd received intensive training in firearms and other weaponry, defensive tactics, forensics, surveillance, crime-scene processing, interrogations and federal law.

That was followed by six weeks of OSI-specific training in counterintelligence, antiterrorism, technology protection, cyber crimes and military law. After that came a probationary year as a rookie, when Cleo investigated everything from murder to fake IDs produced by troops old enough to fight and die for their country, but not old enough to buy beer.

In the years that followed, she did get to work some cloak-and-dagger-style ops, most notably in Honduras and Kuwait during the first Gulf War. She might still have been working them if her stubborn independence and hardnosed investigative techniques hadn't gotten her crosswise of a number of superiors, General Barnes included.

She wasn't sure who had been more relieved when she'd decided to part company with the air force and go into business for herself—her immediate supervisor at the time or the Old Man. She knew it irritated the hell out of Barnes that he'd never quite broken her to rein—almost as much as it had galled him to lose one of his field agents. Not that the general would admit it, of course. He'd bite through the stem of the Meerschaum he always kept clamped between his teeth first.

Which he looked in imminent danger of doing when his exec escorted Cleo into his office.

Barnes was a tall, spare man who carried every one of his years of service on his craggy face. Today he wore a set of the new blue-and-gray-striped camouflage utilities Cleo had heard were being tested for wear by air force personnel in the field. No one had asked her opinion about a possible shift from the browns and greens of the standard battle-dress uniform, of course. Good thing. She thought those blue stripes made the Old Man look like an oxygen-deprived zebra.

"Afternoon, sir."

The *sir* was instinctive. So was the urge to whip up a salute. Damn! There was more of the military officer still skulking around in her than she wanted to admit.

"What's good about it?" Barnes growled.

Uh-oh. Things were not going well in OSI land.

"Get Donovan in here," he barked at his exec. Gesturing Cleo to the chair in front of his desk, he shoved a folder in her direction. "While we're waiting, you might as well take a look at this."

"This" was an OSI file on one Captain Douglas Caswell, tanker pilot, currently deceased. Cleo absorbed the details like a sponge sucking up water. Born Minneapolis. Graduated University of Minnesota near the top of his class. Completed undergraduate pilot training in 1997, tanker training the following year. Upgraded to command pilot in minimal time. Earned an Air Medal and one oak-leaf cluster during initial Afghanistan surge, another cluster for support of Iraqi operations.

Pretty impressive, until you got to the index of cases in which Caswell was named as either a contact or a possible suspect.

"Busy guy," Cleo murmured, skimming the executive summaries. "Investigated for possible black marketeering in Turkey. Named as suspect in a computer porn case, but never charged. Believed to be the instigator of a regular poker game."

Her brows lifted.

"Since when does the OSI investigate poker games?"

Barnes shifted the Meerschaum from one corner of his mouth to the other. "Since Captain Caswell relieved a senior senate staffer of roughly six thousand dollars during a congressional junket."

Her lips pursed in a silent whistle. The captain played for high stakes. Flipping the file open, she was treated to a digitized image of what she assumed was formerly Doug Caswell's skull.

"We're waiting for the autopsy report," Barnes informed her. "Preliminary indications are he took two .45 slugs to the back of his head."

Ouch! One would have done the trick very nicely, thank you. Whoever put the captain down had wanted to make damned sure he never got up again.

"The shots were fired at close range, from a silenced pistol."

"Where and when?"

"Monday night, between 7:00 and 8:00 p.m., London time. Caswell was at his apartment a few kilometers from Royal Air Force Base Mildenhall."

"Any witnesses?"

"No."

"Suspects?"

"None so far, but given the captain's extracurricular activities, the list could turn out to be a long one."

"What about forensics?"

"The Brits are still working the ballistics on the bullets. They also lifted fingerprints and DNA from the apartment, but I suspect this shooter was too smart to leave his behind. I don't suggest you hold your breath."

Cleo didn't intend to. Nor did she intend to go into any situation blind. "There's an OSI detachment at RAF Mildenhall. They have responsibility for working cases like this, in conjunction with the local constabulary. Why did the Brits request reinforcements?"

The pipe made another shift. The general's eyes narrowed until his glance was a skin-searing laser. "That's what I'm sending you and Donovan to find out."

As if on cue, the exec rapped on the door and stuck his head in. "Major Donovan's here, sir."

He stepped aside and Jack strode in. Tall, tanned, with tawny gold hair and those ridiculously thick, gold-tipped lashes fringing his blue eyes. Like the general, he was in BDUs, but his were the standard green and brown that looked baggy on most everyone else but molded themselves to Donovan's muscular frame. The pants were neatly bloused in his shiny black boots, the sleeves rolled up to reveal the scattering of sun-bleached blond hair on his arms.

Cleo's stomach did a funny little flip-flop. Pretty ridiculous, considering she'd spent several quality hours with the man just two weeks ago. Maybe the fact that they'd both been naked and breathing real hard at the time had something to do with her suddenly constricted blood flow.

"Sir."

Donovan tipped a nod in his boss's direction, but his eyes were all over Cleo. A happy sound thrummed at the back of her throat. It stayed there until Barnes yanked his pipe from his mouth and lanced the stem at her like a sword.

"The last case you worked cost the air force a cargo ship and tons of munitions, North. Don't blow anything up on this one!"

2

"So what gives?"

Cleo had waited until the C-5 Galaxy ferrying them to England had leveled off before letting loose the barrage of questions Jack had been expecting.

"What's the real story behind this London gig?"

He slid her a sideways glance. Damn, she looked good! Her hair was longer than he remembered. He liked how she'd brushed the heavy mass to one side of her face in a smooth sweep. And he'd forgotten those gold flecks in her brown eyes. Funny how two solid weeks penned up in a windowless room with analysts from a half-dozen intelligence agencies could fuzz the small details.

The important ones were etched clear and sharp, though. Like the busy, curious mind that never shut down. Not to mention the skill with which the woman could lock her legs around him and just about shut *him* down. The mere thought of those calves of steel hooked around him put a sudden, serious kink in Jack's gut.

"C'mon, Donovan. You know something about the Caswell case I don't. Probably several somethings. Spill 'em."

"I don't know much more than what you read in the file. He was a man of many interests, not all of them legit."

"Which of those interests got him crosswise of British Intelligence?"

"Take your pick. Gambling. Pandering. Usury. Turns out he's staked a few locals to loans at rates that would make Chase Manhattan drool. MI6 has had him on their radar for several months now."

She made a rude noise. "But they waited until he ate two bullets before calling us in? Typical."

Jack bit back a smile at that all-encompassing "us." Cleo never missed a chance to remind him she operated independently now. Yet she still slipped up every so often and included herself as part of the establishment. You could take the woman out of the uniform...

The kink in Jack's gut got tighter.

That's exactly what he intended to do. At the first possible opportunity, he'd have Cleo out of what passed as her uniform these days, flat on her back and gasping out those breathless groans that made him crazy.

"How's your father?" he asked, as much to keep himself from losing it right here in the passenger pod of the C-5 as to dodge her questions. "Have he and Wanda recovered from the visit by those thugs who shot up their den?"

"Dad has. Wanda's still pretty shaken up. She's soothing her shattered nerves by knocking down the wall between the dining room and the kitchen. This case saved me from having to go shopping for light fixtures with her. I would have accepted half my usual fee for that alone."

"Did you?"

She grinned, her eyes gleaming. "No."

Jack couldn't help himself. Sliding a hand under that silky spill of mink-brown, he wrapped his fingers around her nape. A quick tug got them as close as their seat belts would allow.

"That's what I love about you, North."

"My expense account?"

His hand caressed her neck. The small, soft hairs tickled his palm. Heat flowed from her skin to his.

"Your expense account," he murmured, his mouth brushing hers, "and those snuffly little grunts you make in your sleep."

"I do *not* snuffle."

"Yeah, babe," he countered, brushing his lips against hers, "you do."

Cleo's breath hitched. Trust Donovan to pick a

noisy transport, with troops sitting just a few rows back, to get her wet.

She was entertaining serious thoughts of dragging him to the forward lavatory, wedging inside and qualifying for entrée into the air force's version of the mile-high club when Donovan blew out a breath and sank back in his seat.

"What about you?" she asked when some of the heat had subsided. "What's been happening in your life the last few weeks, aside from hunts for illegal arms dealers?"

"With you in Dallas? Nothing."

"No late-night calls from Kate?"

Instantly, the smile went out of Jack's eyes. Cleo could almost hear the shutters slamming.

She tried not to feel hurt, told herself everyone had some cross to bear. Hers was Waffling Wanda. Donovan's was his ex-wife, who tended to forget such minor matters as *divorce* when she went on one of her binges. The difference was Cleo could vent to him about Wanda. Donovan wrapped his guilt over his ex's condition in stony silence.

Cleo had heard the vicious, ranting messages Kate had left on Jack's answering machine a few weeks back. She'd offered to help then and been shut out. This time was the same.

"Kate's dry," he answered with a shrug that said he didn't want to talk about it.

She let the subject drop, and tried to let the tiny niggle of hurt go with it.

At seven-ten the next morning, the C-5 put down at Royal Air Forces Base Fairford, a NATO joint-use base about a hundred miles west of London. RAF Mildenhall, where Caswell had been stationed, lay to the north of the capital, but the runway was temporarily closed due to maintenance on the approach lighting system. That was fine with Jack and Cleo. Their instructions were to make contact with their British counterpart before heading up to Mildenhall.

Lady Marston was the widow of a British member of Parliament and a longtime undercover operative for MI6, the United Kingdom's counterpart to the CIA. She was also the sister of a client who'd hired Cleo to track down a missing employee, plunging them all into a tangled web of murder and international intrigue. *Smart, elegant* and *lethal* pretty well described Johanna Marston, Cleo mused. Not to mention filthy rich, she added when she got a glimpse of the shiny silver Rolls the intelligence agent had sent to pick them up.

"Lady Marston's compliments," the chauffeur said with a regal bow. "She's been called to Paris but is expected to return early this afternoon. She suggests you rest at her London flat until then."

Since it was just past two in the morning Washington time, Cleo jumped at the suggestion. A few hours' sleep sounded good. The idea of stretching out between clean, ironed sheets with a certain OSI agent might also have had something to do with the smile she sent the driver's way.

"Lead on, Macduff."

"It's McDowell, madam."

"Lead on, McDowell."

Jack settled beside her on the cloud-soft leather. He'd changed out of his uniform before they departed Washington. His button-down Oxford shirt and lightweight summer sport coat still looked crisp and neat. Cleo's cream-colored linen jacket, on the other hand, showed the effects of eight-plus hours in the air. So did her hair and face, she knew. She couldn't wait to hit the shower. And the sheets.

The Rolls zipped along the M4 at a good clip, conveying Cleo and Jack through the rolling uplands of the Cotswolds and on into Berkshire. The countryside was dotted with charming, carefully preserved medieval villages and hedges green with the tender shoots of spring. Between the hedges lay fields glowing a brilliant yellow.

"What is that stuff?" she asked the driver.

"Rapeseed, madam."

"And that is?"

McDowell permitted himself a smile. "The source of much of our cooking oil. What doesn't go for canola oil is used to feed farm animals."

The gold seemed to go on forever, blanketing

every undulating hill that wasn't being grazed by sheep or cattle. Eventually it gave way to the inevitable urban sprawl of the capital. The Rolls inched through the heart of London, skirting Regent's Park before winding south through Hyde Park to the cobbled streets and swanky mansions of Belgravia.

Lady Marston's flat took up the top two floors of a columned Georgian masterpiece. Cleo managed not to gawk when the private lift opened onto a reception area trimmed in mahogany and hung with gilt-framed portraits, but the sitting room beyond took her breath away. It was done in soothing neutrals—creams with splashes of gold and deep purple for accent. The subdued color scheme formed a perfect backdrop for the ornate Victorian furnishings.

The sitting room, formal dining room, study, kitchen and servants' quarters were downstairs, the housekeeper informed them as she led them up a wide, curving staircase. The master suite and guest rooms occupied the upper story.

Jack and Cleo followed her down a hall lined with more portraits. He held on to his briefcase, but a footman trailed behind with their bags.

"Do you wish to rest and freshen up after your journey?" the housekeeper inquired. "Or would you prefer to breakfast first?"

The prospect of a hearty English breakfast made Cleo's stomach sit up and take immediate notice. Mouth watering, she envisioned rashers of thick-sliced bacon. Fat, glistening sausages. Fried tomatoes and moist little mushrooms with their pointy caps. A wedge of that mysterious black stuff the English labeled black pudding. Then there were all those luscious jams to slather over toast or crusty rolls.

She was ready to vote for food first when the housekeeper stepped aside. One glimpse of the canopied bed triggered an instant brain dump. All she could envision at that point was Donovan, sans clothing and cocooned inside those brocaded curtains with her.

Evidently Jack was thinking along the same lines. "Why don't you send up some coffee, juice and rolls?" he suggested while the housekeeper showed them the bath and adjoining bedroom. "We'll let you know if we need anything else."

"Certainly, sir."

With a polite nod, she waited until the footman had deposited their luggage and followed him out. Jack caught the waistband of Cleo's jeans and yanked her into his arms almost before the door closed.

There was nothing gentle about this kiss. Unlike the one on the C-5, this was hard and hungry. And bristly, Cleo discovered as her chin yielded several layers of skin to his dark gold whiskers.

"You need a shave," she muttered when she got some of her breath back.

"Yeah, I do." His thumb made a pass over the tender spot. "You want first dibs at the bathroom?"

"It's all yours. I'll wait for the coffee."

"I'll make it quick."

Shrugging out of his sport coat, he tossed it on a skirted chair. His shoulder harness and 9 mm Sig Sauer followed. When he started on the buttons of his shirt, Cleo's adrenaline spiked again. She would have been all over the man if the phone hadn't rung at that moment.

It was the housekeeper, calling to inquire whether she wished orange or tomato juice.

"Orange," she answered, her eyes on Jack's tight butt as it headed for the shower.

"Very well, madam. I'll bring the tray up straightaway."

Damn! With a last, regretful glance at Jack's behind, she waited for the tray.

When it arrived he was scraping the last of the shaving cream from his cheeks. Cleo wiggled out of her jeans and top, poured him a cup of coffee and joined him in the bathroom. The strangled sound that erupted from his throat put a smirk on her face.

Men were *so* predictable. This particular male, anyway. One glimpse of bare breasts had him breathing fast. The lacy hipsters got him hard.

Which is exactly what Cleo had intended. Taking immense satisfaction from the way his entire body went taut, she handed him a delicate china cup.

"My turn."

Using a hip, she nudged him aside. She had a

toothbrush stuck between her lips and toothpaste frothing on her teeth when Jack thumped the china cup down on the vanity. One quick tug on his zipper and his pants dropped to the carpet.

He was primed and ready. So ready Cleo just about choked on her toothpaste. She got a glimpse of a truly magnificent erection in the mirror. Only a glimpse. Then he hooked his thumbs in the skimpy briefs and dragged them down over her hips. A second later, he was dragging Cleo down with them.

"Jack!" she got out through the froth. "Wait!"

"Why?"

With a fleeting thought of the canopied bed, she managed a quick swish, tossed aside the toothbrush and sank onto the plush carpet. It was the same misty green as the walls and soft as a cloud.

Donovan, on the other hand, wasn't soft at all. Every spot Cleo touched felt tough and sinewy, and she made it a point to touch every inch she could reach with her hands and tongue and teeth. By the time she'd worked her way down to his belly and back up again, her breath rasped in her throat. His was a hoarse growl.

"God, I've missed you, Cleopatra Aphrodite."

She grunted at the use of her despised middle name, then gasped as he nipped at the tendons of her neck.

"You know," she got out, "you're the only person who's called me that and lived to tell about it."

His response was a deep, chesty laugh that would

have melted Cleo on the spot if she hadn't been so distracted by the knee he hooked between hers. Prying her legs apart, he slid into her. Slowly. Inch by tantalizing inch.

Cleo arched to meet him, enjoying every second of the deliberate entry. He filled her, withdrew, corded his muscles and pushed in again. She figured she was good for about two hours of this deliciously erotic stimulation.

To her profound disgust—and Jack's considerable amusement—she lasted only until the third thrust. The heat that flamed under her skin was her only warning. Suddenly, the muscles low in her belly contracted. Pleasure shot through her in swift, jagged jolts.

She tried to pull back, tried to scuttle away, but her frantic wiggles only increased the friction. With a long groan, she rode the tight, spiraling waves.

"Sorry 'bout that," she got out on a shaky laugh a few moments later.

"Not a problem." Propping himself up on his elbows, Donovan gave her a smug grin. "I've got enough staying power for both of us."

"Is that right?"

Smiling, she traced a lazy fingertip over the old bullet wound on his shoulder. Still smiling, she gathered her strength and concentrated it all in a hard, swift pull of her vaginal muscles.

"Christ!"

His breath exploded on a hiss. His lower body

jackknifed. To Cleo's intense satisfaction, Donovan's staying power didn't hang around much longer than hers had.

They didn't leave the bedroom until midafternoon. By then they'd zoned out for a few hours, tested the springs on the canopied bed and devoured the contents of the breakfast tray.

The rolls had hardly made a dent in Cleo's now-ravenous hunger. Her stomach was in loud, angry revolt when they descended the stairs. The housekeeper met them with the news that Lady Marston had phoned from her vehicle and should arrive at any moment. The ever-so-efficient housekeeper also indicated she'd prepared afternoon tea.

"Will you and Special Agent Donovan take it in the garden?"

Tea in the garden with Special Agent Donovan. It reminded Cleo so much of the characters from her favorite childhood mystery game that she had to bite back a flip request for cocktails in the library with Colonel Peacock.

"That sounds lovely."

Actually, it sounded more than lovely. With a fervent prayer of thanks for the English institution of afternoon tea, she did serious damage to the three-tiered silver tray of dainty cucumber sandwiches, flaky pastries and chocolate truffles. Nor did she ignore the scones. She downed one swimming in clotted cream, another slathered with strawberry preserves. She eyed a third, but magnanimously left it for Jack.

He polished it off, stretched out his legs and leaned back in his wrought-iron chair. May was too early for many of the shrubs in the garden, but tulips and crocuses provided a riot of color and lilac bushes dripped fragrant blossoms. The fat blooms formed a lush backdrop for Jack's rugged good looks.

"Okay," Cleo said when he'd made himself comfortable. "General Barnes gave me the idiot treatment back in Washington when I asked why the local OSI couldn't handle Minnesota Fats's murder."

"Minnesota Fats?"

"Caswell was born in Minneapolis, liked to play for high stakes, ergo..."

She'd attached nicknames to people for as long as she could remember. Radio Man. Assault Rifle Guy. Waffling Wanda. Jumpin' Jack Donovan. Gulping back a grin at the genesis for that one, she scooped the last bite of scone from his plate.

"C'mon, Jack. Do you have any idea why the Brits requested additional investigators?"

"Not just any investigators," a cool voice answered from behind them. "I made sure the request specifically named the two of you."

Their hostess glided through the glass doors leading to the flower-filled garden. Cleo had last seen the slender brunette on the veranda of the naval hospital in Naples, where the survivors of the explosion of the U.S. Motor Vessel *William H. Pitsenbarger* had been flown. Despite having just abandoned a burning ship, the British agent had looked sleek as a cat in a black leather jumpsuit that clung to her trim curves.

Today she was crisp, businesslike and stunning in a severely tailored pin-striped pantsuit and cinnamon silk blouse that could only have come from Dior. Trying not to lust after that incredible blouse, Cleo rose to take the hand Johanna offered.

"So sorry to have run out on you two," the British agent apologized. "I must say, you're looking remarkably fit after your flight over. Did you get in a spot of rest?"

Her gaze zeroed in on the whisker burn left by Jack's bristles. Amused, she answered her own question.

"Yes, I see you did. Of a sort."

"Of a sort," Cleo echoed, swallowing a grin.

Her gray eyes dancing, Johanna Marston gave Jack a warm handshake, slid into a chair and rang for a fresh pot of tea.

"In answer to your question," she said while waiting for it to be delivered, "I asked my superiors to request the two of you by name because I have firsthand experience as to your competence."

"And?" Cleo prodded. She knew there was more behind the request than that. There had to be. British

Intelligence wouldn't bring in hired guns without good reason.

"I also saw how well you worked together."

"And?"

Unruffled by Cleo's persistence, their hostess looked from her to Jack. "Nor could I fail to note the sparks you struck off each other. I thought perhaps you might jump at the chance to team up again." Her mouth curved. "And so you have."

Donovan answered that one with a lazy drawl. "Much as we appreciate your matchmaking efforts, what do you say we cut the bull? What's the story, Johanna? Why is MI6 so concerned about a murdered air force pilot?"

"We're more concerned about who murdered him and why. Your Captain Caswell was a man of many interests."

"So we've discovered."

Johanna's sable lashes shielded her eyes for a moment. When her gaze lifted, it was hard and sharp.

"Then perhaps you can discover why the bullets the medical examiner dug out of his skull appear to have been fired by a model 1911 Colt pistol."

"Why is that so significant?" Jack asked. "The Colt .45 is one of the most popular handguns of all time. As the model number indicates, it was first manufactured in 1911 and was used by our military forces in both world wars. It's since been copied by gun manufacturers all over the world."

"The ballistics on these bullets indicate they were fired by a special lot of Colts manufactured in 1939 and purchased by our government under the Lend-Lease Program," Johanna said crisply. "The bullets themselves are also somewhat unusual."

"How so?"

"All metals were scarce during the war, as I'm sure you appreciate. Lead, especially, was quite difficult to acquire in sufficient quantities to meet demand. As a result, bullets issued to our regular military forces contained two to four times the normal amount of zinc to make up for the shortage of lead. The bullets that killed Captain Caswell, however, were heavier and far more destructive. I've been informed they were issued exclusively to our Special Forces and certain…"

She hesitated, choosing her words carefully.

"Certain agents charged with conducting clandestine operations behind enemy lines."

Aha! Cleo thought. That explained MI6's involvement in a case that would normally be handled by the locals. The ballistics tracked the murder weapon back to one of their own.

Lady Marston confirmed as much in the next sentence. "By a rather laborious process of elimination, we determined that these rounds were most likely fired by a Colt .45 issued to one Grenadier Sergeant Clive Gordon. Gordon was listed on the rolls of the Grenadier Guards, Kentish division, but had been recruited by SOE—our Special Operations Executive. It was the counterpart to your Office of Strategic Services."

Cleo was familiar with both. Like all air force OSI agents, she'd studied case histories of the daring, incredibly dangerous operations conducted by SOE and OSS agents during World War II.

"Sergeant Gordon, his sidearm and the Dakota transport he was aboard disappeared over the English Channel sometime in March 1943. Neither the plane nor the bodies of the personnel aboard were ever recovered."

"But Gordon's weapon was?"

"Apparently. And we should very much like to know how it came to be used to kill your Captain Caswell."

When the Americans decided to take advantage of the late afternoon sunshine and motor up to RAF Mildenhall, Johanna didn't try to dissuade them. They were well rested—very well rested, from all appearances—and she was feeling the effects of her over-and-back dash to Paris.

She saw them off on their mission without a qualm. She hadn't lied to them. She'd merely declined to reveal certain pieces of information they didn't require for the conduct of their investigation.

What she did feel, though, was a distinct pang of envy when she recalled that whisker burn on Cleo's chin. Drifting into the formal sitting room, she lifted her gaze to the portrait over the marble-fronted fireplace.

Bartholomew St. Ives Marston. DSO. DLI. Stiff-spined, square-shouldered, so handsome Johanna's breath caught on an old, familiar ache.

"We felt the same heat once, didn't we, my darling?"

The memory of it warmed her now. The passionate fire of their courtship and early marriage. The flame that burned so hot and bright during his years as a barrister. The steady glow that carried them through his terms in Parliament and Johanna's frequent absences as she rose through the ranks of the intelligence community.

The smoldering embers of those last, awful weeks when Barty had died a little more each day, right before her eyes. She'd lost him five years ago and still missed him dreadfully.

Her work kept her busy but came nowhere close to filling the hole. Nor had the two discreet affairs Johanna had indulged in since Barty's death provided more than temporary ease.

The ache would always remain, she suspected. A constant reminder of her husband and the rare, uncluttered love they'd enjoyed.

Stifling another pang of envy for the Americans she'd drawn into this delicate and potentially dangerous web, she returned to the garden for more tea.

3

Jack and Cleo's escape from London took forty minutes. Once outside the urban sprawl, he locked on to the M11 heading north and opened up the rental he'd had delivered to Lady Marston's flat. Since he'd charged the vehicle to his air force expense account, it was a fuel-efficient Ford Taurus. On her own, Cleo would have ordered up a sporty Jag or Aston Martin.

Not that she gouged her clients. Her fees were at the high end of the industry standard, but only because she'd earned a reputation as one of the best in the business.

Those fees were negotiable, though. She'd hunted down a lost turtle for her six-year-old neighbor for the quarter the kid insisted on paying her. She'd also protected a woman from her vicious, knife-wielding ex—for the token fee of a dollar. On the other end of the scale, she insisted on appropriate payment for her skills from well-heeled clients.

For all General Barnes's bluster when it came to negotiating fees, the United States air force tended toward the low end of Cleo's scale. Still, she wasn't about to complain.

She was feeling mellow at the moment. The scones and cucumber sandwiches had semisatisfied her nagging hunger. Jack had satisfied pretty much every other appetite. And this murder case was looking more interesting by the minute.

Lolling back in her seat, Cleo enjoyed a landscape of rolling green hills dotted with postcard-perfect villages. When they turned onto the A11 and zipped past Cambridge, she caught a glimpse of the university's spires poking above the trees. The turnoff for the air base came some kilometers past Newmarket. Prominent signs directed them to RAF Mildenhall. Another sign pointed to RAF Lakenheath, a satellite base not far from Mildenhall.

As they neared the gate, Cleo squinted through the windshield at the tanker coming in on final landing. The big, gray-skinned Boeing 707 airframe skimmed the fields to the east of the town, its boom raised for landing.

"Looks like they finished the maintenance work on the runway lights."

"Looks like."

Jack's gaze narrowed on the distinctive yellow-

and-black tail markings of the 100th Air Refueling Wing. He'd done some hurried research on the 100th ARW before leaving D.C. and had been impressed by its history.

Originally activated as a heavy-bomb group, the unit had arrived in England in early 1943. Crews manning the B-17 Flying Fortresses saw heavy action during the war. So heavy their unit earned the grim distinction as the Bloody Hundreth.

After the war, the group rotated back to the States and experienced the same fluctuations as other military units. Deactivated during periodic force drawdowns. Reactivated at different bases across the country. Assigned various missions over the years.

The 100th had returned to the U.K. forty-eight years after departing, this time as the United States Air Force's sole air refueling wing in Europe. As such, its aircraft flew missions in support of just about every ongoing operation in Europe and the Middle East.

Now, apparently, a pilot assigned to the 100th had been blown away by bullets fired from a Colt .45 lost during the years the wing had been originally based in England. The coincidence would have been intriguing—if Jack believed in coincidence.

Throw in the murder victim's recent e-mail to a sergeant in regular contact with a suspected terrorist cell, and the case took another, deadly twist. No one outside the air force and CIA knew about those contacts as yet. General Barnes had charged Jack with making sure no one else did while the sensitive investigation was ongoing.

Unfortunately, that included Cleo. Her civilian status no longer gave her access to the inner sanctum. Jack only hoped he didn't have to remind her of that fact. She tended to get pissed about small matters like being sent into an op blind.

He eased his conscience by reminding himself they were going into this one together. He'd be right beside her, watching her every step. That was the plan, anyway.

It seemed to be working so far, but Jack didn't kid himself. His previous efforts to keep Cleo on a leash had required skill, cunning and every dirty trick in the book.

The commander of Mildenhall's OSI detachment was waiting for them. Flame-haired and freckled, Major Paul Morrison had a firm handshake and a chilly smile for the headquarters type muscling in on his turf.

"It's been a while since Kirtland, Donovan."

"Yes, it has."

"Care to tell me why General Barnes doesn't think I'm capable of conducting this murder investigation?"

"The general thinks you're eminently capable or you wouldn't be in command of this detachment. You know how it works, Morrison. Certain cases get additional attention. This is one of them."

"Why?" The edge was still there. "What makes Caswell so special?"

"He had his fingers in a lot of pies. Ms. North and I are here to help you sort through them."

Morrison's frosty smile warmed a few degrees when it shifted to Cleo. "It's good to finally meet you. I've, uh, heard about you for years."

The telltale "uh" had Jack shifting his gaze out the window. Cleo merely grinned.

"Heard, or seen?"

"Seen," the major admitted sheepishly. "That Victoria's Secret ad still pops up on our computers occasionally."

The lingerie ad seemed to follow her wherever she went. It had been discovered during her rookie days and had zipped around the globe to OSI computers everywhere. Evidently it still made the occasional appearance.

Not that Cleo minded. She'd been a curvy size four when she'd done that shoot. She couldn't squeeze into a size four now with a shoehorn but didn't object to basking in the memory of those glory days.

"I understand you got the ballistics back from the constabulary," Jack drawled, steering Morrison's attention back to the small matter of Doug Caswell's murder.

"We also got an advance copy of the autopsy. Not much to add to the preliminary report, other than the make of the weapon that fired the slugs. Turns out it was a Colt .45, part of a special lot manufactured for the British forces and purchased using Lend-Lease funds."

Jack nodded but didn't mention they'd already been given that information. "What does the list of possible suspects look like so far?"

"A who's who of crime in the local area," Morrison replied with a grimace. "Since we've started digging, the rats have been scurrying out of the woodwork. The Mildenhall constables took statements from several who admitted they would have offed Caswell if they'd thought they could get away with it. We lined up a couple more here on base. Want some coffee while I run through the list?"

When Jack and Cleo had mugs in hand, Morrison waved them to a seat and pulled out a black notebook.

"The leader of the pack right now is a local thug by the name of Michael Woodhouse. He's got a rap sheet as long as your arm for assault, dealing and B and E. The constables found several pieces of expensive electronics in Caswell's flat that traced to Woodhouse. Naturally, Woodhouse couldn't produce receipts for any of it."

"Naturally."

"Seems Woodhouse felt Caswell screwed him royally on the resale. The man groused to his pals he was going to carve the captain into little pieces."

"Does he have an alibi for the time of the shooting?"

"Claims he was with his girl. She backs him up."

"Surprise, surprise," Jack drawled. "Who's suspect number two?"

"Betty Talbot, a local, uh, entrepreneur. She's got priors for solicitation, prostitution and lewd acts with barnyard animals."

"Goats, donkeys or horses?" Cleo asked.

"All of the above." Morrison cracked a grin. "One of the constables said they'd heard a rumor about a prize bull, but it was never substantiated."

"Holy cow!"

Jack groaned. Undaunted, Cleo slipped in another atrocious pun. "What's her beef with Caswell?"

"She claims he hired her to perform at a party, then failed to pay in full for services rendered. Ms. Talbot made several very vocal promises to castrate the bastard the next time she laid eyes on him."

"Did she lay eyes on him the night he was murdered?"

"She says no, but you could poke a Bradley Fighting Vehicle through the holes in her alibi."

Jack jotted a few notes in his own black book. "Number three on the list?"

"A barmaid at the Hare and Hound by the name of Yasmin Indali."

"Indali?" His head came up. "Indian or Pakistani?"

The question was casual. Too casual to anyone who knew him as well as Cleo did. She tipped him a narrow glance while Morrison consulted his notes.

"Her parents immigrated from Pakistan. Apparently this woman and Caswell enjoyed an intimate relationship until he dumped her. Ms. Indali is now four months pregnant."

"Uh-oh," Cleo murmured. "Hell hath no fury…"

"In this case, the real fury is the father. He's old-school conservative and thoroughly outraged over the stain on his daughter's honor. When I interviewed her, she was running real scared."

"Of what?"

"I'm not sure. Could be her father, who lodged a complaint against Caswell with the wing commander. Could be her brother, who's vowed vengeance. Could be just because we came knocking on her door."

Nodding, Jack made another note in his book. Morrison ran through three more possible suspects in the local community before turning to the two from the base. One was an airman who'd purchased a vehicle from the captain, only to have it fall apart on him a week later. He'd demanded his money back and been refused.

Another was a lieutenant colonel who had lost his shirt in one of Caswell's high-stakes poker games. They were both in the same squadron, which subjected the colonel to possible charges of fraternization and gambling with a subordinate…if not murder.

"We'd like to talk to these folks."

"I figured you would. I've got interviews set up for you for tomorrow morning here at our offices. I've also arranged for the inspector from the local constable's office to meet us at the crime scene before we start talking to folks."

"Thanks. Can you make me copies of the interviews you've conducted so far, as well as the autopsy and forensics reports?"

"I've got them ready for you. One more thing. The 100th Air Refueling Wing commander asked me to bring you by his office. He wants to brief you on certain classified elements of the 100th's mission that Caswell had access to." Morrison's glance slid to Cleo. "I'm sorry, Ms. North. Headquarters advises you're not cleared for that level of briefing. You can wait here if you like."

Cleo had never been into waiting. And this exclusion business was starting to become a real annoyance. She'd have to see about getting her security clearances reinstated when she got back to the States, she decided. Particularly if she was going to keep working cases for the air force.

"I'll take the car into town and check into our hotel," she said with a shrug. "Mind dropping Donovan off when you're through with him?"

"Can do."

Although Jack could have reserved them rooms in the Visiting Officers' Quarters on base, they'd opted instead for the centuries-old inn Johanna Marston had recommended. One, it gave them more freedom of movement. Two, Johanna's description of blackened timbers, antique-filled rooms and a three-star restaurant had won Cleo's instant vote.

Jack hesitated a moment before handing over the keys to the rental car. He'd ridden in vehicles piloted by Cleo before.

"Left side of the road, remember."

She was tempted to flip him the bird. She settled for flipping her fingers under her chin in a gesture almost as expressive.

Cleo made it into town with only two or three close encounters of the fender-bending variety.

Mildenhall was a comfortable if somewhat scruffy mix of old and new. Fast-food places and apartment buildings sprouted up like mushrooms on the outskirts. Not surprising in a town that supported a major military installation, with another air base only a few miles away. The town center was more picturesque and included a square marked by an ancient stone cross, a few shops and a massive Romanesque cathedral.

Cleo had to ask directions twice before she found the Thistle Inn. The rambling, half-timbered structure sat on a side street—only a few blocks from the Hare and Hound, she noted with a sudden leap of interest.

That was where Captain Caswell's pregnant girlfriend worked. She and Jack might just have to wander over that way later this evening.

She squeezed the Taurus into the inn's minuscule

parking lot and lifted their bags from the trunk. Jack's was considerably heavier than hers. Wondering just what the heck he'd packed in there, Cleo carried them into the reception area. They'd booked two rooms, but after their session between the sheets this afternoon she had no qualms about altering the arrangements to a single suite.

"Would you like me to make a reservation for you in the dining room?" the well-endowed matron at the front desk inquired as she handed over a key. "We're serving a tasty rack of lamb tonight."

"Yes, please."

"What time do you wish to dine?"

Cleo checked her watch and booked a table for seven-thirty. Declining assistance with the carryalls, she climbed a creaking set of stairs. The two-room corner suite lived up to Johanna Marston's promises. Blackened beams, an honest-to-goodness fireplace and ancient wooden floors that dipped and curved like a roller coaster.

The bathroom, though, was strictly twenty-first century. Cleo filled the claw-foot tub and sank to her chin in lavender-scented bubbles, and then dried off with fluffy towels warmed on electric rods. Wrapping a towel around her, she aimed a blow-dryer at her hair.

She then raided the minibar. Paced for a while. Tried the TV. Restless and more irritated by the minute at being cut out of the loop, she hooked up her laptop and decided to do a little Googling.

She never ceased to be amazed at the information floating around out there on the Internet. Sure enough, a search for Grenadier Sergeant Clive Gordon turned up a written order dated June 29, 1938, listing him and others in his company promoted that month. A search on the Colt .45 returned more than five hundred thousand results. Not unexpected for a weapon that, as Jack had indicated, was one of the most popular handguns of all time.

Curious as to how an American-manufactured .45 had made it into the ranks of British troops, Cleo clicked up information on the Lend-Lease Program. She'd heard of it, of course, but hadn't realized Franklin Delano Roosevelt had instituted the program as a means to circumvent earlier, isolationist laws enacted to keep the United States out of the war in Europe. Determined to aid beleaguered Britain, FDR arranged the loan of fifty U.S. navy destroyers decommissioned after World War I. In exchange, Churchill granted the United States ninety-nine-year leases to bases at various ports of call in the Western Hemisphere ranging from Jamaica to Newfoundland.

As the storm clouds darkened and America's involvement appeared more and more likely, FDR nudged his nation's industrial base toward a wartime production capacity by expanding the Lend-Lease Program to include *new* ships, aircraft, trucks, tanks and other armaments. By the time Truman ended the program in 1945, almost fifty billion dollars' worth of war material, food and financial aid had made its way to British Commonwealth countries, the USSR, China and forty additional allies.

And somewhere among all that stuff, Cleo mused, was the Colt .45 used to murder Captain Doug Caswell.

The data dump had absorbed her interest, but with the snap of the computer lid her restlessness returned. She checked her watch, paced a while and finally said what the hell.

She was tired of waiting for Jack. The Hare and Hound drew her like a beacon on a foggy night.

She left the room key at the front desk, along with a note informing Donovan where she was headed. A few minutes later she strolled into the Hare and Hound.

It was your quintessential English pub, all oak beams, stucco walls and tables the size of postage stamps. Hunting scenes, shots of local points of interest and framed portraits of the royal family papered every inch of the walls. The aroma of curry and fresh fried fish and chips battled for supremacy with a thick pall of cigarette smoke.

Ignoring the instant feed-me noises her stomach started making, Cleo claimed a table in the corner. The waiter who approached had golden skin and dark, liquid eyes. Was this Yasmin's brother? The one who'd vowed vengeance against Minnesota Fats?

"Yes, madam?"

"I'll have a pint of Banks."

She took the brand name off the coaster on the table, but should have known it wouldn't be that simple. The Brits took their ale seriously.

"Bitter or easy?"

"Easy."

"Cask, keg or smoothpour, madam?"

She took a wild stab. "Keg, please."

He relayed the order to the tall, turbaned bartender. Yasmin's father, Cleo guessed. He was smiling at a customer and looked at home behind the counter, but she knew all too well appearances meant nothing. The most cold-blooded killers could project warm friendliness.

Her waiter returned with the foaming pint and Cleo took a cautious sip. The ale went down smooth and creamy and tasted faintly of hops. She downed another swallow and settled back to wait.

Her patience was rewarded when a barmaid came out of the kitchen carrying a heaping plate. The young woman's stomach was gently rounded under her apron and an ugly purple bruise darkened one side of her face.

Cleo's fist tightened on her glass. Had papa or bro taken a fist to the pregnant woman? If so, they sure as hell should answer for it.

Biding her time, she caught the waitress on her way back to the kitchen. "What was that you just delivered? It looked delicious."

"Curry chicken pie with chips, madam."

"Is that on the menu?"

"Yes, it's just here." Bending, she pointed to the entry. Up close her bruise was even uglier. "It's a house specialty."

"So I see." Cleo lowered her voice. "Are you Yasmin?"

The question brought sudden and unmistakable fear into the girl's dark eyes. "How do you know my name? What do you want?"

"I'm Cleo North, a private security consultant from the United States. I'm here to help investigate Captain Caswell's murder. I'd like to talk to you, if you have a few moments."

"I cannot." The waitress threw a frightened glance over her shoulder. "Not here."

"At my hotel, then. I'm staying at the Thistle Inn."

"No! They know me there. My father…"

The tremor in her voice made Cleo long for the chance to have a little heart-to-heart with the barkeep.

"I can help you," she murmured. "Just talk to me."

Yasmin wavered, threw another glance at the bar and conceded in a whispered rush. "Come round to the back of the pub after you finish your ale. I'll slip out and meet you in the alley."

With a nod, Cleo handed back the menu. She downed the rest of her Banks slowly, yet could still feel the kick as she gathered her purse and paid the tab.

The pub was starting to fill up when she left. Yasmin's brother was showing two new customers to Cleo's table almost before she reached the door. She wandered outside to a slowly gathering dusk fragrant with the scent of lilacs. A few steps took her around the bushes and into the alley that ran between the pub and the building behind it.

"Here!"

Yasmin huddled in the shadows. Cleo located her primarily by the stark white of her apron.

"I can't stay long," the young woman whispered, nervousness threading her voice. "My father will notice I am gone."

"Did he do that to your face?"

"Papa? No!" Genuine shock overlaid her fear. "He wishes only to protect me."

"Then who beat you?"

She put a shaking hand to her bruise. "Two men stopped me on my way home yesterday. They said Doug had placed bets with them on races at Newmarket. They'd traced the calls to my mobile phone."

What a sleaze, Cleo thought in disgust. Using his girlfriend's cell to play the horses instead of his own.

"These men didn't believe me when I said I knew nothing about the bets," Yasmin whispered. "One of them hit me. He said he would come back, that he'd make sure these debts were paid in full."

"Did you call the police?"

"No! The constables have already questioned my father and brother about Doug's murder." Gulping, she tried to hold back her tears. "I didn't... I couldn't..."

Cleo gave her a few moments to recover. "How did you explain that bruise to your family?"

"I told Papa I fell down the stairs," she said miserably. "I couldn't tell him about this other. I couldn't! He would kill these men for hurting me! I've shamed him enough already. I won't have him go to prison because of Doug's debts."

"You need to think about this, Yasmin. If Caswell was placing bets illegally, his bookies won't want any calls traced back to them. You've got to notify the police, tell them Caswell used your phone to..."

"Too late for that, sweetheart."

Cleo whirled, her eyes narrowing as she recognized one of the men who'd entered the pub just as she was going out. Thin, wiry and cocky as all get out, he sauntered forward. Light spilling through the pub's rear window glinted on the pistol he held gripped in his left hand.

It was a 9 mm, she noted. Not as powerful as a .45, but every bit as lethal.

"She's got the right of it, Yasmin. I can't 'ave the constables breathing down me neck, now, can I?"

Her face pale with terror, the young woman crossed her arms over her middle in a protective gesture as old as time and backed away.

"I didn't tell the police about the calls Doug made! I swear I didn't!"

"Yet here you are, singing to this bird about 'em. I knew I couldn't trust you to keep your mouth shut."

Cleo edged sideways, putting herself between the gunman and Yasmin, drawing his attention.

"You need to think about this, bud."

"Sod that." His lips curled. "I already done my stretch at Dartmoor. They put me in the cage, they did. For weeks on end. I'm not going back to that hole."

Cleo spotted another figure coming around the corner of the building and knew she had to move now, before this guy's pal got into position. She was gathering her muscles when the back door to the pub opened.

"Papa! Stay back!"

Cleo was already in the air. She hit the little sleaze with the full force of her body. Just before she smashed him to the pavement like a cockroach, he got off one wild shot.

She felt an instant of searing heat, a sudden blinding agony. Yasmin screamed, her father bellowed with rage, and Cleo's world went black.

4

When Jack and Paul Morrison left the office of the commander, 100th Air Refueling Wing, Jack knew considerably more about tanker operations than when he'd gone in. Unfortunately, he'd gained next to nothing that would help him in the investigation of Captain Doug Caswell's murder.

Despite the captain's questionable dealings off duty, he'd evidently been one hell of an aviator. Caswell had logged hundreds of hours in the air in support of operations in Afghanistan, hundreds more since Iraq kicked off. His co-pilots and boom operators had nothing but praise for the pilot's cool eye and steady hands during refueling operations.

Jack could only imagine what it took to keep the KC-135 steady during those hairy moments when some two hundred thousand pounds of highly flammable fuel streamed from the tanker to the fighters nuzzled up to its belly. One air pocket, one scrape of metal against metal, and the tanker would have exploded in a ball of flames.

"I forgot to congratulate you, by the way," Morrison said, pressing a remote on his key chain to unlock the doors of his car.

Jack slid into the passenger seat and glanced at Morrison. "For…?"

"For making the list for promotion to lieutenant colonel. Two years early, yet. If anyone deserves to make LC below the zone, you do, Donovan."

"Thanks."

The compliment rekindled the fleeting glow Jack had enjoyed a few weeks ago when the Old Man had informed him he'd made the list. Right before he threatened to bust Jack's balls if he didn't get Cleo on a leash.

The general's instructions on *this* op had been even more explicit. Heads as well as balls would go on the chopping block if former special agent North caused a permanent rift in relations between the United States and its staunchest ally. Jack had damned well better…

The ping of Morrison's cell phone cut into his thoughts. The OSI detachment commander answered, listened for a moment, then winged a frown at his passenger.

"We'll be right there."

Morrison flipped the phone shut, his freckled face grim. "That was the Mildenhall Command Center. A call just came in for me from the local police. Cleo North has been shot."

Jack's terror was instant, icy and all-consuming. Like a giant fist, it gripped his heart and squeezed.

"How bad?"

"She took a bullet to the head." Morrison twisted the wheel. Tires screeching, he jerked his vehicle in a one-eighty. "She's at the Lakenheath Medical Center. They're working on her now."

Jack didn't utter a word during the breakneck drive to the satellite base some five miles from Mildenhall. He was out of the car before it stopped rolling at the entrance to the emergency room. Vaulting through the doors, he sprinted to the desk and flashed his gold shield at the receptionist.

"Cleo North. GSW to the head."

"Yes, sir. She's in examining room two. But you'll have to wait. The physicians haven't… Sir! Wait!"

Ignoring the protests, Jack slammed through a set of swinging doors and raced down a hall bordered on one side by curtained cubicles. The first three were empty. The curtains were partially drawn on the fourth.

He tugged it aside, felt his insides freeze. Cleo lay still and lifeless on a gurney. Blood coated one side of her face and drenched what he could see of her linen blazer.

Jack's hand fisted on the curtain, almost yanking the ball bearings out of the track. Their tinny rattle popped Cleo's eyes open.

"'Bout time you got here, Donovan."

He was so frozen he didn't react, *couldn't* react.

"I kept telling the docs I was good to go," she said in disgust, "but they wouldn't release me until you showed. Took you long enough," she grumbled, levering upright.

He saw the bald patch then. Three square inches shaved clean, with an inch-long wound in the center puckered together under a clear plastic strip.

"Jesus, Cleo."

"It's just a scratch. Honestly. The bullet barely broke the skin. They didn't even have to put in stitches."

She swung her feet over the side of the gurney.

"The locals insisted on bringing me here, although I told them I wasn't military. Evidently the E.R. here at RAF Lakenheath has some kind of joint-use agreement with the civilian communities in the area."

When she started to hop off, Jack unfroze enough to push forward and wrap a restraining hand around her arm.

"What happened?"

"A slimy little shit who used his fists on Yasmin Indali got off a shot before I dropped him." Thoroughly disgusted, she shook her head. "I can't believe I miscalculated the angle of my attack so badly."

Jack dragged in a long breath. Terror still churned in his bowels, but anger was beginning to work its way through the fear.

"When you left Mildenhall, you were going to check into our hotel and wait until I finished with the wing commander. How the hell did you hook up with Ms. Indali?"

"I got tired of waiting and took a walk."

The reply stoked his anger. The careless shrug that accompanied it locked his jaws. Cleo didn't seem to notice.

"Let's get out of here. I'll tell you all about it on the drive back to our hotel."

Bridling his temper, he trailed her down to the central nurses' station, where she corralled the medical coordinator and signed the appropriate forms. Major Morrison met them on the way out. His gaze zeroed in on Cleo's bandaged bald patch as he provided a quick update.

"I just got a call from Chief Inspector Berry, head of the West Suffolk Constabulary. Evidently you and Ms. Indali's father took down two hired enforcers for an illegal gambling syndicate Berry's been after for some time. Indali beat one of them to a bloody pulp. The other is currently spilling his guts in return for a promise to serve time at some institution other than Dartmoor. Berry's ecstatic. He says he has enough now to bust the entire syndicate."

"Glad I could be of service," Cleo replied with a

grin. "Did the inspector establish any link between those two slime-buckets and Captain Caswell's murder?"

"Not yet. They both claim they had nothing to do with it and there's no evidence tying them to the shooting."

When they exited the hospital, Jack blinked in surprise at the inky darkness. He couldn't remember if dusk had turned to night before the frantic drive to the hospital. Hell, he couldn't remember anything about that drive except the terror that had coiled in his gut.

The last remaining tentacles of fear had pretty well melted by the time Morrison pulled up to the Thistle Inn. Jack's anger was still simmering, though. He had to put it on hold again when they entered the lobby and found Yasmin's father waiting for them.

His face grim beneath his turban, Indali rose to greet Cleo. "I rang the hospital. The nursing matron said they'd released you, so I came here."

He surveyed her bloodstained clothes and curled his bruised, skinned knuckles into fists.

"You saved my daughter's life. You have my most profound gratitude, Ms. North. I'm sorry you were injured in the act."

"I'll bet this little scratch doesn't hurt me as much as those knuckles do you."

"I take great pleasure in the pain. Again, I thank you, Ms. North. Yasmin is most precious to me."

Precious enough to murder the captain who dishonored her? Cleo didn't think so. Not after tonight.

"Here is my card," the man said. "If I can ever be of service to you, please ring me at once."

"I will."

"And you are welcome at the Hare and Hound anytime, you and your friends. As my guest."

"Thanks."

"We should take him up on that offer," Cleo murmured as the pub owner bowed and departed. "You should have seen the chicken curry pie at his pub. It was topped by a pastry puffed a good three or four inches high."

Jack's jaw torqued again. The woman had just taken a bullet to the head and all she could think about was food.

"Did you check in here at the inn before you took off for the Hare and Hound?"

His curt tone drew a quick glance. "Yes, I did. We're on the second floor. I left the key at the desk."

Spinning on one heel, he stalked to the desk and retrieved the key from the receptionist. When he returned, he put a hand in the small of Cleo's back.

"Upstairs."

"Why don't we eat something before we go up?"

"Later."

The prod was anything but gentle, the tone brusque. Cleo's brows snapped together. She threw a glance at the dining room and looked ready to dig in her heels.

"We need to talk," Jack bit out. "Now."

They took the stairs without looking at each other. Entered the room in silence. Turned and squared off.

"All right, Donovan. What are you so pissed about?"

"You couldn't wait one hour? One fucking hour?"

She opened her mouth, clamped it shut again and did an obvious mental ten-count.

"You were off doing your thing with the wing commander. I couldn't see any point in sitting around here."

Her tone tried for calm and reasonable. Jack was feeling anything but.

"So you went in without a backup or a clear assessment of the situation and got yourself shot in the process. Jesus Christ, North, did you leave your smarts back in Dallas? We're supposed to be working this as a team."

"First," she said icily, "getting shot is an occupational hazard in our line of work. Second…"

"There is no second," he snarled. "You're working an air force investigation. We're paying your fees, we're calling the shots."

Anger leaped into her face, but she made an effort

to control the situation. "Calm down, Donovan. We can't discuss this if you're all hyped up."

Her attempt to handle him only fueled Jack's fury. He knew he was taking those moments of sheer terror out on her. But he also knew he had to press the point or there'd be no holding her back.

"There's nothing to discuss. This is an air force op, North. You play this by the rules, or you don't play it at all."

A furious hiss split the air. Blood rushed to her face. Even the shaved patch of scalp turned red. Without another word, she shoved past him and stalked into the bedroom. A quick shrug got her out of the bloodstained linen blazer. Wadding it into a ball, she tossed it in the wastebasket, scooped up her carryall and thumped it on the bed.

Jack observed the activities from the door, his teeth clenched. "Don't be stupid. You just took a bullet. If you're going to walk on this op, wait until tomorrow."

"No way. I'm out of here. I don't need you *or* the air force *or* your bullshit about us being a team."

"It's not bullshit, dammit. We have to work together."

"Come off it, Donovan!" Scooping her makeup kit off the dresser, she threw it into the bag. "Did you think I didn't note your sudden interest when Morrison dropped Yasmin Indali's Muslim-sounding name?"

Christ! He should have known she'd pick up on

the vibes. Jack tried to negotiate his way through that minefield.

"You know there are certain classified matters I can't discuss with you."

"I understand that. I accept that." She slam-dunked a pair of folded jeans on top of the makeup kit. "What I'm having a hard time with is that you don't seem to feel you can discuss *anything* important with me, classified or un—"

"Like what?"

"Like your ex-wife, for starters."

Jack went still. He could almost feel the old wounds start to bleed.

"You know about Kate." He hated the stiffness in his voice but couldn't keep it out. "The problems she has."

"I also know your guilt over her condition is rip-ping you apart." Her holstered Glock hit the jeans. "Why don't you get help?"

"I did. We both did. Several times."

Whirling, she rounded on him. "Then talk to me! Tell me how I…"

She stopped, her breath hitching. The red washed from her face and left it a sick white.

"Oh, hell."

"What?" Alarm shattered Jack's rage. "Cleo, what's the matter?"

"I turned around too fast. It made me…a little dizzy."

A little dizzy, hell! His heart thumped as her eyes

went glassy. Cursing, he leaped forward and caught her as she started to topple.

"Just a scratch, huh? Didn't even need stitches. You think you're so damned tough."

"Shut up, for God's sake!" She put up a shaking hand and fingered the plastic bandage. "I don't need you bellowing in my ear at the moment."

He forced the near panic out of his voice. "You sure it's just a scalp wound?"

"Yes."

"Did the docs give you any painkillers?"

Nodding, she gestured toward her purse. Jack dug out a flat pack, tore the plastic shield and popped two capsules into his palm. Retrieving a bottle of water from the minifridge, he thrust it and the pills at her.

"Here."

She downed the capsules without argument. That told him almost as much as the gray cast to her face.

"Now, lie back and get some rest. We'll finish this discussion later."

She gave up the fight and sank back on the pillows. Jack retreated to a chair and kept a close watch until the color returned to her face and her breathing steadied. The knots in his neck muscles didn't relax, though, until she gave a snorting huff, rolled over and buried her face in the pillow.

Uncoiling his limbs, Jack dragged the spread over

her. He knew from experience Cleo woke up surly at the best of times. If her head still hurt when she came awake later, the woman would have all the warmth and charm of a she-wolf poked with a sharp stick. Deciding he needed fortification before that happened, he went into the other room to raid the peanuts from the minibar.

He discovered several hours later that he'd underestimated the potential for disaster by exponential degrees. Cleo not only came awake snarly, she sprang out of bed primed for murder.

Much of that was his fault. *He* was the one who gave in to hunger pangs and called room service. *He'd* ordered full dinners for two, knowing how much Cleo could pack away. *He'd* shushed the waiter when the man rolled in the loaded cart. Tipping him generously, Jack said he'd handle the setup himself.

Unfortunately, *he* also forgot about the thick rug laid over the creaking floorboards. The damned cart snagged on the edge of the rug, tilted and sent half its load to the floor.

The plate covers landed with a clatter. China and glass shattered. Jack lunged forward to catch the coffeepot before it went over and ended up hitting the floor with the rest of the contents of the cart.

"Goddammit!"

The crash jolted Cleo straight up in bed. She heard

the muffled shout, tried to process its source, but her brain felt as though it was wrapped in gauzy cotton. Reacting on pure instinct, she rolled out of bed and looked about wildly for a weapon.

Her Glock. Where the hell was her Glock?

She couldn't remember where she'd put it, couldn't seem to shake the haze from her head. Cursing, she scrambled for her purse.

The Glock wasn't in it, and a heavy thump in the other room had her clawing through the contents in search of another weapon, any weapon. Her keys. The sharp tips could gouge and rake with vicious results.

She had the tips speared through her fingers like spikes and was running for the bedroom door when it suddenly opened. Still in a haze from sleep and the painkillers, Cleo saw only a dark silhouette framed in the doorway.

Dropping into a crouch, she brought her hand up. She didn't realize a flat case dangled from the key, didn't know she'd squeezed its center until it gave a small whir.

"What the hell…?"

The figure in the doorway threw up an arm and staggered back.

Jack! That was Jack!

She sprang up and started toward the doorway. Two steps later, she came to a dead halt.

She saw Jack's lips draw back in a snarl, heard him

spit out a curse. All she could do was stand there, blinking in confusion. Somehow, some way, the entire upper half of Donovan's face had disappeared.

5

"Doreen calls it a moon-spinner."

Flicking away a tuft of carpet fuzz, Cleo bit into the remains of a Yorkshire pudding. The once puffy pastry was flat as a tortilla. What wouldn't be after taking a direct hit from a hundred and eighty pounds of Donovan?

"Doreen got the idea from the Soldiers' Support Lab at Natick. Supposedly, they're experimenting with light-refracting fibers for use in camouflage gear."

Scowling, Jack rubbed his forehead. "That woman's a menace."

Cleo took another bite of her Yorkshire tortilla and eyed the red bands circling his forehead. They complemented the bruise that had blossomed on his left temple, where the constricting filaments had burst a couple of small capillaries before Cleo managed to saw through the strands.

Tough. After his play-it-my-way tirade earlier, he deserved a few bruises.

Legs crossed under her, she hunched forward and picked through the few pieces of unbroken crockery for another edible morsel. A gooey pink-and-white blob snared her attention.

"What's this?"

Jack studied the mess for a moment. "I'm guessing it used to be strawberry trifle."

Hooking two fingers, she scooped up a taste. "God, that's good!"

She dug in again, savoring the mushy mix of sponge cake, strawberry puree, heavy whipping cream, Amaretto and several other ingredients she couldn't identify.

"We do have spoons, you know."

"You eat your way, Donovan, and I'll eat mine."

The smart-ass retort brought their fierce and as-yet unfinished argument instantly to mind.

Jack lost his look of sardonic amusement. Cleo lost her taste for trifle. Swiping her fingers on one of the napkins she'd salvaged from the mess, she slumped back against the armchair behind her.

"We need to settle things between us. I can't work with you if you continue to feed me only what you think I need to know."

"Can't or won't?"

"Take your pick."

His eyes locked with hers. She could read him like

a PalmPilot now. Her muscles tightened as she anticipated his response. Sure enough, By-the-Book Donovan shrugged.

"Then we don't work together."

"That's what I figured you'd say." Dusting her hands, she got her feet under her and started up. "Well, it's been fun, big guy. I'll be out of here first thing in the—"

"Unless you update your Air Force Form 2583," he cut in. "You need to request a National Security Agency check and have your government security clearances reinstated."

She wasn't about to admit she'd been thinking along the same lines. She wouldn't give him such an easy win.

"You know how I hate filling out forms. My damned 2583 ran to fourteen pages the last time I updated it."

"That's what happens when you're born abroad and spend most of your life jaunting around the world. You rack up a long string of addresses that require verification, associates who need screening, foreign contacts who have to—"

"I know the drill, Donovan. I just don't like doing it."

"It needs doing." He leaned forward, his blue eyes intent. "If you want us to be a team."

"That's not all that needs doing."

He got the message. She could see him fighting to stay in there, to keep the doors from slamming.

"I've been thinking about what you said. I admit I have a tendency to pull back whenever Kate's name comes up."

"You don't just pull back. You shut down. Totally and completely." She gestured to the flat case she'd tossed on the coffee table. "It's like you wrap yourself in Doreen's magic threads and disappear."

"I know, I know." He scrubbed a hand over his jaw. "I guess I don't want to drag anyone else into the viper pit with me."

That hurt. More than Cleo had imagined it could.

"Funny, I didn't think I was just 'anyone.'"

His hand dropped. "I didn't mean it like that."

"No? Then maybe you'd better explain just what you did mean."

He smiled then, obviously trying to ease the tension. "If you weren't sporting a bald patch on your head, I'd show you. We always communicate better when we're naked, North."

"Yeah," she replied slowly. "We do."

Jack wasn't the only one who'd done some thinking. Cleo let out a long breath. This wasn't going to be easy. She just hoped it was right.

"I think maybe we should hold off on sex for a while."

"Do you?" His smile stayed in place. More or less. "Why?"

"Think about it, Jack. We know that works for us."

"Yeah, it does. Pretty damned well, too."

"But we can't rely on *naked* and *sweaty* as the solutions to every problem. We have to come up for air sometime."

"Why not worry about that if and when it happens?"

Good question. She was still fumbling for an answer when Donovan leaned across the mess and caught her chin in his hand.

"You scared the crap out of me when I saw you on that gurney tonight, North."

"Yeah. So?"

"So I knew then it was more than sex between us, Cleopatra. You're in my head. In every part of me."

Her eyes narrowed. "Are you just saying that to get laid?"

"Is it working?"

"No. Yes. A little."

Smiling, he made a slow pass along her jaw with his thumb. "I'm not real good at this, Cleo. God knows I made a mess of things with Kate. But I'm willing to give it a shot if you are."

She wanted it spelled out. "Give what a shot?"

"Us. You and me."

"Let me get this straight. You're willing to go without sex for as long as it takes to figure out just what the heck we have going for us?"

"Those are your conditions, not mine."

She was still mulling things over when someone rapped on the door.

"Oh, jeez. If that's room service, they're *not* going to be happy about this mess."

Jack didn't appear worried about room service, but his training and instincts went too deep to respond to any late-night knock on the door without exercising basic precautions. Approaching the door from an angle, he ignored the peephole. No agent worth his salt would block the pinprick of light at the hole and present such a prime target to someone sighting a gun on it.

"Yes?"

"It's Paul Morrison."

With a surprised glance at his watch, Jack twisted the locks. "What's up?"

"I got called out on another case and… Good God! What the hell happened to your face?"

"I made the mistake of disturbing a certain former OSI agent's slumber," Jack drawled.

His eyes widening, Morrison shot Cleo a startled look. When he took in the broken crockery and spilled dishes, his lips rounded in a silent whistle.

"Whoa! Remind me not to get crosswise of you."

She pushed to her feet, all too well aware that Donovan had just added another chapter to her ridiculously exaggerated reputation among the OSI community.

"What's going on?"

"The West Suffolk constabulary ran the calls made on Yasmin Indali's mobile phone, as you requested, and I picked up the printout. I'd planned on dropping a copy off at the front desk for you, but they told me you'd ordered room service a little while ago so I brought it up."

"Any interesting calls on the list?"

"Several. We won't know if Ms. Indali made them until we talk to her tomorrow, of course, but they have Caswell's stamp all over them."

Sliding the computer-generated list out of its envelope, he stabbed a finger at one of the numbers circled in red.

"This one's to an off-base wine importer known to rebottle products to avoid stiff import taxes. These are to deep-water salvage and dive-boat operators. And here's one to Ms. Talbot, made just two days before Caswell was shot."

"Interesting," Jack said. "We'll check them out tomorrow, after we view the crime scene and finish the interviews you've got lined up for us on base."

The walk-through of Caswell's flat provided insights into his taste in music, wine and nudie magazines, but no clues as to who might have offed him. The interviews with the two military men known to have a grudge against Caswell, on the other hand, opened several new leads.

With her hair parted on the opposite side and combed over to hide her patch of bare scalp, Cleo played spectator while Jack conducted the interviews. The airman who'd purchased a used car from Caswell didn't have any details to add to his previous statement. The officer who'd lost a bundle to the captain in a poker game proved more fertile.

Lieutenant Colonel Sikes served as director of operations for one of the squadrons assigned to the 100th Air Refueling Wing. His flight suit molded a tight, lean body. His face was tanned above the checkered scarf tucked into the green Nomex bag.

He sat silent while Jack ran through the ritual of identifying the persons present and the purpose of the interview. Once the preliminaries were completed, he preempted any questions with a blunt statement.

"Yes, I knew gambling with a junior officer violated Article 134 of the Uniformed Code of Military Justice. And yes, some of our games ran to big-dollar pots. I offer no excuse for my conduct."

The colonel's curt, almost belligerent attitude didn't surprise Cleo. She knew just enough about the tanker world to understand they were a breed apart. They had to be, to strap themselves into the cockpit of a flying gas tank containing upward of two hundred thousand pounds of highly flammable jet fuel. It took good hands and iron nerves to keep their giant KC-135s or KC-10s steady while some fighter jock nuzzled up and, as one of the more polite expressions went, sucked at the hind tit.

"Talk to me about Caswell," Jack said. "Tell me

about the man, not the officer perpetually on the lookout for a quick buck."

"You can't separate the two. Caswell could be a real sonuvabitch if you owed him money. But I've also seen him stuff his entire winnings into an envelope and pass it to a boom operator whose daughter needed braces. It took me a while, but I finally figured out Doug enjoyed the game more than the outcome."

"How about his personal life?"

"He operated in the same mode. He chased after that girl in town, Yasmin something…"

"Indali."

"Right, Yasmin Indali. Christ, he was hot for her. Mostly, I suspect, because her father was so protective. Doug said the old man practically locked her up at night. He figured he'd have to hack his way through a chastity belt before he finally bagged her."

Cleo was feeling a distinct lack of sympathy for the murdered captain. It dipped another notch when Sikes finished his recital.

"Once Doug had finessed her into bed, he lost interest and dumped her. The bastard bragged to the whole squadron about scoring a kill."

"Did Caswell also brag about how he cleaned out your bank account?" Jack slipped in.

The colonel's shoulders went stiff again. "The word got around."

"So that's when you confronted him and told him to shut his mouth or you'd shut it for him."

"Yes."

Sikes bit out the single syllable. Jack let it hang there until the colonel chopped a hand through the air.

"My wife knows I play occasionally but has no idea of the stakes. I didn't want it to get back to her that I'd lost the equivalent of our son's college tuition. So yes, I told Caswell to shut his friggin' mouth. And no, I didn't shut it for him. Someone else took care of that."

He hesitated, obviously reluctant to dig himself in any deeper. Again Jack waited.

He was good at that, Cleo thought. She tended to get impatient and pull statements from witnesses. Donovan let silence work for him.

"Caswell offered me a way out of the hole," Sikes related after a moment. "Said he was working some scheme that could make us both rich. All I had to do was go with him and interview a couple of boat captains. He knew I was dive-qualified, figured I would understand the lingo and know whether or not they were giving him the straight skinny on what it would cost to search for some wreck."

Jack didn't so much as flick an eyelash, but Cleo could sense his sudden interest. Her own antennae had snapped straight up, too.

Several of the calls made on Yasmin's phone had been to salvage-and-dive operations, she recalled. And Caswell had been killed with a pistol lost over the English Channel more than sixty years ago.

Had the captain recovered the Colt .45 from the murky waters, only to have it used against him? The irony of the possibility intrigued Cleo.

"Did you accompany Caswell when he went to talk to these boat captains?" Jack asked.

"No. We were both flying heavy schedules. We were never down long enough at the same time to make it over to the coast."

"And he didn't tell you the specifics of this scheme or what he wanted to salvage?"

"No, but…"

Again the colonel hesitated.

"Doug did mention that he'd talked to the base historian. I don't know if it was in conjunction with this project or some other wild scheme, but I got the feeling the two were somehow connected."

"We'll check it out."

"The base historian?"

Cleo, Jack and Paul Morrison exchanged wry glances. Most cases worked by the OSI took unexpected twists and turns. This one was proving no exception.

"I didn't even know we *had* a historian here at Mildenhall," Morrison admitted, reaching for the phone. "I'll get my secretary to track him or her down."

While he relayed the request, Jack pulled the computer printout from his briefcase and took another look at the calls made from Yasmin's cell phone. Four of the numbers had been identified as salvage-or-wreck diving operations. Cleo leaned over his shoulder and recited the locations.

"Dover, Folkestone, Portsmouth, Weymouth."

Their glances zinged to the map of Great Britain prominently displayed on the wall behind Morrison's desk. All four were port cities.

"The call to Dover lasted longer than the others," Cleo commented, noting its strategic location directly across from the French port of Calais. "Almost twenty minutes."

"Want us to make the contact?" Jack asked when Morrison returned to his office.

"Sure, why not? The West Suffolk police are so grateful for the break on the gambling and extortion ring, I'm sure they won't mind if you bring them a new lead on the Caswell murder. Neither will I, for that matter."

Jack pulled out his cell phone and centered it on Morrison's desk. It was one of those new clear-streaming video jobbies, with e-mail capability and a direct satellite uplink to secure channels. The last time Cleo had been with Jack when he placed a call, General Barnes's face had suddenly materialized on the two square inches of screen and just about scared the crap out of her.

Evidently the person on the other end of the call didn't possess the same state-of-the art technology, since the screen remained blank. But his voice came through the speaker, lilting and pitched high to be heard above what sounded like a whistle of wind.

"Mulholland Wreck and Reef Dives."

"This is Special Agent Jack Donovan. I'm with the USAF Office of Special Investigations."

"Yes?"

"I'm following up on a call made to this number two weeks ago, at 10:17 a.m. on Thursday, April 22. We think the call might have made by an American by the name of Douglas Caswell."

"Seems I recall the captain mentioning a call from some Yank."

"The captain?"

"Captain Mulholland. Master of the *Argos II*."

"Is he available?"

"Not at the moment. But he'll be surfacing any minute. The seas are getting heavy."

"Will you have him contact me? My number is—"

"Jay-sus!"

They heard a roar, like a freight train charging through a tunnel.

"I can't talk now!"

The connection went dead.

"Well," Cleo said into the small silence that followed, "that was interesting."

"Very," Jack agreed. His gaze went to the wall map again. "What do you say we take a drive down to Dover after we talk to this base historian?"

He was all set to tuck the videophone into his pocket when it started to ping. Jack hit Receive, and this time the screen filled with Johanna Marston's worried face.

"I just heard about Cleo. Is she all right?"

"She's fine. She's right here, in fact."

Jack stepped aside to allow Cleo access to the tiny camera built into the phone. With a nod and a wave, she assured Johanna she was still in one piece.

"I'm relieved to hear it. I got quite a start when word came through you'd been shot."

There was a delicate pause while neither woman commented on the fact that the MI6 agent was keeping apprised of her guests' activities.

"I spoke to Chief Inspector Berry of the West Suffolk constabulary just now," Johanna continued. "He indicates you've turned up an interesting new lead in the Caswell case. He mentioned some calls to salvage captains."

"That's right."

"I'm looking at the list of calls now."

Somehow, Cleo wasn't surprised Marston had already obtained a copy of the list and made the link between a transport lost over the English Channel and an opportunistic captain's calls to salvage operators.

"We were just talking about them," Jack conceded, edging back into the camera's angle. "The one to Dover looks interesting."

"Yes, I see it lasted quite a bit longer than the others. Shall I assist you with the follow-up? I'm motoring down to my country house in Kent later this afternoon. It's a bit out of the way, but I could pop over to the coast and speak with the person Captain Caswell rang."

Cleo and Jack exchanged glances. They both knew the polite query masked an interest in the case the British intelligence agent had yet to share.

"Tell you what," he said. "You follow up on those calls. Cleo and I will work the other leads that have opened up here."

"What are they, if I might ask?"

"We'll tell you about them when we get together to compare notes."

Marston conceded the game of you-show-me-yours-and-I'll-show-you-mine with a smile.

"Very well. Why don't you join me in Kent this weekend and we'll do that? My house is in the village of Bethersden, about eight kilometers from Ashford."

Jack's glance zinged to the map again. "Kent, Ashford, Bethersden. Got it. We'll let you know if we can make it."

6

Johanna dispensed with the Rolls for the drive to the country. Instead, she had McDowell bring round the Morgan and load her suitcase in the boot. With her case stowed, the chauffeur ran a loving hand over the roadster's curved fender wings.

"She looks as good as if Sir Bartholomew had just put his polishing cloth away."

"Yes, she does."

With bittersweet memories pulling at her, Johanna tied a scarf over her hair and settled behind the wheel of the 1961 convertible. Barty had restored the sports car with his own hands, sweating over every bolt, every spoke on the wire wheels. Normally Johanna couldn't bear to take it out and sully the burgundy finish he'd always kept polished to a mirror shine.

Today, though, she intended to wrap her hands

around the leather-covered wheel, put her foot to the floorboards and let the wind blow away the edginess that gripped her.

Much of it had to do with this bloody Caswell case. It was like some dark thing at the bottom of a pond, putting out tentacles that sucked at the unwary. Johanna was swimming through the murky water blind. As were the two Americans.

And there was the other source of her restlessness. Cleo and Jack. They were so mad for each other, so very right for each other, although neither seemed to have recognized yet just how well they fit.

Swallowing a sigh, Johanna bid goodbye to McDowell and keyed the Morgan's ignition. The engine turned over with the well-mannered growl that had always elicited an answering hum from Barty. She ached to get the car on an open road and release its power, but she had one stop to make first.

"Lady Marston." The nurse who let her into the closed ward beamed at her. "How good to see you again."

"And you, Mrs. Forrester."

"Have you come for another visit with Mr. Potts?"

"Yes, I have. How is he today?"

"Much the same, I'm afraid. His daughter was by earlier. He didn't recognize her, poor thing."

Johanna's heart sank, but she had to give it another go. "I'll just have a chat with him, shall I?"

"Yes, of course. He's in his room. Shall I brew up a spot of tea?"

"I shouldn't want to put you to any trouble."

"It's no trouble at all. The kettle's already on."

Ushering Johanna down the hall, the nurse broadcast her arrival to the small, wizened figure in a hand-knit sweater that appeared five sizes too large for him.

"Mr. Potts, sir! Have a look at who's come to visit."

With an effort that seemed almost too much for his thin neck, Phillip Potts lifted his head. His clouded blue eyes showed not the faintest flicker of recognition.

"It's Lady Marston," the nurse said with bracing cheerfulness. "You mind your manners, now, while I fetch some tea and biscuits."

Johanna crossed the room and sat on the edge of the neatly made bed. "Hello, Phillip. It's good to see you again. We had a nice chat a few days ago, if you'll recall."

His forehead furrowed while he searched what had once been one of the most brilliant minds in the Special Operations Executive.

A forerunner to the intelligence service Johanna now operated in, SOE had been established in 1940 and disbanded shortly after the war. During its brief years of operation, the unit had conceived and executed some of the most daring intelligence-gathering operations ever mounted. Phillip Potts had been the architect of one of those operations.

With a quick glance at the empty hall, Johanna

lowered her voice. "We talked about the war. Do you remember?"

The paper-thin lips moved, but she couldn't understand the unintelligible mumble.

"You were SOE," she reminded him softly. "Grenadier Sergeant Clive Gordon was one of your operatives."

MI6 had come by that bit of information almost by accident. Initial puzzlement over the World War II-era bullets used to kill Captain Caswell had led the Suffolk investigators to firing test records buried deep in the War Ministry's archives. A day and a night of digging had linked one of those tests to a weapon issued to Grenadier Sergeant Clive Gordon.

As soon as the name had been entered into the computers, a red flag popped up at a special office in MI6. That's when Johanna's superiors had sent her to interview this unbearably frail ninety-two-year-old civil servant.

She edged closer, until they were almost knee to knee. "Do you recall Sergeant Gordon? His posting records say he went into action with the First Kent Grenadiers, but in fact he was detached from his unit in 1942 and assigned to your special cadre at Wolverhampton. Round Peg, it was called."

Something flickered in the cloudy eyes. Mindful of his fragility, she took both his hands in hers.

"That was the code name for your cadre. Round Peg. You were charged with fitting those pegs in square holes. Tell me how you did it, and what happened to…"

He mumbled again. She thought she detected "top secret" before he pulled free of her hold. Praying she hadn't lost him, Johanna dug in her pocket for her credentials.

"I'm MI6. You can trust me."

"MI6."

The confusion cleared, and for a moment the keen mind that had once directed a stable of covert operatives looked through the foggy eyes.

"Tell me about Grenadier Sergeant Gordon," Johanna urged. "The last time I was here, I reminded you he was aboard a troop transport that went down in the Channel. Can you tell me why he was on that aircraft? Where was he—"

"Here we are!"

The nursing matron bustled in with a tray holding two cups and a china pot nestled in a crocheted tea cozy. Johanna smothered a curse as the light in Phillip Potts's eyes dimmed, then died completely.

The nurse left after depositing the tray, but the damage was done. Try as she might, Johanna couldn't coax another sound through the papery lips.

For a good part of the drive to Dover, Johanna puzzled over the link between a dead American pilot and a weapon issued to a sergeant lost over the Channel more than sixty years ago.

As she neared the coast, though, she forced her thoughts from a war fought before she was born to one whose aftermath was still being felt. The individual she now intended to interview had been serving in the Royal Navy as a clearance diver during the Iraq War when one of the mines he was clearing had detonated.

Her eyes on the chalky hills and green dales bordering the motorway, Johanna reviewed the file she'd pulled up on Petty Officer Sean Mulholland. A graduate and one-time instructor at the Defence Diving School at Horsea Island, Portsmouth, he'd served in the Royal Navy for more than nineteen years. His active military career had ended in the clear aqua waters off Iraq, but the explosion hadn't kept the man out of the water permanently.

After extensive surgeries and long months of recovery and rehabilitation, Mulholland had purchased his own boat and begun diving again. Incredibly, he'd also regained his dive status in the Royal Navy Reserves, where he still held rank.

The man now owned a charter service that catered to the increasingly popular sport of wreck diving. A quite profitable charter service, if the figures Johanna had obtained from the Ministry of Commerce were to be believed.

The photo she'd pulled from Mulholland's service records was fresh in her mind as she exited the motorway and began a winding descent to Dover.

In full dress uniform, Petty Officer Mulholland presented a stern, unsmiling portrait.

That image stayed with her while she navigated past the white cliffs famous in song and film to a marina protected by long stone quays. It was utterly and irrevocably shattered when Johanna picked her way down a floating dock to slip number twelve and called out to the individual kneeling beside an inflatable raft.

"Would you tell me where I might find Sean Mulholland?"

Pivoting, the man answered in a whisky-rough growl. "You've found him."

Johanna hid her surprise behind a cool smile. With his red-rimmed eyes, misshapen nose and shaggy hair, Mulholland looked more like a recent prison parolee than a spit-and-polish former petty officer.

"I'm Johanna Marston. I rang earlier and spoke to your mate. He said you'd be available to chat with me."

When Mulholland swiped his hands on a rag and rose, she couldn't fail to note the tattooed anchor showing beneath the rolled-up sleeve of his black T-shirt.

She also noted how the sweat-stained cotton stretched over an extraordinarily well-muscled chest. Surprised and somewhat annoyed by an unexpected flutter deep in her belly, Johanna met his cool stare.

"What can I do for you, Lady Marston?"

She'd purposely refrained from using her title when she spoke to his mate. Interesting that Mulholland had run a check on her, just as she had him.

The society bits and Friends of the Royal Opera Company profile he'd no doubt accessed wouldn't have given him a clue as to her official status, though. Sliding the flat leather case containing her credentials from her pocket, Johanna flipped it open.

"I'm with the Secret Intelligence Service. I should like to query you about a call you received from Captain Douglas Caswell on Thursday, April 22."

Mulholland's gaze narrowed on her shield, then made a deliberate journey from her hands to the silk scarf knotted around her throat to her face. Johanna endured the unfamiliar and quite irritating sensation of being stripped naked right there on the dock.

Snapping the case shut, she tucked it in her pocket. "Do you recall your phone conversation with Captain Caswell?"

"I didn't, until someone contacted my mate earlier this morning and inquired about him."

"That was United States Air Force special agent Jack Donovan. We're acting in tandem on this case."

Mulholland worked the rag through his hands again. He took his time about it, Johanna thought, as she noticed for the first time the scars webbing his hamlike fists.

"What case?" he asked at length.

"Captain Caswell was murdered Monday past."

"Was he now?" Eyes hooded, Mulholland tucked the rag in his back pocket. "Why is MI6 working a murder? I'd have thought that would fall under the jurisdiction of the local constabulary."

"It does. Will you tell me the purpose of the captain's call, please?"

His shoulders rolled in a shrug. "He wanted to know what it would cost to charter the *Argos II*."

"He wanted to dive on a wreck?"

"He wanted me to locate it first, then dive on it."

"What type of wreck was he looking for?"

"A World War II-era Dakota transport that was lost over the English Channel."

Johanna didn't so much as blink, but her pulse began to race. "Indeed? Did you give him a quote for this charter?"

"No, I didn't."

"Why not?"

His mouth drew down in a sardonic curve. "Do you have any idea how many planes went down during the war?"

"As a matter of fact, I do. The Allies lost 984 aircraft prior to D-day, Germany almost twice that number. That equated to roughly 10.3 losses per one thousand sorties flown."

"You've done your homework, Lady Marston."

"Yes, I have. I must confess, though, I couldn't pin down the precise number of aircraft lost over the Channel."

"Statisticians will give you different answers to that, but they all agree it's well into the hundreds. When you add ships sunk, wrecks from previous wars and losses to storms, collisions and other accidents, you have a veritable scrap heap under those murky waters. As I told the Yank, it would be impossible to find one downed aircraft without the approximate coordinates of where it went in."

"What was his response to that?"

"He said he'd try to fix a search area and get back to me."

A breeze off the sea caught the ends of Johanna's scarf, fluttering them about her face. Impatiently, she brushed them aside. "Did Captain Caswell tell you *why* he wanted to find that particular aircraft?"

"No, he didn't."

Hiding her disappointment, she dug out her card case. "Here's my card. Give me a ring, will you, if anyone else should contact you regarding a search for a missing Dakota?"

Nodding, Sean took the card and slid his thumb over the discreet, raised embossing. Johanna Marston was much like her bit of cardboard, he thought as she made her way back along the quay. Elegant. Sleek. With far more to her than what appeared on the surface.

What did meet the eye was first class, though. Sean allowed himself the pleasure of watching her until she slid behind the wheel of a classic Morgan.

Tucking her card in his pocket, he hunkered down beside the rubber Gemini boat he'd been patching when she'd arrived. With the tang of the polyurethane adhesive sharp in his nostrils, he mulled over SIS's interest in the murdered Yank.

Not for the first time, Sean wondered why the American had wanted to dive on a downed World War II aircraft. The U.K. had passed the Protection of Military Remains Act in 1986 to prevent the abuse of the final resting place of those who died in service to their country. The law protected all ships sunk and aircraft lost in U.K. waters since 1914, including enemy planes and vessels. It was legal to dive on them, but a serious offense to enter them or disturb them in any way. It was even more serious to remove artifacts without specific written permission from the Ministry of Defense.

Sean wasn't about to risk a fine or a criminal charge by violating the law. More to the point, with nineteen years of active military service under his belt, he flatly refused to dishonor the underwater graves of fellow seamen, soldiers or airmen—an issue he made clear to all prospective charters. Caswell had been no exception.

The Yank had mouthed the appropriate responses. He only wanted to locate the wreck, pinpoint its location, take a few pictures. For his uncle, a former Army Air Corps aviator who'd once piloted that exact aircraft.

Sean hadn't believed a word of it. The bloke was too glib, too quick with his explanation. And no one forked over the quid it would take to mount this kind of an operation just to send old Uncle Joe a few pictures.

Now Caswell was dead, murdered according to the sumptuous Lady Marston. His brow furrowed, Sean centered the patch over the tear.

7

After calling ahead to set up an appointment, Cleo and Jack made a visit to the 100th Air Refueling Wing historian. The weather had turned cold and damp, more in keeping with Cleo's memories of an English spring. Relieved now that she'd packed the red wool blazer, she turned the collar up and hunched her shoulders for the short dash to the building that housed the historian's office.

Madeline Ridgeway was nothing like Cleo's image of a historian. A vivacious blonde with a wealth of knowledge about the base and local area, she was eager to share it with her unexpected visitors and disappointed when Jack explained the purpose of their visit.

"I'm sorry, Special Agent Donovan. I can't help you. I've never had any contact with Captain Caswell. I read about his murder in the papers, though. Scary to think that kind of thing can happen in a sleepy little country town like Mildenhall."

"Could he have spoken to anyone else in your office?"

With a rueful grimace, she gestured to her tiny work cubicle. "There isn't anyone else. I'm it."

"What about the base history?" Jack asked, eyeing the spiffy twenty-inch flat-screen monitor on the woman's desk. "Is it all on computer?"

"Yes, it is. It took forever to scan in all the old typewritten documents and correct errors made by the optical reading program, but I had two summer interns to assist with the effort. Nowadays, of course, all reports are submitted electronically, which makes it far easier for me to index subjects and collate data on specific events, missions or operations."

"Who has access to the histories?"

"The unclassified portions are available to anyone. The classified sections require special access."

"What about Second World War records?"

With a click of the mouse, Ridgeway brought up an electronic file emblazoned with a shield showing lions rampant.

"It's all here, beginning on June 1, 1942, when the 100th was activated as a heavy-bomb group, through December 21, 1945, when it was deactivated at Camp Kilmer, New Jersey."

In between, Cleo saw as Ridgeway scrolled

through a chronology, were months of stateside training on B-17 Flying Fortresses, departures for England, assignments to the airfield at Thorpe Abbots in Norfolk, and years of combat missions that earned the unit several Distinguished Unit Citations and the French Croix de Guerre with Palm Leaf.

"We believe Captain Caswell may have been interested in locating the wreck of a plane that went down in the Channel during the war. A troop transport," Jack said.

"We lost a good number of those during the Normandy Invasion and the Battle of the Bulge."

"This one would have gone down earlier, sometime in March 1943."

Ridgeway pursed her lips. "Well, Headquarters Eighth Air Force issued Daily Intelligence Operations Summaries, which compiled the activities of all subordinate units. Some of these reports are available online through the USAF History Office. You could start there. Then there are the wartime mission folders held by the Public Records Office at Kew, just outside London. Most of those, unfortunately, are still on paper. Oh, and you might give Mr. Brill a ring."

"Mr. Brill?"

"Reginald Brill. He's a local history buff and a devotee of the Dak, as the Brits called the Douglas C-47. It began as a hobby for him, but over the years he's collected an astonishing amount of memorabilia and information concerning troop-carrier missions during the war. I consult with him frequently."

She jotted down the name and telephone number, along with the other sources she'd referenced. Jack pocketed the list, thanked her and accompanied Cleo outside.

"Do you get the feeling we're chasing our tails?" she commented once they were ensconced in the Taurus.

"Like we ever do anything else at the start of an investigation?"

"Most investigations don't usually involve World War II troop transports *and* illegal gambling syndicates *and* women who get it on with barnyard animals. Speaking of which…"

"Later," Jack said with a grin. "First I want to put folks to work on those USAF history files."

The call back to the OSI computer ops division took only a few moments. The call to the Public Records Division at Kew took considerably longer.

"Ms. Ridgeway was right," Jack reported with a grimace after terminating the connection. "The mission folders she referenced are still in paper format. The only way to extract information concerning specific operations is through a manual search of the records."

"Maybe this Mr. Brill can help us narrow the search."

"Maybe."

Punching in the number the historian had provided, Jack identified himself and explained the reason for his call. Cleo saw him suddenly tense, felt an answering leap of excitement when his eyes cut to her.

"Thanks," he said into the phone. "We'll drive over now, if that's convenient."

"What?" Cleo demanded when he flipped the phone shut.

"We might just have gotten our first break. Seems our boy Caswell made a personal visit to Mr. Brill only last month, looking for information on Bouncing Bertha."

"Hmm. First Barny and Betty and now Bouncing Bertha. Wonder if they're connected?"

"I doubt it, as Bertha last saw action in 1943."

"So you think this might be the transport Caswell wanted to locate?"

"Could be," Jack replied, his blue eyes gleaming with the thrill of the chase. "It very well could be."

Big and ruddy-faced, Reginald Brill looked even less like the stereotypical image of a historian than Madeline Ridgeway had. The retired railroad engineer lived some miles northeast of Mildenhall and stored his collection of memorabilia in a rusted Quonset hut sitting in the middle of a wheat field behind his house.

"This was the crew-briefing shack," he told Cleo and Jack, leading them through the drizzle toward the corrugated metal structure. "And just there, you can see a patch of the old runway."

They followed his pointing finger to an upended chunk of concrete poking above the new growth of wheat.

"I was just a young cawker then. Not more than six or seven. But I can still remember when lorries loaded with paratroopers would roll up. The Daks would taxi in from their dispersal points, the crew chiefs would hustle the troopers aboard, and the aircraft would lumber down the runway like big dray horses. Once airborne, they'd join up in perfect V formations. The whole sky would get dark with them."

Shaking his head at the memories, Brill led them around to the hut's entrance. A faded, hand-painted sign above the doors displayed the letters TARFU. Brill pushed a key into the padlock hanging from the rusted hasp and put a shoulder to the warped wooden door to force it open.

"Here we are, in TARFU Town."

Cleo had to ask. She suspected TARFU was a derivative of *SNAFU*. "Situation normal all fucked up" was still a favorite expression among the troops. But she couldn't quite make the translation.

"Okay, I'll bite. I know *SNAFU*. What does *TARFU* stand for?"

"It's troop-carrier talk," Brill explained with a twinkle in his eyes. "For 'things are *really*, uh, fouled up.' Mind the step, now."

Cleo dutifully minded the step. The next moment her jaw dropped in astonishment. Gaping, she let her gaze roam the remnants of the once-busy airfield Brill had collected and put on display inside the Quonset hut.

Old aeronautical maps lined one wall. A row of metal lockers marched along the other. Two battered wooden desks were positioned beneath a limp windsock hanging from a crossbeam. Wire hangers displayed moth-eaten leather jackets decorated with patches, while posters depicted aircraft nose art, mostly female and pretty much naked.

But it was the photographs that drew Cleo's fascinated gaze. They filled every square inch of the south wall of the hut. Faded, black-and-white shots of crew members with arms hooked over one another's shoulders. Pilots leaning out cockpit windows to give a thumbs-up. Ground mechanics with their hat bills pushed up and grease streaking their faces.

Then there were the planes. Brill had collected dozens of pictures of the twin-engine Dakota C-47, known universally as the Gooney Bird. Some rolled down the runway. Others were in flight, towing gliders or trailed by a stream of paratroopers. A number of photos showed planes that had been shot all to hell. One was missing half a wing. Another had a hole in the fuselage that looked big enough to drive a jeep through.

The most gripping photo, though, showed a transport engulfed in flames, spiraling down into the sea. Brill noted how the stark, black-and-white photo held her riveted and offered a quiet explanation.

"That was taken by a combat photographer during the invasion of Sicily in July of '43. What a TARFU that was."

"How so?"

"The details weren't unclassified until long after the war and you won't find many books that talk about it, but that was when the bastards at headquarters issued the 'crew return only' order."

"Meaning they couldn't bring their load of troops back to base?"

"Precisely. They had to drop their sticks, whatever the cost."

When Jack came to stand beside Cleo, Brill's gaze returned to the photo.

"The Sicily invasion was a two-pronged operation. In the first prong, Daks towing gliders filled with troops were routed to a low-altitude release two miles off shore, near Syracuse in the British sector. Unexpectedly strong headwinds blew up at the release point and carried the gliders out to sea. More than three hundred British aviators and ground troops drowned that day."

"Christ," Jack muttered.

Brill nodded, his face grim. "One of the loadmasters told me years later that his pilot saw what was happening. He got on the radio, begging for permission not to release his glider. His request was refused."

"Because of the crew-return-only order?"

"Yes. The loadmaster said his pilot was crying when he gave the order to cut the tow rope."

Cleo's stomach knotted. She'd spent enough years in uniform to know even today's sophisticated navigational aids and secure satellite communications couldn't completely negate the confusion that came with massive, multiservice joint operations. Mistakes happened. Troops died. Forces were hit by friendly fire. But try explaining that to the next of kin of those crews.

"And that number of dead doesn't include those who were aboard transports hit by enemy fire," Brill added, nodding to the C-47 engulfed in flames. "Like this one."

"Do you think that's what happened to the Bouncing Bertha? She was hit by enemy fire?"

Brill rolled his shoulders, as if to shake off the memories, and turned. "What's behind the interest in that particular aircraft all of a sudden?"

"We're hoping you'll provide the answer to that."

"I wish I could help. As I told Captain Caswell, I don't have much information on her."

"Just give us what you do have."

"It's right here."

He led the way to one of the file cabinets leaning crookedly against the wall. It was positioned directly under a poster of the nose art from *Tico Belle*. The voluptuous brunette reclined in a come-hither pose that promised all kinds of delights once her crew returned to base.

If they returned to base, Cleo amended silently. She suspected Brill's account of the invasion of Sicily would stay with her for a long time.

"*Here* she is. Bouncing Bertha, tail number 316130. Rolled off the assembly line at the Douglas aircraft plant in July 1942. Arrived in England October of that same year. Originally assigned to troop carrier command, but diverted for use as a special transport."

Jack had been jotting down notes. That brought his head up. "Special how?"

Brill consulted his own notes. "Courier missions. Counter-force insertions. Delivery of gold, counterfeit currencies and supplies to resistance fighters. Basically, whatever HQ decided needed to be done."

Cleo zinged Jack a quick glance. His face showed not so much as a quiver of emotion, but she'd bet her last dime he'd picked up that bit about gold.

"Lost over the Channel on or around March 17, 1943," Brill finished on a gusty sigh.

"Do you know where it went down?"

"Sorry, no. As I told Captain Caswell, I've never come across any reports documenting her loss. Her last flight plan might be included among the mission folders kept at Kew, but I've never gone down to slog through all that paper."

Kew again. Cleo had the feeling that she and Jack were going to spend some time digging through musty old files.

"I told the folks who contacted me after the article came out to try Kew, too."

"What article?"

"It was a nice little piece about aircraft lost over the Channel, part of a series of articles commemorating the sixtieth anniversary of the Normandy invasion. I have a copy of it right here."

He shuffled through the file and produced a laminated, two-column London *Times* article. Jack made a note of the date and author.

"The reporter actually quoted me here," Brill said, stabbing a beefy forefinger at the second column. "It generated quite a few queries when it went up on the *Times* Web site, I can tell you. I got calls from all over, mostly folks wanting information on granddads or great-uncles who flew Daks. That's when Captain Caswell rang me."

Cleo and Jack said goodbye to the retired engineer and departed TARFU Town a short time later.

"Well, we're a few steps ahead of where we were an hour ago," she said as they made their way to the rental vehicle. "We have the tail number, the nickname and a possible source to hunt for Bouncing Bertha's flight plan on the day she went down. We also have the fact that she might have been used to transport gold."

Sliding into the front seat, she clipped her seat belt. Her mind was churning with possibilities.

"That has Minnesota Fats' stamp all over it. No wonder he was checking out salvage operators. I'm not sure I understand why the powers that be would transport gold aboard a slow-moving, unarmed C-47, though."

Shrugging, Jack fastened his seat belt. "Probably because they could go in low and do pinpoint drops."

The reply was casual. Too casual. Cleo twisted to the side and pinned him with a swift look. "What do you know about these airdrops?"

"Not much." He shoved the key in the ignition, cranked the engine and started to put the Taurus in gear. "Let's get back to…"

"Dammit, Donovan!" Reaching across the center console, Cleo yanked the key out of the ignition switch. "You know something. Something you're not telling me."

"Give me the key."

"Tell me!"

"Cleo…"

With an angry hiss, she raked a hand through her hair and flipped the heavy mass to the other side. "You see this little bare patch? I think it earned me the right to whatever the hell you know that I don't."

He hesitated just long enough for her to seriously consider bursting a few capillaries on the right side of his face to match the left.

"I see all that talk about us being a team was just that," she jeered. "Talk."

With a curse, he sank back against the seat. "When we get back to the States, I'm marching you into the Defense Investigative Service's headquarters and *sitting* on you until you fill out those damned forms to reinstate your security clearances."

"All right, all right. Just tell me what we're dealing with here."

"British national gold reserves," he ground out. "Some seven billion dollars' worth."

8

The digits careered around in Cleo's head, one seven and a whole bunch of zeros.

"Talk, Donovan. I want details."

"Give me the car keys. I'll tell you what I can while we drive back to Mildenhall."

"Don't give me this *what I can* crap. I want the whole story."

"You'll get what I give you," he fired back.

Fuming, Cleo tossed him the keys. That was Donovan. Toe the line. Play by the rules. Unless and until he decided circumstances warranted tossing the rule book out the window, of course. Evidently he hadn't reached that point with her yet.

Tapping an impatient foot against the floorboards, she waited until he got the Taurus in gear and on the road. When the fields were rolling by in neat, soggy checkerboards, he unfolded a tale right out of Ian Fleming's *Goldfinger.*

"You know Germany invaded Poland in September 1939."

"Yes. Tell me something I *don't.*"

Ignoring the sarcasm, he plowed ahead. "After Poland, most of Europe fell like dominoes. Finland in March 1940, then Norway, Denmark, Holland, Belgium. The French and the British fought on until Dunkirk in June of 1940. The Nazis marched into Paris shortly after that."

"At which point they turned their attention to an invasion of England."

"Right. Those were desperate days for the British. They were standing alone against Hitler. He'd signed a nonaggression pact with Stalin. The U.S. hadn't yet entered the war."

"Officially," Cleo put in, drawing on her recent research regarding the Lend-Lease program.

"Officially," Jack concurred. "But the Battle of Britain took a hell of a toll. Publicly, Churchill declared he and his countrymen would fight to the last ditch and hedgerow in defense of their country. Privately, the government had already prepared for the worst by transferring England's gold reserves to safe havens in Canada and the U.S."

"Seven billion dollars' worth?"

"Give or take a couple million."

The idea of that much gold making its way across

an ocean swarming with enemy subs made Cleo forget her pique enough to ask how the heck the Brits had accomplished that feat.

"In small shipments delivered by fast merchantmen and warships to ports in Halifax and Quebec. At the ports, the gold was loaded onto heavily guarded boxcars and transported to a special vault in Montreal. Later shipments went to Chase Manhattan in New York City and were used as partial payment for items purchased under the Lend-Lease program. The entire transfer was all done in absolute secrecy and, amazingly, not one ship ferrying gold was sunk."

She couldn't even begin to imagine how much gold equated to seven billion dollars back then.

"Okay, so how do we get from reserves shipped to Canada and New York in '39 and '40 to a U.S. Army Air Corps transport that went down over the Channel in '43?"

"Most of the gold remained in Canada and the U.S. for the duration of the war. After the Battle of Britain ended and Hitler scrapped his invasion plans, though, England pulled some of her reserves back for wartime purchases."

"Some?"

"Estimates vary, but a recently declassified Bank of Canada report indicates Ottawa held three billion at war's end. The U.S. about 2.5."

Cleo would be the first to admit she didn't have a head for math. The rest of her anatomy was just as numerically challenged. But even she could make that calculation. Seven minus 5.5 still left a *big* chunk of change floating around out there.

"What kind of wartime purchases required payment in gold?"

"Just about every kind. The European economy was in shambles. Hitler had delinked the mark from the gold standard, making it useless in international trade. Currencies in countries Germany invaded likewise lost their value. Adding to the problem, each side froze the assets of both individuals and corporations suspected of contributing to the enemy's war machine. Neutral countries like Portugal, which produced critical supplies of tungsten needed by both sides, demanded payment in gold, U.S. dollars or Swiss francs."

International trade and banking practices were an aspect of war Cleo had never really thought about. Evidently a certain tanker pilot had, though.

So, apparently, had Jack.

"You knew Caswell was sniffing around these gold shipments before we left Washington, didn't you?"

"I knew he had accessed Web sites related to World War II gold transfers."

"Care to tell me just how you knew that?"

He squeezed out another nugget of information. "Caswell had visited certain other Web sites we're keeping an eye on, so we put an electronic tag on his computer."

"Dammit, Donovan! You could have clued me in to some of this."

Dragging his gaze from the road ahead, he shot her a level look. "I didn't have any evidence that Caswell's sudden interest in the gold was in any way connected to his murder. I still don't."

But they were getting closer. Cleo could feel it in her bones. That didn't quite make up for the fact that Jack was still feeding her only what he thought she needed to know, however.

Pissed all over again, she crossed her arms and spent the rest of the drive back to the inn sorting through the data they'd accumulated. When they pulled into the parking lot, Jack checked his watch.

"It's just a little past two. I'm thinking we might drive to Kew and have a look at those mission folders. Depending on how long that takes, we could head down to Johanna Marston's place in Kent from there."

"Ha! Now it's 'we' again. You're sure good at switching that pronoun off and on, Donovan."

"Is that a yes, North?"

"Yes."

The car door slammed behind her with a satisfying thud.

Cleo acted as navigator for the drive to Kew.

The map showed it to be a small town located on the outskirts of London on the River Thames, one

Underground stop from the village of Richmond. According to the map legend, Kew was the site of a former royal residence whose grounds included extensive gardens and massive Victorian glass conservatories. Now open to the public, Kew Gardens had earned a spot on the list of UNESCO World Heritage Sites.

Cleo caught a glimpse of the gardens' ornate wrought-iron gates as Jack turned onto what appeared to be the town's one major thoroughfare. The Public Records Office sat just off the main street.

Cleo had pulled up the PRO's Web site on Jack's super-cool little cell phone-slash-computer, so she knew it constituted the national archives for England, Wales and the United Kingdom. She also knew it acted as a repository for England's oldest and most famous public document, the Domesday Book.

Luckily, they'd hit the huge, ultramodern complex on one of the days the PRO remained open for extended hours as a convenience to folks bitten by the genealogy bug. The visitors' center was a soaring, open structure of glass and marble. Their footsteps echoing on the polished floors, Jack and Cleo joined a long queue of ancestor-hunters seeking information on the use of the center's computers and possible search sources.

When it was their turn, Jack produced his credentials, identified both Cleo and himself, and asked to see the 1943 mission folders for headquarters, Eighth Air Force.

The attendant typed in a quick search. "Those records are still in paper format, sir."

"Yes, I know."

"I'll have to get permission for you to go down into the archives. If you'll just wait a moment, please."

He returned with his supervisor in tow. After scrutinizing Jack's credentials, she escorted them to an elevator.

"I'm sorry we haven't put these records online yet," she apologized as the elevator whizzed downward. "We've approached your government about a possible joint effort in that regard."

That prompted a question from Cleo. "I'm curious. Why are you holding United States Army Air Corps records? Shouldn't they have been shipped back to the States after the war?"

"The American forces were stationed on British soil," the recordskeeper reminded her gently. "Your aircrews flew out of RAF bases, and their missions were often directed by or at least coordinated with RAF planners. The records of those missions hold as much historical significance for us as they do for you."

"Oh. Right."

Feeling a tad stupid, Cleo said nothing more until the elevator door whirred open. When they stepped out, she couldn't help murmuring to Jack that it looked as if they'd just landed in library heaven.

Like the reception area upstairs, the archives were state of the art. Long halls with floors polished to surgical-ward sheen led past room after room of meticulously filed and labeled documents. Security cameras were mounted at regular intervals along the corridor, as were smoke detectors and fire-suppression units.

"Do you keep videotapes of the security sweeps?" Jack asked, eyeing the red eye of a camera.

"For a short time. Thirty days, I think, unless something occurs to generate a permanent record. I'll ring our security chief and verify that. If you'll just sign in here, please."

The sign-in sheet was electronic, one of those pads with an attached stylus now so popular in supermarkets and department stores. Cleo's pulse kicked up at the sight, but before she could comment Jack was already making the request.

"We'd also like a record of all persons accessing this room in the past thirty days, if that's possible."

"Yes, of course. I'll check on that while you have a go at the mission folders. It was 1943 you wanted, wasn't it?"

"Yes."

"I believe 1943 occupies eight cabinets. They're just here."

Cleo was still gulping down that "eight" when she stepped into a room equipped floor-to-ceiling with lateral filing cabinets. The area was so clean and so austere, she couldn't shake the eerie sense she'd just entered a morgue. The sensation intensified considerably when the records keeper issued a warning.

"You might want to have a care when you go through these folders. Musty old records like these have been known to contain certain, shall we say, surprises."

"What kind of surprises?"

"Oh, nothing very dire," she answered with an apologetic smile. "Just mold, insect droppings and the occasional bird skeleton."

When she left to attend to their requests, Cleo eyed the cabinet with a distinct lack of enthusiasm.

"You don't have rubber gloves on you by any chance?"

"I've got some in my carryall," Jack replied, looking only slightly more thrilled at the prospect of digging through bird skeletons. "If either one of us hits anything that looks, smells or feels dead, I'll go retrieve a couple pairs."

"Deal."

Approaching the cabinet with some caution, Cleo pulled out the top drawer. It opened noiselessly, a smooth, silent slide of metal bearings. The odor wasn't all that bad, she decided after a wary sniff. Almost identical to the scent of the past that had permeated Reginald Brill's reconstructed TARFU Town.

Going up on tiptoe, she skimmed the labels affixed to the dozen or so accordion folders inside the drawer. "Looks like they're in chronological order. These are for January 1 through 3."

"Well, hell! All those folders for just four days?"

"Guess there was a lot of air activity going on in early 1943."

"Now we know why Brill never boogied on down here to wade through these folders. Let's find March."

Cleo skipped a few drawers, tried another and kept on going. Two cabinets later, she hit March. Folders dated the 17th started toward the rear of the drawer. Cleo extracted one thick folder and passed it to Jack. Carrying the second to the table in the center of the room, she flipped back the musty lid.

The first document she pulled out bore the daunting title of *Headquarters U.S. VIII Fighter Command, Narrative of Operations, Intelligence Summary Number 147.* It ran to twelve pages, including maps.

"Look at this," she muttered, rifling the pages. "The military runs on paper, even in the middle of a world war."

Despite her whining, she found the report riveting. The first page provided a statistical summary of sorties flown by aircraft type. Number of each type of aircraft lost. Number damaged. Number of personnel MIA. KIA. WIA.

The statistics were sobering enough. The brief mission narratives that followed added blood-chilling drama to the numbers.

Target-Support, 1st ATF, 2nd Division: Tutow.
355th Fighter Group, Colonel Jenkins leading.
43 P-51s up 1002 hours, down 1500 hours. Nil
abortive sorties.
Made landfall-in east of Cuxhaven 1150 hours
at 21,000 feet. Two motor vessels sighted SE of
Heligoland at 1145 hours. Both strafed, one left
burning.
Rendezvoused in Warnemünde area with three
combat wings of B-24s escorted by P-38s and
P-47s, 1225 hours at 24,000 feet. Light to mod-
erate flak along route. Target acquisition 1320
hours. Bombs dropped.
Two B-24s seen going down in Wismar area,
no chutes. One unidentified plane spun in east
of Quakenbrück, 1345 hours. Landfall-out, IJ-
muiden, 1350 hours, at 19,000 feet.

Reluctantly, Cleo returned the document to its
folder. As riveting as these summaries were, she was
looking for information relating to troop carriers
and transports, not missions flown by fighters and
bombers.

"Nothing on C-47 sorties in this one," she reported
after checking the contents of the entire folder.

"This one, neither."

They worked their way through the next two folders, then two more. They didn't find any bird bones
or insect droppings, thank God, although the last

folder in the drawer had a suspicious smell. Her nose wrinkling, Cleo shoved it at Jack's chest.

"This one's yours. I'll start on the next drawer."

She had the drawer half open when she spotted the rat. It was perched atop the folders, staring at her with bright, glassy eyes.

"Ugh!"

Reacting on pure instinct, Cleo sent the drawer crashing into the cabinet and jumped back a good three feet.

"What the…?"

That was all Jack got out before the drawer exploded.

9

The steel cabinet contained most of the explosion, but not the fire. Thick white smoke poured through twisted metal. Flames whooshed out behind it.

"Get a fire extinguisher!"

Shouting the order at Jack, Cleo yanked down her blazer sleeve and tugged at the drawer handle. She couldn't have said what drove her more at that instant: a blind, instinctive need to save those precious documents, or the wild notion that someone had rigged an incendiary device to keep her or anyone else from getting to them. All she knew was that she had to rescue those files.

She got a good grip on the drawer pull with her sleeve-covered hand, but the dammed sides were too warped to give. Bent double to avoid the smoke, she wrestled it open a few inches and ·

reached inside. A few folders. If she could save just a few folders...

She got only one out before Donovan came barreling into the room. "Get out of the way!"

Shoving the extinguisher under his arm, he aimed the nozzle at the flames leaping from the drawer. Nothing happened.

"Hell!"

He shook the canister. Checked the nozzle. Aimed again.

Still nothing.

"Jack! Does it have an on-off valve?"

"Yes, it has a valve," he snarled, dodging the flames. "I switched it on."

"Try again."

They realized the valve had been tampered with about the same time they realized the overhead fire-suppression systems hadn't activated. By that time smoke had blanketed the room and flames were licking at other cabinets.

Grabbing Cleo's arm, Jack dragged her into the hall and searched the corridor. "There's a house phone. I'll notify the front desk."

"And I'll try these other alarms."

To free her hands, she stuffed the charred remains of the folder she'd extracted under the flap of her red blazer and into the waistband of her jeans. Charging down the hall, she broke the glass and yanked the handles on little red boxes. The first one was dead.

The second set up a loud screech. The third added nicely to the din.

Whirling, she raced back to Jack. She reached him just as the elevator arrived. The door opened on a stunned records keeper and equally startled uniformed security officer. The guard sprang into instant action. The librarian gave a heartbroken little moan and did the same.

It took almost an hour for fire-response teams to extinguish the blaze. Once it was under control, the on-scene investigators requested statements from Cleo, Jack and various personnel from the Public Records Office—most of whom gave her evil looks whenever she glanced in their general direction. Destroying precious historical documents obviously ranked right up there with first-degree murder in their minds.

The on-scene investigator went over Cleo's statement a final time before releasing her. "We've notified the arson division, Ms. North. They'll have a team here straightaway. You're sure you didn't catch a glimpse of any wires or explosives when you opened that drawer?"

"Only a dead rat."

"Yes. Quite. In our Public Records Office."

His tone implied she'd just insulted the PRO, the town of Kew and British janitors everywhere.

"The woman who took us down to the archives

explained that old records sealed up for long periods often contained dead birds or insect droppings."

Since he appeared unconvinced, Cleo dropped the matter and switched subjects.

"We—Special Agent Donovan and I—also think the fire-suppression systems on that floor were tampered with."

"Yes, he mentioned that to me. The arson team will have a time with that now, won't they?"

"I expect so."

"It may take several days for the team to sift through the debris and determine the exact cause of the explosion. If you'll leave me your address and a number where you can be contacted, I'm sure they'll want to talk to you personally."

Cleo gave him her cell phone number and Johanna Marston's address in Kent. Jack provided his number as well and requested a call from the arson team as soon as they got a fix on the explosive device used.

"I'll have them ring you straightaway, sir."

"You're racking up quite a record," Jack commented as he and Cleo ducked under the cordon and made their way back to the Taurus. "A ship loaded with munitions last month. World War II operational summaries tonight. What's next on your agenda?"

"I don't suppose it would do any good to point out that I wasn't the direct cause of either of those explosions."

"I'm not the one you'll have to convince."

"Oh, hell! You're not going to call Barnes, are you?"

"You think I'm going to let him hear about this back channel? Not hardly. I like my balls right where they are, thank you very much."

"At least wait until I duck into... Dammit, Jack!"

It was too late. He already had the screen flipped up and the general's exec centered on the tiny, two-inch screen.

"Ms. North and I need to speak to the Old Man."

"He's in a meeting, sir. Should I interrupt?"

Cleo made frantic no-no-no signals. Jack ignored them.

"Yes."

They'd reached the Taurus by the time Barnes's craggy face filled the screen. Cleo could tell he wasn't happy by the way his teeth were bared above his pipe stem.

"This better be good. I just walked out of a meeting with a four-star."

"I'm not sure I'd term it 'good,' sir."

Jack angled the camera built into the phone to catch the building behind him, still surrounded by emergency vehicles, fire trucks and TV-news vans.

His bushy brows hooking inward, Barnes squinted into the screen. "What's that?"

"Britain's national archives."

"*What!*"

The thunderous roar had Cleo wincing. She had to remind herself she wasn't under the general's direct command anymore. Even when she had been, she'd survived his frequent and furious broadsides. Still, her shoulders went back and her chin came up in anticipation of the question Barnes now barked.

"Was North involved in this?"

Jack kept a straight face, but Cleo caught the smirk in his reply. "Yes, sir."

The bastard was enjoying himself!

"You're gonna pay for this," she hissed furiously as Barnes yanked the pipe out of his mouth and bellowed through the screen.

"Dammit it all to hell, I *told* that woman not to blow anything up!"

Enough was enough. Thrusting out a hip, Cleo bumped Jack aside and stuck her face in the camera. "Major Donovan has neglected to make one minor point, sir. I did *not* cause this explosion. Well, I did by opening the drawer, but someone else rigged it."

"Who and why?"

Jack edged back into the camera angle. "We don't have the answer to that yet. But we think it's related to the Caswell murder."

Cleo derived intense satisfaction from watching the Old Man struggle to make the leap from a dead air force captain to an explosion at the British national archives.

"Go secure," he barked at Jack. "I want to know what the hell's going on over there."

"Yes, sir."

With a glance at Cleo that was half apology and half tough nuggies, Donovan picked up the phone, switched off the screen and walked far enough away to converse without being overheard.

Pretending supreme disinterest in their conversation, Cleo leaned against the Taurus. The Public Records Office was still cordoned off, but the emergency vehicles were starting to depart and the crowd had thinned. Most of the news crews had departed as well, except for one enterprising reporter who shoved a mike in the face of the woman who'd escorted Cleo and Jack down into the archives. Looking harried, the librarian stabbed a finger at Cleo.

Oh, crap.

One of the cardinal rules of private security work was to maintain as low a profile as possible. Having your face splashed all over the evening news made it tough to blend into the background when protecting a client or shadowing a suspect. Government investigative agents operated under the same general principles and usually used a public affairs type to interface with the media.

With no public affairs officer in sight and Jack still hunched over his cell phone twenty yards away, Cleo resigned herself to the inevitable.

Sure enough, the reporter scurried across the parking lot a few minutes later, trailed by his camera and sound crew. "Ms. North, Harold Fields, BBC News.

Is it true you're a private security consultant from America?"

"That's correct."

"And you were in the archive room where the explosion occurred?"

"Also correct."

"Why were you there?"

Duh. Why did anyone visit a records repository?

"I was conducting research."

"On what subject?"

If he hadn't already elicited that information from the PRO folks, Cleo wasn't going to provide it.

"I can't discuss the details. Client privilege. You understand, of course."

He understood but didn't like the answer.

"I heard one of the fire inspectors say you spotted a rat in the drawer. Is that true?"

She'd already gone down that road once with the on-scene investigator. She wasn't about to insult British national housekeeping standards again.

"Excuse me, I see my associate has finished his phone call. We have to leave."

The reporter tried to glom onto Jack, but he referred all queries to the local authorities and quickly disengaged. A few moments later, he had the Taurus heading down Kew's main street.

"What did you tell that reporter?"

"That I was doing research and almost got my head blown off," she retorted, offended that he would even ask the question. "What did you tell the Old Man?"

"Pretty much the same."

"Did he know we were hunting for information on a C-47 that went down in March 1943?"

"He does now. He's going to turn up the heat at his end, see what our air force historians can come up with. Too bad about those mission folders," he added on a note of sheer frustration. "We were getting so close at this end. One more file and we might have had a hit."

Cleo chewed on the inside of her lip. She was tempted to let him suffer, especially after the way he'd offered her up to Barnes like a sacrificial lamb, but curiosity was eating her alive. Sliding a hand under the rear flap of her blazer, she extracted the charred folder.

"Ask and ye shall receive."

"Jesus, North! Did you waltz off with a public document belonging to the national archives?"

"I *saved* a public document belonging to the national archives from certain destruction. I fully intend to return it. After I read it. I'd let you know what's in it, Donovan, but I wouldn't want you to compromise your lofty principles in any way."

His lofty principles didn't survive beyond a glance at the date on first page.

"March 17." His voice took on a rough edge. "Are those the stats for Troop Carrier Command?"

"Looks like."

"Out of what bases?"

She skimmed the list. "Exeter, Merryfield, Weston and Upottery."

"Get to the summaries. Look for…"

"Hey, who pulled this report out of the fire? You drive, I'll go through the document, and if you're nice to me—*very* nice to me—I might tell you what's in it."

Donovan shot her an evil look but didn't have a whole lot of choice in the matter. They'd hit the suburbs right at rush hour. The Friday evening rush hour. Vehicles of every size and description clogged the road leading south as what looked like every second Londoner headed to the country for the weekend.

While Jack wrestled with the crawling, stop-and-go traffic, Cleo slumped in her seat and started in on the summaries. She'd intended to merely skim them, but as before, the stark drama they contained reached out and grabbed her by the throat.

Left England at the Bill of Portland, 21 ship formation.
No. 2 lead downed over Gibraltar.
Landed and regrouped, Sebkra d'Oran.

It took her a while to figure out the missions referenced in this intelligence summary involved troop transports en route to Africa in preparation for the invasion of Sicily to follow. The image of that burning transport hovered in her mind as she read summary after summary.

A brief entry on the next page jolted her upright in her seat.

On course 213 degrees magnetic, 1500 feet, hit cloudbank 1723 hours. Dropped to 700 feet, spotted lone C-47 below spinning into Channel. USAAF markings. Last digits of tail number 3-0. No chutes.

"Jack! What was Bouncing Bertha's tail number?"

"Three-one-something." Reaching into his coat pocket, he tossed her his notebook. "I wrote it down."

Her blood pumping, Cleo thumbed to the notes he'd taken during their conversation with Reginald Brill.

"Here it is—316130. It's her, Jack! It's her. Bouncing Bertha."

He wrenched his gaze from the traffic crawling along on all sides of the Taurus. "How do you know?"

"Listen to this. A C-47 left Upottery at 1420 hours and departed England via the Bill of Portland, whatever the heck that is. It flew on a course of 213 degrees magnetic for fifty-five minutes, hit a cloudbank and dropped below the clouds. At 700 feet, the pilot spotted another transport spinning into the Channel. The last two digits of her tail number were three-zero. What he didn't spot was any chutes."

"Bingo," Jack said softly.

"Yeah," Cleo echoed, fingering the file. "Bingo."

Her spurt of excitement was already fizzling. The war had become too real to her, and Brill's photo of that C-47 spiraling into the sea was now seared in her mind. Verifying that the crew and passengers aboard Bouncing Bertha had met a similar fate didn't give her the thrill she normally felt at fitting together the pieces of an investigation.

"We still don't know what turned Caswell on to that particular aircraft," Jack cautioned after a moment. "Nor do we have any hard evidence Bouncing Bertha was ferrying gold."

"But the circumstantial evidence is piling up. Lieutenant Colonel Sikes said Caswell was working some get-rich-quick scheme that involved an underwater wreck. We know Caswell contacted Brill looking for information about Bouncing Bertha, and you said he'd hit several Web sites that detailed the shipment of British gold reserves."

She cocked her head, gave him a curious glance. "You never did tell me why the OSI put an electronic tag on Caswell's computer, by the way."

"I couldn't…until I talked to General Barnes a while ago."

Before Cleo could get huffy about how long it had taken him to convince the Old Man to include her on the inside team, Donovan dropped a bomb.

"Caswell recently contacted a sergeant who's been

supplying information on air force tanker operations to a terrorist cell."

"What!"

"The sergeant is a devout Muslim. He's also one of ours. We got him court-martialed, took a couple of stripes and helped him broadcast the fact that he was thoroughly pissed at the air force. The leader of a known cell approached him via the Internet less than a week later."

"God! They must have thought they'd found a diamond mine."

"They did. Our man fed the bastards all kinds of misinformation regarding tanker operations. Cruising speeds. Refueling procedures. Rendezvous checkpoints. They gobbled it up like candy and kept coming back for more."

"Yikes!"

A handful of fanatics had wrought unbelievable devastation with commercial airliners carrying sixty or so thousand pounds of fuel. The mere thought of what they could do with a tanker hauling three times that amount of aviation fuel made Cleo's throat go tight.

"That's how we nailed 'em," Jack continued with fierce satisfaction. "They got greedy, left a computer trail we finally managed to trace to an apartment in Istanbul. The Turkish authorities took the bastards down earlier today."

Which was why General Barnes had cleared

Donovan to tell her about the operation. So much for being part of the inside team.

"Was our boy Fats involved with these terrorists?"

"We don't *think* so. The sergeant flew with him a few years ago. Caswell e-mailed him, said he'd heard about the court martial, wanted to know what the deal was. Before the sergeant could respond, someone put two slugs into the back of the captain's head."

"Man, this case just keeps getting weirder and weirder."

"Yeah, it does."

Cleo gnawed on the new information like a coyote on a thighbone. A possible link to terrorists added a whole different complexion to the Caswell case.

"That's why the Old Man sent you to London, isn't it? This terrorist connection."

"Yes."

"I knew it had to be more than the murder. So what's the plan now the cell's been busted? Is Barnes calling you home?"

"We discussed that."

"And?"

"And I told him I was into this investigation now and wanted to see it through."

"I bet that went down well."

He slanted her a quick glance. "It went down better than when I told him I had some personal business to attend to after we wrap up the investigation."

"After?"

"Aren't those the ground rules? Hands off until we figure out what we have going for us besides sex."

"Right. Those are the rules."

They'd made sense to Cleo when she'd suggested them last night. They still made sense, she lectured herself sternly, but she was suddenly impatient as hell to get the investigation over and done with.

"It's after six. You've been playing chauffeur all day. Why don't you pull over at the next rest stop? We can grab something to eat and I'll drive for a while."

10

Jack should have known better than to turn the wheel over to Cleo. The woman made the Federal Law Enforcement Academy's offensive and defensive driving courses seem like circus rides for six year olds.

He started grinding his teeth around the exit for Sevenoaks. By Maidstone, his jaw felt as though an oral surgeon had gone to work on it. Without anesthetic. By the time they left the M20 at Ashford and followed the signposts for Bethersden, he needed a drink.

They'd called Johanna Marston to let her know they were on their way and to get directions. Jack didn't think he'd ever been so glad to see anything in his life as the George Freehouse sitting at a bend in the road.

"Go past the pub," he directed. "The road curves around a church. Take the first right after the church."

"Got it."

"Jesus, North!" He braced an arm against the dash as she feathered the curve. The dark bulk of the church went by in a blur. "You planning to get back on your side of the road any time soon?"

"When did you get to be such a wimp, Donovan?"

"I've been asking myself the same thing for the last fifty kilometers. Turn here. Here!"

She had to slow for the two-lane country road and take it down another few notches when pavement gave way to dirt.

"I can't see Johanna's chauffeur bumping that shiny Rolls along a dirt track. Are you sure we took the right turn?"

"Pretty sure." Breathing easy for the first time in an hour, Jack peered through the soft May night. "I think I see lights up ahead."

The two-story structure was set off the road, bathed in moonlight that painted the stone facade a pale gold. The sturdy shutters at the windows and the vines arching over the front entrance would have given it the look of a farmhouse if not for the circular drive and half acre of landscaped lawn fronting it. Rampant stone lions, each with a paw resting on shields, sat atop brick pillars at the entrance to the drive. Jack winced as Cleo breezed past a pillar with all of two inches to spare.

The front door of the manor house opened almost before she killed the engine. Johanna Marston appeared in the spill of backlight, elegant even in a short-sleeved shirt and jeans.

"I've been watching for you. Did you have a pleasant journey?"

"Yes."

"No!"

Brows lifting, their hostess glanced from one to the other in some amusement.

"Let me offer you a word of advice," Jack drawled, reaching for the bags he'd tossed in the back seat. "If Cleo offers to drive you anywhere, take the train. Or the bus. Or grab a bicycle."

"I'll remember that." Laughing, she stood aside for them to enter the house. "Shall I show you to your rooms so you can freshen up or would you care for a drink first?"

"A drink," Jack said with real feeling. "Anything around eighty proof will do."

"I think I can supply that." As her guests passed her on their way inside, Lady Marston's aristocratic nose wrinkled delicately. "Have you been to a fire? Your clothing has rather a smoky tang to it."

"Long story," Cleo said. "We'll tell you about it inside."

Shelving her curiosity, Johanna showed them into a hall paneled in aged oak and thick with the scent of the lilacs bunched in a copper watering can.

"You can put your... Good gracious, Jack! However did you get that vicious bruise on your temple?"

"Longer story."

He wasn't up to explaining the moon-spinner until he'd washed down the chalky taste Cleo's driving had left in his mouth.

"Where shall I put these bags?"

"Just leave them there on that hall bench, why don't you? We'll carry them up later."

As directed, Jack deposited the leather totes on a high-backed pew that looked like it might have come from a Gothic cathedral and followed the two women down the hall.

He wasn't real up on architecture or interior decorating. His Washington condo contained only what was needed for basic life support. It was obvious even to him, though, that Johanna Marston had furnished her country home with an eye toward color and comfort.

Gleaming golden oak floorboards creaked under his feet. Mullioned windows refracted the lamplight in the library she escorted them into. Hunting prints, brass coaching horns and a collection of drinking steins decorated the walls. The leather sofa and chairs were man-size and well worn, as were the leather-topped stools drawn up to the bar.

"Will you do the honors, Jack?"

"My pleasure," he said, eyeing the bottle of Glenlivet perched on the shelf of a massive, intricately carved sideboard. "What would you ladies like?"

"I'm having a gin and tonic. My glass is just there, on the bar. You might top it up."

"Cleo?"

"I'll have some of that Glenlivet. Neat."

Frowning, Johanna caught Cleo's elbow and angled her toward the light. "I see you're sporting a sticking plaster. Is it the gunshot wound from last night?"

"Yes. It's just a scratch. I'd forgotten all about it."

With a careless shrug, Cleo raked her fingers through her hair. A small flip settled a swatch of glossy brown over the bald spot.

The gesture had Jack's hand fisting on the bottle of Scotch. As much as Cleo hated her full name, it fit her like a spandex bodysuit. Ninety-nine point nine percent of the time she came across as Cleopatra, warrior queen and absolute ruler of all she surveyed.

Every once in a while Aphrodite, the ultrafeminine goddess of love, beauty and sexual rapture, made an appearance. Like now, when she covered the bare patch with a casual gesture that held just a hint of self-consciousness. Or when she pranced around in silk boxers or lacy hipsters.

The memory of those hipsters telegraphed an urgent message from his brain to the lower half of his body. The response took a little longer to make its way back north.

Forget it! Cleo had drawn a line in the sand last night. No peeling those hipsters over her trim, tight buns until they'd figured out what they had going for them besides lust.

He'd made a start on it tonight, when he'd convinced the Old Man to let him stay on the Caswell case. Jack had pretty well used up his entire BS supply on that one. He was also fairly certain Barnes hadn't bought a word of it. The general had terminated the call with the acid warning that Special Agent Donovan had better get his ass in gear or he'd end up with his dick in a sling.

Words to live by, Jack mused as he passed Johanna her gin and poured healthy measures of the finest single malt Scotch known to man for himself and Cleo.

"Speaking of nasty little wounds," Cleo said to Johanna after they'd clinked glasses and downed satisfactory swallows, "how's your brother doing?"

"Alex? Quite well, actually. Marc says he's regained a measure of mobility. It's still rather hard to take in," Johanna admitted with a rueful smile. "Six months ago I was an only child. Now I have twin brothers and a sister-in-law."

"What?" Cleo squawked. "When did Diane break down and agree to marry Marc?"

"I'm not sure she did agree." Johanna's slate-gray eyes filled with laughter. "He tells me he just put her in his plane, flew her to Las Vegas and kept her, shall we say, entertained until she was too exhausted to resist him any longer."

"That sounds like Marc."

Yeah, Jack thought with a grimace, it did.

Okay, he could admit it. He'd disliked the too-rich, too-handsome brothers Sloan on sight. The fact that one of them of had been suspected of espionage and the other had been hitting on Cleo at the time might have had something to do with Jack's instant and deeply visceral reaction.

"They're coming over for a visit next week," Johanna announced happily. "All three of them. When Marc rang yesterday, I told him you two were here as well. He's quite hopeful they'll arrive whilst you're still in England."

"Whether we're still here," Jack said, steering the conversation around to the purpose of their visit, "depends on what happens with the Caswell case."

"Ah, yes. Captain Caswell."

"What did you find out from the dive boat operator?"

"Not a great deal. He confirmed Caswell rang him to inquire what it would cost to locate and dive on the wreck of a World War II-era transport. Mulholland claims he told the captain it couldn't be done without more precise information as to her location."

"Claims? Didn't you believe him?"

"I have no reason not to. He's a chief petty officer in the Royal Navy reserves, although you wouldn't think it to look at him now. Scruffy sort of chap, really." A crease formed between the black wings of her brows. "Something about him disturbed me."

"Disturbed you how?"

The faintest tinge of red crept into her cheeks. In any

other woman, Jack might have taken it for embarrassment or discomfort. But Lady Marston happened to be a highly skilled agent of Her Majesty's Secret Service. He didn't figure she embarrassed easily.

"Let's just say it occurred to me Mulholland might have decided to eliminate Caswell and go after the wreck himself. As I said, he was a scruffy sort."

Actually, that thought hadn't popped into Joanna's head until this very moment. She wasn't sure where it sprang from, but she *did* know Mulholland's admittedly splendid physique had preyed on her mind far more than it should have since their brief interview.

Perhaps it was time she tried another lover. Someone young and strong and vigorous. Someone like Jack Donovan.

Now there was a man.

Fighting a sharp stab of envy for the woman occupying the bar stool next to hers, she met Donovan's cool blue gaze.

"Why would Mulholland want to go after the wreck himself?" he asked.

Johanna returned his look with one equally steady and unflinching. They were down to it now, the heart of the case that had engaged them both.

"I'd rather hoped you might be able to tell me that. You mentioned you'd uncovered several new leads. You and Cleo."

At the mention of her name, the American thunked her glass down on the counter.

"Thank you, Lady Marston. I've been wondering when I was going to be included in this conversation. Okay, here's the deal. We suspect Doug Caswell found a manifest or information of some sort that convinced him the C-47 carrying your Grenadier Sergeant Clive Gordon was also ferrying a cargo of gold bullion."

The blunt admission took Johanna aback, then forced a laugh that was equal parts delight and chagrin.

"It appears Jack and I may have been in the spy business too long. Like fencers engaged in a deadly duel, we thrust and parry. You hack through things with a broadsword."

"I do tend to get a bit impatient," Cleo admitted without the least hint of guilt or regret. "The last I heard, though, we're all on the same side."

"So we are." Johanna drew in a breath. "You're correct. The plane in question was ferrying gold."

Along with another, less-stable cargo. The tension that had gripped Johanna since being assigned to this case returned with a vengeance, grabbing her by the throat. The thought of that canister breaking open— or being broken into by some greedy treasure hunter like Douglas Caswell—had put her superior at MI6 in a cold, nervous sweat. Johanna allowed none of her thoughts to show on her face as Cleo voiced a question.

"How much gold?"

"Estimates are it would be worth more than five million today."

"Whoa! That's a nice chunk of change."

"Yes, it is."

"And this gold was going where?"

"It was to be air-dropped in two increments to agents operating behind the lines."

Brows knit, Cleo twirled a strand of hair around her forefinger. The motion released a rather strong whiff of smoke that tickled Johanna's nose.

"What about Grenadier Sergeant Clive Gordon? Was he merely a courier, or one of your operatives?"

"He was one of our best."

Round pegs. The courageous men and women dispatched to operate behind enemy lines were round pegs fitted into unbelievably dangerous square holes.

"He made his last contact with his superior just prior to boarding that U.S. Army Air Corps transport. We're certain the C-47 went down over the Channel but were never able to verify the exact date or location."

"We have," Cleo announced. "It was spotted going in by the pilot of another transport that departed Upottery Airfield at 1420 hours on March 17. We've got the magnetic bearing and exact coordinates of the crash."

The polite mask Johanna had perfected over the years slipped. Astonished, she gaped at the American. "However did you unearth those details?"

"We started with a tip from one of Caswell's gambling buddies at Mildenhall, followed the trail to the base historian, who pointed us to a local expert on Dakota transports and ended up digging through the intelligence summaries stored in your national archives at Kew."

"Kew? Good heavens!"

No wonder the woman's hair and clothing stank of smoke!

"I heard a snippet on the radio just before you arrived. It said something about a fire at the Public Records Office. Were you caught in it?"

"Well…"

"She wasn't just caught in it," Jack put in dryly. "She started it."

"I did *not* start it," Cleo countered, knifing Donovan with an evil look. "I merely detonated the device that started it. Unintentionally, I might add."

"Good heavens," Johanna said again.

Still stunned but recovering fast, she pressed the Americans for details. Their stark tale of an explosive device buried inside musty old files, malfunctioning fire extinguishers and a disabled fire-suppression system started goose bumps marching up her arms. But when Cleo made a passing reference to a rodent perched atop the World War II records, Johanna's heart stopped dead inside her chest.

"A rat? You saw a rat?"

"Yes." Scrunching her nose in distaste, the American downed a gulp of Scotch. "I never really appre-

ciated the expression 'beady little eyes' until I pulled
that drawer open."

Johanna was already off the stool and halfway to
the door. "Please excuse me. I must ring my superior
at once. Pour yourself another drink, if you wish. Or
you might catch the late news on television. I'm sure
the fire will be featured on it."

Johanna was right. The story made the late news.
So did Cleo, rumpled red wool blazer, smoke-
streaked face, bald patch, and all.

The reporter who'd cornered her had done his
homework. The caption below her picture identified
her as the president and CEO of North Security and
Investigations, a private consulting firm headquar-
tered in the United States.

"Oh, great," she groaned. "Just how a corporate
exec wants to come across on international television. What do you want to bet I don't get many new
clients out of this interview?"

Any concerns about new clients vaporized a moment later, as the camera cut back to the news desk
and the serious young anchorwoman.

"The incident tonight brought forcefully to mind
the media coverage of documents released by the
Public Records Office in 1999. Once classified top secret, these documents detailed a wide range of devices developed for use by British agents engaged in
clandestine operations during the Second World War.

The devices included such items as papier-mâché logs used to conceal grenades, bombs disguised as cow dung, Electrolux vacuums containing built-in wireless sets, and one-man submarines that could travel more than four hundred miles and carry explosive charges powerful enough to sink a German destroyer."

Pictures of each of the items mentioned flashed on the screen. After the minisub, the anchorwoman reappeared wearing a small moue of distaste.

"One of the more imaginative devices was an exploding rat. Technicians at the former Special Operations Executive stuffed the dead rodents with bombs especially designed to fit their body cavities."

"Holy shit!" The Scotch still left in Cleo's glass sloshed over its sides. "Jack, look at that!"

The diagram of a long, whiskered rodent appeared behind the announcer, complete with detailed written instructions on how to arm and detonate the device implanted inside it.

"From the reports of a dead rodent being spotted just prior to the explosion at Kew tonight, authorities are wondering whether some malicious mischief-maker may have utilized these exact instructions to construct a similar device."

11

A thousand miles across a storm-tossed sea, another watcher paid close attention to the same news report. He tuned into the BBC regularly.

"...authorities are wondering whether some malicious mischief-maker may have utilized these exact instructions to construct a similar device."

"Yes," the assassin murmured, "I did. I did, indeed."

He'd intended to merely remove the material and destroy it. But he'd lingered too long in the vault, waiting for two researchers to leave. He couldn't risk them taking special note of him, couldn't show his face to the security cameras. So he'd resorted to his backup plan and slipped the device inside the drawer when their backs were turned.

He'd calculated the charge carefully. Enough to ignite the files, but not seriously maim or kill.

Not that he drew the line at killing. He'd eliminated

many men. A number of women, too. That's what he'd been trained to do. What he'd excelled at. He'd never taken joy in the act, though. Never felt a thrill at bringing down a target. Even the American captain he'd been forced to eliminate.

His heart cold, the assassin stared fixedly at the screen until the story switched to an accident on a fog-shrouded motorway involving three lorries and five cars. A click of the remote muted the newscast.

Feeling infinitely weary, he rested his head against the hand-stitched tapestry of his chair. His gaze drifted from the screen to the drapes he'd left parted to the stormy night. He liked watching lightning fork through the angry darkness, feeding his memories on the thunder of the sea crashing against the rocks. He'd once carried that same anger inside him, once delivered that same relentless fury.

Now...

Now he killed only because he had to. The rest of the time he spent here, tending his beloved roses and the family that had become his own.

12

Jack and Cleo waited with gathering impatience until Johanna returned to the library.

She made straight for the bar. Splashing another healthy wallop of gin into her glass, she ignored the tonic and took a long swallow before turning to face her guests.

"I've just spoken to my superior. He's given me the green light to share some rather sensitive details concerning the case you're working."

"It's about time," Jack snapped.

"Yes, well, you know how HQ is. Their need to compartmentalize and feed agents in the field only what they think we need to know can really throw a spanner in the works at times."

Cleo gave Donovan a pointed look but managed to refrain from comment as Johanna brought her drink with her and sank into a leather chair.

"I believe I've mentioned SOE? Our wartime organization set up to collect intelligence and conduct clandestine operations behind enemy lines?"

"You aren't the only one who's mentioned it," Jack commented. "We watched the news while you were on the phone. Evidently the reporter who interviewed Cleo made the connection between the incident at the PRO and some recently declassified documents that detailed the SOE's more inventive exploding devices."

"Bloody hell! That was already on the news, was it?"

"It was. The reporter also suggested whoever planted the bomb copycatted it from those old documents."

"Yes, well, that would be one explanation."

"You have an alternative theory?"

Johanna thrust a hand through her dark hair. Even now, after clearance from HQ, it was difficult to put the incredible tale into words.

"We're not sure, but we believe that incendiary bomb—like the bullets used to kill Captain Caswell—may have been developed by a special SOE cadre."

"Believe?" Jack echoed.

"I'm afraid our knowledge of this unit is rather hazy. A V-1 rocket hit the building housing it in the last days of the war. All records were destroyed and most of the personnel killed. The only survivor still living is a Mr. Phillip Potts, and I'm sorry to say, his mind is sadly muddled these days."

Intrigued, Cleo hooked her elbows on her knees. "What was so special about this cadre?"

"It conceived of one of the more daring clandestine operations of the war. Simply put, they created exact doubles of various German officials and Nazi sympathizers, then sent them to replace the originals."

"You're kidding!"

"That was my reaction when I first heard of the scheme. Rumors about it have circulated within our intelligence community for years, but I'd never quite believed them. None of us in MI6 did. Only recently did I learn this cadre not only existed, it actually managed to fit round pegs into square holes."

"Come again?"

"That's what they called their operation: Round Peg. They selected volunteers and reshaped them so they would fit into their targets' skin, into their lives. From what we can gather, it took considerable effort. A team of highly skilled surgeons altered facial and body features of these volunteers. Linguists drilled them in accents and idioms. Refugees and POWs provided intimate details of the targets' preferences and personal habits."

Cleo had conducted enough undercover investigations herself to know how tough it was to maintain a *fictional* cover. She couldn't imagine sliding into a real person's life.

"Who did these folks impersonate?"

"One took over as manager of a munitions factory

in Dresden. Another assumed the duties of a Dutch physician who screened and treated women selected for German brothels. I'm told he provided absolutely essential intelligence prior to the invasion of Holland." She paused, drew in a breath. "One was aboard a U.S. transport that went down in the Channel on March 17."

"Grenadier Sergeant Clive Gordon."

"Yes. There were others, although the exact number is imprecise."

"How did you bring these round pegs home afterward, if you didn't know how many you had or who they were?"

"Four made contact with us. We believe at least two others were killed. In bombing raids, perhaps. Or they might have tripped themselves up and been shot as spies, although no documentation has ever come to light indicating the Nazis knew they had impersonators in their midst."

"What happened to the men they impersonated?" Cleo asked, although she suspected she already knew the answer.

"They were disposed of."

Johanna made no apologies. War was war.

"This operation was all very hush-hush," she continued. "Ultra top secret, as you might imagine. From what we've been able to piece together, the look-alikes were armed with an assortment of well-forged documents and rather ingenious weapons."

"Like exploding rats and cow patties?"

"And," she added after a brief hesitation, "some rather potent itching powders."

"Hey, I've read about those. Our side played with them, too."

Like all AF OSI recruits, Cleo had devoured case studies from the Office of Strategic Services. Organized during World War Two, the OSS was the U.S. counterpart to Britain's SOE and the precursor to the CIA. At its peak, it numbered more than forty thousand personnel, including some seventeen thousand women. Most women served as code breakers. A few, like Julia Child, Marlene Dietrich, and sexy, sultry Josephine Baker, gathered intelligence in the field.

In one of their more bizarre brain farts, the wunderkinds in the OSS special weapons lab developed an irritant for field agents to pass to children in Japanese-occupied China. The kids were instructed to toss the powder at Japanese officers and run away. The officers, it was theorized, would lose face when reduced to frenzied scratching in front of others and thus become demoralized.

"You know," Cleo muttered, "that exploding rat suddenly doesn't seem so crazy. Not as crazy as itching powder as a weapon of war, anyway."

Johanna bit her lip. "I wish that were so. Unfortunately, the powder SOE developed contained an ingredient we now know grows more virulent over time."

"Uh-oh."

"Yes," the Englishwoman said with a helpless shrug. "Quite."

"Just how virulent?"

"If allowed to incubate for extended periods of time, it can cause extreme irritation to the mucus membranes and eventual death to anyone who breathes it. It's also highly airborne. One teaspoonful tossed on a brisk breeze could wipe out a small town."

Cleo let out a slow whistle and left it to Jack to pick up the thread from there.

"So that's why you're so interested in that C-47. It's not the gold you're concerned about, it's what Sergeant Gordon might have been carrying with him."

"Exactly." Her face tight with worry, Johanna hunched forward. "Obviously, someone recovered Gordon's Colt .45 from the wreck of that downed aircraft. We don't know what else was recovered. Our best guess is no one retrieved a canister of this powder. If they had and opened it, there would have been a huge outcry. But you understand how imperative it is that we locate the transport and make sure."

With a huff of amazement, Cleo flopped back against her seat. "And here I thought this case couldn't take any more twists and turns!"

Jack ignored her editorial comment and pinned Johanna with a sharp look. "What's the plan now?"

"My superiors are arranging for a team of divers to search for and dive on the wreck, if and when we locate it. I'm to brief the team when they assemble on Monday. I plan to accompany them on the dive, as well."

"Count us in on that."

"I'll have to get clearance for you to go along."

Ice-blue eyes locked with gray. "Seeing as Cleo and I are the only ones who know the coordinates of the crash site, I doubt that will be a problem."

Promising to make another call to her superiors and arrange matters, Johanna escorted her guests up the well-worn oak stairs. She refrained from comment when Cleo staked a claim to one bedroom and Jack the one across the hall. The ultrapolite expression that flitted across her face suggested she thought they'd chosen separate rooms merely for form's sake.

Cleo had to admit she was having second thoughts about the arrangement herself. Taking sex out of the equation had sounded rational and intelligent and necessary when she'd first proposed it. Making the transition from proposal to actual fact was proving tougher than she'd anticipated.

"You have this floor to yourselves," Johanna said, adding to Cleo's annoying doubts. "I'm below. We had part of the kitchen and back parlor converted to a master suite when Barty—my husband—took ill and couldn't make the stairs. There's a hot-water pot for coffee or tea in your rooms and I left some biscuits, but feel free to raid the pantry if you should get hungry."

After Johanna went downstairs, the tin of thick, chewy macaroons claimed Cleo's immediate attention. A hot shower to remove the smoky stink from her skin and hair came next on her agenda. Wrapped in a plush ruby robe provided by her hostess, she made another swoop at the cookie tin before heading across the hall.

Jack had left his door partly open. He was standing at the window, staring out at the darkness and massaging the back of his neck. The weary slump to his shoulders under the white cotton of his T-shirt roused an unfamiliar need in Cleo.

The urge to soothe and stroke him startled her. Donovan had never stirred those impulses in her before. Lust, yes. Violent explosions of pleasure, definitely. Annoyance and anger, frequently. But this need to comfort Donovan was new to her.

Swallowing the last bite of coconut-covered macaroon, she rapped lightly on his door. "You okay?"

His hand dropped and his shoulders regained their horizontal line. "Yeah. Just tired."

"I can't imagine why. I mean, we arrived in England, what? Just over thirty-six hours ago? We've been a tad busy since then."

"Just a tad," he agreed with one of those slow grins that curled Cleo's toes.

No sex, she reminded herself sternly. There would be no sex.

"And as I recall, you spent most of last night being pissed at me. Did you get any sleep at all?"

"Not much," he admitted.

She chewed on the inside of her cheek. Those unfamiliar urges were still tugging at her. The lust was there, too, swirling around just under the surface, but she figured she could handle it.

"Want me to un-kink those knots in your neck? I got pretty good at massage when my dad and I lived in Bangkok. Pop says I have fingers of steel."

"And that's supposed to reassure me?"

"Don't be such a baby. I'll be gentle with you."

"Yeah, that's what they all say." He hooked a brow. "Do we get naked for this?"

"Nope. In a traditional Thai massage both practitioner and subject remain clothed."

"Well, hell. What's the point?"

"Do you want me to work on that neck or not?"

"Okay. Just go easy with those fingers of steel."

Grinning at his wary expression, Cleo locked her hands and flexed them back. Her knuckles gave with small, satisfying pops.

"We really should put you on the floor and start with your feet to properly release your *sen*."

"If want sin, you should start higher than my feet."

"*Sen*, Donovan. S-E-N. Sit here, on the edge of the bed. We'll just work the soft tissues in your neck tonight."

She scooted around and spread her thighs on either side of his hips. He still carried a smoky tang, not as strong since he'd discarded his Oxford shirt and jacket, but it was there in his hair and his skin. If she closed her eyes, Cleo might imagine leaves burning on a crisp fall day instead of beady-eyed rodents.

"Okay, here's the deal. Thai massage involves two separate processes. First we press the muscles your *sen* passes through, to open the channels."

"What is this *sen*, anyway?"

"Energy, heat, life force. Whatever." She clucked impatiently. "Turn your head back around."

Still wary, he faced front. Cleo pressed her hands to his shoulders. The cotton of his T-shirt was smooth and soft under her palms, but the muscles underneath were strung wire tight. She followed their curve to the base of his neck.

"This might hurt a little."

Despite the warning, Donovan nearly jumped off the bed when she dug in her thumbs.

"Jesus, North! You call that a massage?"

"It'll get better."

"When?" he forced out through gritted teeth.

"Soon. I promise. Just hang in there."

In a traditional Thai massage the practitioner used hands, elbows and feet to work the pressure points and release *sen*. Obviously, Jack wasn't ready for elbows or feet. Her thumbs and palms did the trick, though. She kept the pace of the massage slow, the pressure rhythmical. Gradually, his taut muscles relaxed to the point where she felt comfortable progressing to the next step.

"Now we stretch."

Sliding her arms under his, she brought her hands up and linked them at his nape.

"Just bend with me. Slowly. Slowly."

She tipped his head forward, relaxed the pressure, bent him again. This was the trickiest part. She had to make sure she didn't overstretch the muscles.

"If I did this right, you should feel as though you're floating on air. Are you there yet?"

"Maybe. Almost."

The reply was grudging and muffled against his chest. Easing the pressure, Cleo let him rest a moment.

God, she loved the feel of him. The smooth cotton, the sculptured contours. A pleasure she'd never experienced with Donovan before eddied through her. It was a small joy, this satisfaction of knowing she could ease his aches. Small and fierce.

She bent him forward a final time before untangling her arms. "That's as much as your neck should take for the first session. How are the kinks?"

He tried a few experimental twists and turns. Surprise and relief threaded through his reply. "They're gone."

"Want me to do your shoulders?"

"Go for it."

Hooking a leg under her for leverage, Cleo started on his right shoulder. She went cautiously at first, circling around the hard, ridged scar where the bullet had exited. There was a matching scar on his front side, she knew, where the twenty-point hollow grain slug had ripped into his flesh.

While her thumbs applied pressure, her mind went back to the terrifying moments in Honduras, when she'd had to staunch the blood and patch Jack up. That was their first op together. Almost their last.

This one was starting to look almost as hairy.

"You really want to go on this dive?" she asked, frowning at the back of his head.

"Don't you?"

Her hands stilled, resting lightly on his shoulders. "I'll admit the possibility of burning up my mucus membranes doesn't hold a whole lot of appeal."

The smooth cotton slithered under her fingers as he twisted around. They were face-to-face now, breath to breath.

"There's no reason for you to go, Cleo. If we turn up anything that relates to the Caswell murder, I'll read you in."

Sure he would. If and when he figured she had a need to know.

The thought torpedoed Cleo's tender, nurturing feelings. With a brisk slap on his shoulder, she disengaged and pushed off the bed.

"The OSI is paying me big bucks to work this case, Donovan. I'm not real thrilled at the prospect of hunting for a canister of membrane-scorching powder, but the idea it might be sitting there at the bottom of the Channel, ready to break open at any moment, thrills me even less."

"There's another possibility," Jack pointed out, following her to the door. "Whoever recovered Gordon's weapon from the wreck might have recovered the canister as well. He could be sitting on it, just waiting for the right moment to pry it open."

That possibility didn't give Cleo any more of a buzz than the others had.

"There's also the chance Gordon wasn't packing any itching powder at all," he reminded her. "So *if* we locate this plane and *if* we can get down to it, there's no guarantee we'll find anything at all."

"True. I'll take that warm, comforting thought to bed with me tonight."

Hooking a hand in the V-neck of her borrowed robe, he tugged her forward. "Why don't you take this instead?"

When his mouth came down on hers, Cleo's blood leaped in response. She went up on her toes, fully prepared to wrap her arms around him and put another kink in his neck.

She should have known Jack would play by the rules. It didn't help that they were her rules this time. She almost wept when he broke the contact. Her frustrated groan had his mouth kicking up at the corners.

"Nice to know I'm not the only one feeling the bite. Sweet dreams, Cleopatra."

He sent her back across the hall with another kiss and a pat on her butt.

13

Jack woke the next morning to the trill of birds chirping like a drunken choir. Rolling out of bed, he made for the bathroom across the hall.

He splashed water on his face, slapped on shaving cream and scowled at his image in the mirror. If he'd ever given the matter any thought, he wouldn't have imagined the prospect of an entire weekend at a centuries-old English manor house would make him feel as restless as a prisoner sentenced to ten to twenty at Fort Leavenworth.

He scraped a disposable razor along his jaw, analyzing his mood. Part of it stemmed from this damned Caswell case. He'd spent a good part of last night peeling back the layers, worrying he'd missed a link between the captain and the newly busted terrorist cell, wondering just how the hell Caswell had planned to convert a stash of gold bullion to cash without raising dozens of official red flags. This business about a canister of poisonous powder hadn't exactly contributed to a restful state, either.

Add to those worries a certain hardheaded private security consultant with magic fingers and a body that left him in a constant sweat. It was a mix that would leave *any* man feeling like a caged panther.

He went downstairs a short time later and followed the aroma of fresh-brewed coffee to the kitchen. It was outfitted with gleaming, high-tech appliances and a brick fireplace that looked roomy enough to roast an ox. One glance at the woman seated at the island counter, nursing a mug, told Jack his MI6 counterpart hadn't slept any better than he had.

Her red corduroy trousers and starched white shirt gave her a fresh, crisp look, but the dark smudges under her eyes told another tale. She glanced up at his entrance, erased her frown and summoned a smile.

"Good morning. I didn't hear you come down. Would you like coffee?"

"I would, but don't leave your perch. I'll get it."

"The mugs are just there, beside the coffeemaker. There's fresh cream, too, from the next farm."

Jack passed on the cream, but added his usual sugar dump. When he took the stool at right angles to Johanna's, she nudged a plate across the black granite counter.

"My housekeeper doesn't come in on weekends, but she left some fresh baked Bath buns in a tin. Can you make do with these for now? I'll cook up eggs and bangers when I hear Cleo stirring."

The reference to Cleo and bangers in the same sentence almost had Jack choking on his coffee, but he managed a credible response. His first bite of the yeasty muffin stuffed with berries and spices had him wondering how many he could down without making a pig of himself. He was on his second swallow when Johanna's cell phone pinged.

She glanced at the number on the LCD screen but evidently didn't recognize it. With a murmured "excuse me" to Jack, she flipped up the cover.

"Johanna Marston speaking."

A moment later, her frown snapped back into place.

"Oh, no! When did this happen?"

Her glance whipped to Jack. Tight lines appeared at the corners of her mouth. As the seconds ticked by, the knuckles on the hand gripping the phone turned white.

"You're certain that's what he said? Just that? Nothing more?"

Her stool scraped against the brick floor. The phone jammed to her ear, she began to pace.

"Yes. Yes, I will. Someone will get in touch with her straightaway. Thank you, Mrs. Lancaster."

She slapped the phone shut, frustration in every line of her slender body. "Bloody hell!"

"Bad news?"

"Do you remember me mentioning Mr. Potts? Mr. Phillip Potts, the lone survivor of the special cadre I told you about?"

"The one who's gone senile?"

"Yes. He suffered a massive heart attack and died last night." Her gaze lanced into Jack. "His nurse said he became agitated while watching the late evening news."

Slowly, he lowered his mug. "Let me guess. He saw the story about Cleo and the explosion at Kew."

"Evidently. His nurse says she went to get his medication. When she returned, he was slumped in his chair, dead."

Cleo entered the kitchen in time to catch the tail end of that. Face scrubbed clean, clingy black T-shirt tucked neatly into her slim jeans, she gave Johanna a quick glance.

"Who was dead?"

"Phillip Potts, the elderly gentleman I told you about last night. From the SOE special cadre."

"He saw you on TV," Jack said with a wry twist of his lips, "and checked out."

The Bath bun Cleo had snagged from the tin on the counter hovered halfway to her mouth. She thought about refuting Donovan's unsubtle suggestion she'd offed the gentleman and decided it was unworthy of response. She made the connection, though. She could hardly miss it.

"Coffee. Black. Please."

She directed the request at Jack since he was nearest the pot and directed another at Johanna. "Tell me what happened."

"Essentially what Jack said. Mr. Potts was watching the news, became agitated and suffered a heart attack when his nurse hurried off to get his medication. I was just about to tell Jack that Mrs. Lancaster—the nurse—indicated Mr. Potts kept repeating one word over and over. Jarlsberg."

"Jarlsberg? You mean like in the cheese?"

"I'm not sure what it means. I only just got word of all this."

Cleo was already sifting through possibilities. "Well, there *is* one connection that leaps instantly to mind." She sketched an air circle with her bun. "You use cheese to bait a rat trap, right?"

"Actually, we use bacon or some other form of meat here on the farm. It works better for rats."

"Just go with me. These look-alikes the special cadre sent in had to use something to lure their targets into a trap, right? Maybe Potts was trying to tell us this Jarlsberg was the bait. Or the target," she added, her mind racing.

"It's certainly an angle to explore."

"Here's another," Jack said as he delivered Cleo's coffee. "Johanna, you indicated the transport that went down in the Channel was ferrying gold to resistance fighters. Isn't Jarlsberg a form of Dutch cheese?"

"I believe it's Norwegian." Something seemed to click in Johanna. She sat up straighter, her brow furrowing. "It's possible Mr. Potts wasn't referring to anything edible. Jarlsberg could well be a family name or town in Norway."

"Did you have operatives working with the Norwegian resistance?"

"Yes, of course. And there's a chance Grenadier Sergeant Gordon was intended to become one of them. I seem to recall that his mother was born somewhere in Scandinavia. I'll have our people check the parish records at the village where he was born."

Excitement threaded her voice, but she felt obliged to issue a caution.

"We must remember that Mr. Potts had become confused with age. Perhaps he saw an advert about cheese before or after the newscast that played on his mind."

"That's easy enough to check," Cleo pointed out.

"Yes, it is. I'll have our folks at headquarters run a replay of the programming from last night. I'll also put them to work on this new information. For all we know, there might well be something buried in old SOE files that links exploding rats and cheese."

Cleo would love to have a look at those old files herself. The deadly serious business of gathering intelligence had come a long way since early spymasters strapped cameras onto homing pigeons and planted explosives in cow dung. Technology would never substitute for ingenuity, though. Not in the world of undercover agents and clandestine operations.

"In the meantime," Johanna continued, "headquarters has informed me they're sending a dive master down later this afternoon. He's bringing computerized Admiralty charts and wants to get a fix on the search area to determine what equipment will be needed for the dive on Monday."

Cleo reached for another sticky bun. "While we wait for this guy, I'll do some serious Googling and see what kind of hits I get."

Within hours, she'd gathered more information than she'd ever expected to know about rat traps, bait and Count Wedel Jarlsberg, whose descendents still resided on the Oslo fjord where the cheese that bore his name was first made. The Jarlsberg family traced its history back to the Vikings. Hundreds of descendants still populated Norway, Argentina and, Cleo discovered with an excited yip, Minnesota.

"Jack! Look at this." She stabbed a finger at the screen. "There are Jarlsbergs in Minnesota. That's where our boy Caswell was from."

"So it was."

His tone suggested Minnesota was a big state. Cleo wasn't about to give up on the lead.

"What are the odds there's a connection there somewhere?"

"Pretty slim, but it's worth a check."

Fishing his cell phone out of his shirt pocket, Jack contacted OSI operations and asked them to dig deeper into Douglas Caswell's background and family history.

They were still waiting to hear back when they joined Johanna for a hearty lunch of green pea salad, cold cuts and custard pie. They ate in the kitchen, at a table set in an alcove that gave a view of the rolling green fields behind the manor.

"The threads are starting to form a loose weave," Cleo said between forkfuls of salad. "Too loose to see any pattern yet."

"Perhaps not as loose as you think. HQ rang whilst you were on the computer. I was correct. Parish records confirm Clive Harold Gordon was born to one Harold Gordon and Eva Sondestrom. The records don't list her country of birth, but the name certainly has a Scandinavian ring."

Jack pounced on that. "Which would have made Eva's son a perfect candidate for Operation Round Peg. Gordon probably visited relatives on his mother's side. Maybe learned to speak her native tongue. He'd fit right in."

"Yes, so it would seem."

"Have your people spoken to any of Gordon's relatives?" Cleo asked. "They might know something about his death that we don't."

"According to army records, Gordon was an only

child and both parents died before the war. He lists no other close relatives."

"No wife or kids?"

"He lost his wife and only son in the Blitz."

"Ouch."

Johanna nodded. "As tragic as that loss was, though, it would explain why he was chosen for Operation Round Peg. He had no one to come home to, you see."

"And no one to comment on his altered appearance," Jack observed.

"Yes, quite. As for tracking down relatives on his mother's side, I hardly see how it would help at this point. None of them could have known Sergeant Gordon was aboard that transport. Official army records show simply that he was reported MIA, presumed KIA, in March 1944."

"Oh. Right. Operation Round Peg was ultra hush-hush."

"Exactly. We just began to dig into Gordon's death after your Captain Caswell was murdered with a Colt .45 once issued to him. It's the Colt that worries us, and whether or not someone might have recovered it from the wreck."

"Along with certain other souvenirs," Cleo murmured, poking a fork at the creamy green-pea salad. "I have to admit the idea of a canister full of nasty stuff resting on the ocean floor gives me the willies. Let's hope this dive master they're sending down here knows his stuff."

"I'm quite confident he will," Johanna said briskly. "Royal Navy divers are among the most experienced and highly skilled in the world."

They were also among the most highly tasked, Johanna learned soon after opening the door a little more than an hour later.

Her first reaction to the man on her front stoop was surprise. Her second, suspicion.

"Mr. Mulholland. What are you doing here in Bethersden?"

Her address hadn't been on the card she'd given him. Johanna was sure of it.

"Captain Daggett sent me."

Dag sent him? This salty sea dog?

"I'm sorry, but I was told to expect a navy dive master."

"I *am* navy. Retired reserve. I'm required by law to maintain my qualifications for a period of twelve years, during which time I'm subject to recall to active service."

She knew that, Johanna thought on a wave of irritation. She would have imagined, though, that members of the retired reserve would be required to maintain their military appearance as well as their qualifications.

Mulholland's eyes were no longer rimmed with red, but his too-long hair curled untidily over his shirt collar and his sea captain's hat was crushed and ringed with salt. He needed a shave, Johanna thought with a moue of distaste. And a good tailor.

"Captain Daggett taps me for special missions when he doesn't have an active team immediately available," Mulholland informed her, his tone edged with impatience. "Do you want to see my master's certificates, Lady Marston?"

"That won't be necessary. I'll ring Captain Daggett, however, before we discuss the specifics of this operation."

"Very well." His mouth twisted. "Shall I wait here on the steps, then?"

The sarcasm thinned her lips. "No, of course not. The library's just down the hall. If you'd care to step inside, I'll... Oh, there you two are."

Jack and Cleo came down the hall at that moment, drawn by the sound of voices. Johanna made the introductions.

"Captain Mulholland, this is Cleo North, a private security consultant from the States, and Major Jack Donovan of the United States Air Force Office of Special Investigations. Jack, Cleo, this is Sean Mulholland, captain of the *Argos II*."

Jack threw Johanna a quick look, which she answered with an almost imperceptible lift of her shoulders. His expression neutral, Donovan offered Mulholland his hand.

"I believe I spoke briefly to your mate yesterday morning."

"Yes, he told me."

Sean had served with enough officers in his nineteen years of service to take this one's measure in a swift, all-encompassing glance. Donovan carried himself with an air that said he was comfortable in his skin. His grip confirmed Sean's impression. It was hard, but not the bone-crunching vise of a man with something to prove.

By contrast, his companion's no-nonsense grip surprised Sean. It told him this Cleo North was used to operating in a man's world and good at it.

And easy on the eyes while she was about it. He liked the way her jeans molded trim hips and the long, endless legs American women all seemed to be equipped with. Liked, too, the thick-lashed brown eyes that returned his intent scrutiny without the least hint of apology.

"I saw you on the BBC last night," he said. "You looked as though you'd had a time of it in Kew."

Rueful laughter crept into her eyes. "I did."

Sean blinked, taken aback by her smile. She was cracking, the American. Not in the same class as Johanna Marston, but cracking.

"Would you take Captain Mulholland into the library?" the lady asked in that cool, Oxbridge way of hers. "I'll join you in a moment."

Johanna waited for the three of them to enter the library before retreating to the privacy of her office. Some moments later, the operations center at headquarters patched her through to Roger Daggett's home.

Dag had been Barty's closest mate at Eton. They'd continued their friendship afterward and expanded the tight circle to include their spouses. Dag and his wife, Eleanor, had spent almost as many hours at the hospital as Johanna had during those last, terrible weeks.

He came on the phone moments later, his rolling Yorkshire accent as familiar as it was dear. "Hello, Johanna. Did my dive master arrive?"

"Yes. I thought you were sending me a navy man, Dag."

"I did."

"An *active*-duty navy man."

"Unfortunately, the two other chaps I would trust with this dive are currently in opposite corners of the globe."

"But Sean Mulholland? However did you come up with him?"

"Mulholland served under me aboard the *Suffolk*. He's…"

A door banged, followed by girlish shrieks of laughter. Dag's granddaughters, Johanna thought, belatedly remembering this was Saturday afternoon.

"Sarah," he barked. "Pamela. Take it outside."

There was more laughter, a giggling "Aye, aye, sir," then another slam.

"As I was saying, Mulholland served under me aboard the *Suffolk*. You won't find a better man for this mission. Apparently this Yank air force officer who was murdered thought so, too. Mulholland said the captain had contacted him about locating this wreck we've all become so nogged about. Sean is convinced the American was after more than souvenir photos of the wreck."

There was a pause, a direct probe.

"I vetted Petty Officer Mulholland with my superiors before I tagged him for this operation, Johanna. Is there a problem?"

How could there be, if Dag vouched for him?

"No. It's simply that he's, well, a bit scruffy."

"Gone to the dogs, has he? It won't affect his work, I assure you. If anyone can locate this transport you're looking for, it's Mulholland."

"Is he aware what might be aboard the wreck?"

Neither of them would get into specifics over an unsecure line, but Johanna needed to know how thoroughly Mulholland had been briefed.

"Yes," Dag confirmed, "he is. I wouldn't ask any of my men to make a dive like this without explaining the risks."

14

"You say these documents indicate the C-47 was spotted going in by another transport that left RAF Upottery at 1420 hours, March 17, 1943?"

"Right."

Cleo flipped through the pages of the charred Intelligence summary. She, Jack and Johanna were crowded around the desk in the library, oblivious to the sunshine spilling through the windows. All eyes were on Sean Mulholland as he attempted to determine a starting point for the search for the missing transport.

"The spotter plane flew a course of 213 degrees magnetic for thirty-five minutes," she read, "and departed England via the Bill of Portland. What is that?"

"Portland Bill is a narrow, rugged peninsula," Mulholland informed her as he entered the data into the sleek, titanium-cased computer he'd carried in with him. "Thomas Hardy described it as the Gibraltar of Wessex."

Cleo found the contrast between the high-tech laptop and the man hunched over it fascinating. He reminded her of Goose, the former Special Ops type who acted as her personal trainer. Both were big, tattooed and muscled up. Where Goose shaved his head and decked himself out in biker's leather and chains, though, Mulholland sported a shaggy mane streaked with silver at the temples, a faded red polo shirt, and an attitude. Cleo couldn't quite pinpoint the reason behind it, but she noticed his faint, almost imperceptible Irish accent lost some of its lilt whenever he addressed Johanna.

Like now, when he responded to her request to know what data he was calling up.

"Weather reports."

Johanna's eyes narrowed at the terse reply. She'd drawn Cleo and Jack aside and told them to disregard her earlier doubts about Mulholland. A man whose judgment she trusted implicitly had vetted him for this mission. She still hadn't warmed up to the captain, though. That much was obvious from the nip to her voice.

"They've input weather reports from that far back, have they?"

"Yes."

A man of few words, Captain Mulholland. Also

like Goose, Cleo thought. She edged closer, fascinated by the way the skipper's big hands manipulated the keys.

"What are you looking for? Wind speed and direction?"

He nodded, his eyes on the screen. "I'll need both to determine how far the transport traveled in thirty-five minutes."

The desired information was painted across the screen a few moments later. Mulholland switched to a navigational computation program and pasted in the pertinent details.

"If we factor in the flying time," he said, the keys clicking, "the C-47's cruising speed of one hundred and seventy five miles per hour, the pilot's course after he left his home base, and a headwind of fifteen knots, we come up with an approximate set of coordinates."

A nautical chart depicting the Channel painted across the screen.

"That's it?" Excited, Cleo squinted at the dot flashing some miles off the southeastern coast of England. "That's our search point?"

"Not quite. We also have to consider currents at that time of year and how badly our wreck broke up when it went in. If we input a maximum scatter pattern…"

The dot became a circle.

"We also have to consider the cargo load the spotter was carrying."

"According to the report, he was ferrying troops

and equipment to North Africa in preparation for the invasion of Sicily."

The keys clicked again. "We'll give him a max load of six thousand pounds, which will slow his cruising speed and widen the search area."

The circle doubled in area, bursting Cleo's bubble. "I'm no sailor, but that looks like a big patch of water."

"It is. We're looking at an area covering more than a hundred square miles."

Surprisingly, Mulholland didn't seem daunted by the prospect of combing all those square miles of ocean.

"In the days before side-scanning radar, it would have taken us a month or more to cover an area that size. Now we can do it in a fraction of that time. That's the good news."

"And the bad?"

"This is one of the most traveled parts of the Channel. There are scores of known wrecks in the area, probably three or four times that number buried in silt and as yet uncovered. We have a job ahead of us to find our wreck among all those others."

He hit Save and copied the chart to a backup disk before shutting down the laptop. His next words further dimmed Cleo's hopes for a quick find.

"This is just a preliminary fix. I'll need to bounce the working parameters against more precise Admiralty Raster charts, our Royal Navy course plotters and Receiver of Wrecks databases. I also want to talk to a couple of RAF chaps I know." Shoving his computer into a padded carrying case, he turned to Johanna. "I'll ring you when I've determined whether or not we have enough to mount a dive expedition."

"When do expect that will be?"

"Late tonight. Tomorrow morning at the latest. If it's a go, I'll move the *Argos II* down to Weymouth and direct the crew to assemble there. It's the closest port to the search area."

"Very well."

"If we do launch a search, I want to shove off at first light Monday morning. You'll need to be aboard by then." His gaze fixed on Johanna's face. "If you're still set on tagging along."

The grudging remark brought her chin up and a chill to her voice. Very much lady of the manor, she gave a regal nod.

"Yes, Captain, I am."

"We all are," Jack put in, either in an attempt to calm the rough seas or draw Mulholland's fire.

Reluctantly, Cleo nodded her assent. The fact that the last ship she'd boarded had exploded and sunk might have had something to do with her lukewarm enthusiasm.

"Do you have room for us?"

"The *Argos II* can handle up to twelve divers. You'll find the accommodations adequate."

Tipping two fingers to the bill of his misshapen cap, he followed Johanna out.

Jack used the interval before her return to make a call to OSI headquarters. The research division was still digging into Captain Caswell's childhood and connections in Minnesota, but they had turned up detailed information on Bouncing Bertha—including the names of the crew members who went down with her, her call sign and the serial number etched into the instrument panel.

"Good. Tell them to e-mail me the data right away. The painted tail number and unit markings will have long since disappeared, but we can ID her by the serial number—if the metal instrument panels haven't rusted away, too."

Uh-oh. If metal airframes could rust, so could metal canisters. Cleo put the thought on hold, as Jack's shoulders stiffened.

"When?"

He turned his back, the phone cradled against his ear. It was an instinctive move, one that Cleo had no difficulty interpreting. He was shutting her out. Again.

"Give me the number. I'll contact her."

She said nothing as Jack ended the call and punched in a phone number. He stood rigid, obviously waiting for an answering machine to cycle through its recorded message. Cleo could hear the faint beep from where she stood.

"This is Jack Donovan. I was told you were trying to reach me. I'm in England." He lifted his wrist, confirmed the time. "It's 1520—3:20—here. Call me when you get this message."

After giving his cell number, Jack snapped the instrument shut. Cleo measured the seconds while he stared at the books lining the library shelves. Just enough of his profile showed for her to see that his jaw had locked.

His ex, she thought. That call had to be about his ex. Cleo had witnessed firsthand how the woman could tie him in knots with just a phone call.

She was damned if she'd break the stony silence, though. He had to take the first step, had to make the decision to include her in his life.

He did, finally, but it was pure pain to watch. He rolled his shoulder as if trying to shift an immense weight, jammed his phone in his pocket, and turned.

"Kate's counselor called OSI headquarters, trying to locate me. Evidently Kate has missed her last two sessions. They want to know if I have any information as to her whereabouts."

"Do you?"

"No."

"Okay, so you tell them so."

His jaw worked. "You don't understand. This counseling is court-mandated, required as a condition of her suspended sentence for that DUI. She misses another session, they'll revoke the suspension and issue an arrest warrant."

Cleo bit back the suggestion that a good long

stretch in the county lockup might help the former Mrs. Donovan see what her drinking was doing to her.

And to Jack.

"You're right, I don't understand. Why is this your problem?"

"We were married for more than twelve years, Cleo."

"And you've been divorced for, what? Three? Four?"

"It's not that easy."

"I'm beginning to see that."

She was treading carefully here, or trying to. The truth was, Cleo found it hard to relate to the guilt Jack hauled around with him like an anchor on a chain. She pretty much subscribed to the get-on-with-it philosophy of life. Career-wise, she'd made the transition from air force investigator to private security consultant without looking back. Romance-wise, she'd made several similar transitions.

The Texas Ranger outfielder she'd fallen for had lasted almost two years. The lawyer she'd subsequently dated had lasted considerably less than that. The first bust-up had left her sad, but not bruised. The second she'd forgotten about when Jack Donovan reentered her life.

It was sobering—and more than a little humbling—to realize Jack hadn't made the same swift transition. Whatever he and Cleo had, whatever it was that sizzled and spit whenever they got within twenty yards of each other, didn't fill the hole his ex-wife had carved in his heart.

Kate was still there. For better or worse.

Cleo wanted to understand. *Needed* to understand. Jack's sense of responsibility for his ex-wife baffled her, though. Almost as much as her father's obvious devotion to Wishy-Washy Wanda. Donovan and Patrick North were both such strong men, yet they'd tied themselves to such weak, helpless women.

Cleo felt like an Amazon by comparison. Tough, well armored, self-sufficient. Until this moment, she'd always considered those desirable attributes.

Now she couldn't help wondering if she came across as too tough, too self-sufficient. Maybe Jack believed, subconsciously or otherwise, that she was Kate's alter ego. An adrenaline junkie who got off on the thrill of the hunt. A woman who went for the throat instead of folding in a crisis. Someone who didn't need him, except in the field, when they were working an op. God knew, they'd never done anything else together.

Was that what fanned their greedy hunger for each other? The constant high that came with action and excitement and danger? Would they feel the same on a Saturday morning, raking leaves in the back yard or cleaning out closets? Not that Cleo did either, but she *did* get restless between jobs.

Would Jack?

Johanna's return forced Cleo to put the insidious thought on the back burner.

* * *

It moved front and center again later that evening.

They got the call from Mulholland a little past six. The search was a go for Monday morning. Faced with a flurry of preparations and the drive down to Weymouth the next day, Cleo, Jack and Johanna opted for dinner at the local pub and an early night.

The George boasted both a public house and a restaurant separated by a well-stocked bar. Deciding on a drink before dinner, the newcomers joined the crowd in the public house.

The proprietor paused in the act of drawing a pint and beamed a welcome across the smoky bar. "Lady Marston! It's good to see you again."

"You, too, Bill."

"It's been a while since you've been down to Bethersden."

"Indeed, it has. May I introduce my houseguests? This is Cleo North and Jack Donovan. They're from the States."

The proprietor's eyes widened with recognition. "Aren't you the one they interviewed on BBC news last night? About the fire up at Kew?"

"Yes."

"Do they know yet what caused the fire?"

Arson investigators had confirmed the presence of an explosive device, but the information hadn't been publicly released yet. Cleo dodged the question with a laugh.

"Whatever caused it, it got my attention."

The admission drew a chuckle from a farmer in muddy Wellingtons. "I saw that bit on the news about the rat. Load of rubbish, if you ask me, all that nonsense about exploding rodents and guns made out of bicycle pumps."

"No, it's true," another pub customer argued. "Didn't you read the stories back a few years ago, after they declassified those SOE documents? Opened my eyes, those stories did."

Johanna deftly avoided being drawn into the discussion. "What would you care to drink?" she asked her guests. "Bill stocks a beer made from hops grown locally and fired in an oast house right here in Bethersden."

"Sounds good to me."

The local brew was dark and nutty and packed a solid punch. Cleo downed one pint in good order but declined a second. When Johanna declined as well, they left Jack in the company of the men at the bar and claimed a table. Within moments, the farmer had co-opted Donovan into a game of darts.

He lost the first game with unimpaired good humor. He wiped the floor with the farmer in the second. Pints were emptied and refilled, cigarette smoke blued the air, and noise levels shot through the roof as the championship game kicked off.

It was a man thing, Cleo and Johanna decided with some amusement, a primal flex of muscles.

"My Barty was every bit as bad. We could never come in for a pint without someone issuing a challenge. And he never failed to rise to it."

Cleo had admired the British agent's classy looks and cool under fire, but this was the first time she'd been allowed a glimpse of the woman behind the shield.

"You miss him, don't you?"

"Every day." A sigh feathered through her lips. "You would think the ache would ease with time, wouldn't you? It merely moves to a different place."

Like Jack and Kate. They'd loved, married and divorced. Yet neither could let go.

"How long were you and Barty together?"

"Eighteen years. I met him just a week after I came up from university and took a position with the government. Two weeks after we met, we dashed off to the south of France for a weekend honeymoon."

The noise from the bar was hearty, giving Cleo the cover she needed to ask the question hovering in her mind.

"So you were married all the time you worked for your present employer?"

"Yes."

"And that never presented problems?"

"Most assuredly it did. I was gone quite frequently those first years, when he was still working his way through the ranks at his law firm. More than one superior took him to task about what was expected of me as an up-and-coming barrister's wife. Barty couldn't tell them what I did, of course."

Cleo played with the cardboard coaster. "How did it work for you when you *were* home? How did you turn off the, er, government employee and turn on the wife?"

"The same way every woman does. And every man. We females aren't the only ones who compartmentalize our lives. Barty tried hundred of cases before he left the bar to enter politics, some of them quite gory and disturbing. He couldn't wait to put off his robe during our time together. We'd spend it on mutual passions. The opera. Our garden. Our friends, here and in London."

She cocked her head, eyeing Cleo shrewdly. "Are you worried about you and Jack? That what you feel for each other is all flash and no heat?"

"Oh, the heat's there."

It was most definitely there. All Cleo needed was a glimpse of Donovan's cocky grin as he put a dart in dead center to feel it stir.

"Whether we can sustain it when we're not in the field, feeding off each other's energy, is another question."

She expected Johanna to sympathize, or at least show understanding of her doubts. She didn't expect the British agent to choke on her beer. Laughing, Lady Marston dabbed at the froth with a paper napkin.

"Oh, Cleo! Surely you know you'll generate a different sort of energy altogether when you're not in the field."

"No, I don't know. That's part of the problem. Jack and I have never been together when there weren't security breaches or murders or ships full of high explosives involved."

"Truly? You've never stolen away for a fortnight at a seaside cottage or a romantic weekend in Paris?"

"We spent a couple of days in a cave in Honduras, waiting for an extraction while druggers prowled the jungle all around us."

"That hardly qualifies as a romantic holiday."

Cleo's lips quivered. "Actually, it turned out to be pretty special after I patched the bullet hole in Jack's shoulder. The man has amazing powers of recovery."

"So do you," Johanna said with a nod toward the clear plastic Band-Aid buried under her swatch of hair. "Perhaps you might get a chance to test those powers whilst we're searching for our missing transport. I suspect we'll put in long days at sea, but we'll spend the nights ashore in Weymouth. It's an old town, and very quaint."

"I wish," Cleo muttered.

She was a private person, unused to baring her soul. So damned self-sufficient, she thought wryly. But Johanna's remarks about her husband and this odd little island of quiet in the midst of all the noise pulled a reluctant admission from her.

"Jack and I have sort of put the physical side of our relationship on hold."

"I sensed there was a deliberate cooling off. How very stupid of you to allow that to happen."

"Hey, it wasn't all me. Well, it was, but that's not the issue here."

Johanna was too polite to blow a raspberry, but her expression did it for her.

"It's complicated," Cleo argued, fiddling with the coaster. "Jack shuts me out at times. On certain issues. It pisses me off."

"I imagine so. I imagine it also hurts."

"More than I thought it could."

"So you've decided to deny yourself—and him— the pleasures of the flesh until you achieve a higher mental and emotional plane."

"Something like that."

There was the look again, the facial raspberry.

"What, you don't think that's the right approach?"

"Oh, Cleo, I wouldn't presume to offer you advice. You have to sort this out for yourselves, you and Jack. But…"

Johanna bit her lip, her natural reserve clearly at war with her emotions.

"What?" Cleo asked again.

"I'll tell you this. I wasn't prepared for Barty's death. Despite the months of treatment, despite those last weeks of excruciating pain, I didn't want to let go. I still don't."

Reaching across the table, she laid her hand over Cleo's. "I'd trade everything I own, everything I hold dear, to potter about in the garden with him one more time. Or curl up next to him again for one night."

Her long, perfectly manicured nails dug in. "That's all I would ask for. One night."

15

Johanna's quiet grief stayed with Cleo during the drive back from the George. It was still in her head when she caught Jack later that night in the hall.

He was returning from the shared bathroom. He'd stripped down to his khakis, had a damp towel slung around his neck and wore the tight, closed expression Cleo was coming to associate with his ex-wife.

"Did Kate's counselor get hold of you?"

He nodded, confirming her guess. "She called just after we got back."

She folded her arms across the front of her sleep shirt. It was her favorite, a well-worn Dallas Cowboys T-shirt that skimmed her lacy hipsters and bare thighs. One foot tapped the smooth floorboards. She wasn't going to ask, but the message was clear. Special Agent Jack Donovan risked serious bodily injury if he didn't elaborate.

"The counselor reiterated the message I got earlier," he said. "Kate's missed two sessions and hasn't answered his calls. She hasn't shown up for work this past week, either."

"What about her friends? Any of them heard from her?"

"She doesn't have any. None that I know of, anyway. I got hold of her crisis contacts from AA, but she hasn't called any of them."

"Has she ever disappeared before?"

Jack's harsh laugh cut through the hall like a serrated blade. "A few times."

Cleo tapped her foot again, weighing her options. She could wait for Donovan to open up and share his burden of worry and guilt. That's what she'd demanded of him. What she thought she wanted.

Or she could bulldoze her way in. As Johanna had pointed out so poignantly, life was too damned short to wait for the planets to perfectly align.

"Okay, here's the deal. I called Goose a while ago. He's just finishing up a job in San Diego. He says he can jump a plane for Cincinnati in a few hours and look for Kate. If you want him to," she tacked on when Jack stiffened. "You know Goose. He's good."

Jack had met Cleo's trainer and sometime backup when she'd provided event security for film star Marisa Conners in Santa Fe. Donovan had witnessed firsthand Goose's ability to think fast and move even faster. If there was anyone who could be trusted to find Kate and do it quickly, it was Goose.

"I told him we'd call him back."

"This isn't your problem, Cleo."

"Hmm." She laid a finger against her chin. "How about we call it our problem?"

When he didn't answer, she pushed harder.

"You can't work this long distance, Jack. Not with everything else we have going on here. Let me put Goose on it."

The hands grasping his towel showed white at the knuckles. She could almost hear the timbers groan and chains clank as the drawbridge lowered a scant few inches.

"Okay."

"You'll have to talk to Goose," she said quickly, before the barriers could go back up again. "Fill him in on Kate's background and binge cycles."

The memories chased across his face like shadows. Cleo smothered a curse and sincerely hoped she and Kate Donovan never came face-to-face.

"It's your call, Jack, but I think we should do this."

"We, huh?" To her intense relief, the shadows slowly dissipated. "I'm not the only one who turns that plural on and off at will."

"What's good for the goose..." she tossed back airily. "Speaking of which, he's standing by waiting to hear from us."

His mouth tipped into a wry smile. "We'd better settle your consulting fee first. I don't know if I can afford you."

She didn't make the mistake of offering him a freebie. The drawbridge would rattle right back up again.

"You'll have to cover Goose's expenses. My agency fee, on the other hand, is negotiable." She moved in a step, laid her palms on his chest. "*Very* negotiable. Why don't you make me a starting offer?"

Surprise swept across his face, followed hard by caution. "Is this a test?"

"Sort of. Are you open to a change of ground rules, Donovan?"

"I *might* be." Still cautious, he frowned down at her. "You want to spell them out first?"

Her palms skimmed his bare chest. His skin was warm, the swirls of hair ticklish. "I've been thinking about what you said."

And about Johanna's quiet, aching grief.

"We know this works for us." She touched her mouth to his shoulder. "And this…"

She moved her lips across the smooth curve, felt a starburst of heat in her belly.

God, she must have been insane to deny them both this searing pleasure! Or more addled by that bullet graze than she'd realized at the time.

"You were right," she murmured against his skin.

"It doesn't make sense to impose artificial restraints. I vote we toss the rules and go with what works."

His muscles quivered, sending another streak of fire through her veins. She was ready to jump him right there, was already working the snap of his khakis, when he stopped her cold.

"Too late, Cleo."

"Huh?"

"You've convinced me. Just going with what works isn't good enough."

Well, hell! That wasn't what she expected to hear with her hand inside his pants.

"You want more," he said quietly. "I do, too."

Her heart gave a little bump. "How much more, Jack?"

"Everything you have to give."

The bump was harder this time. A solid smack of muscle against bone. She was sure he must have heard the whap because he flipped the towel over his head, collared her and drew her into him.

"I love you, Cleopatra. It's taken me a while to separate that particular emotion from the lust and irritation and downright fury you rouse in me, usually all at the same time."

They were hip to hip now, heart to heart. She could feel the hard muscles of his stomach against the back of her hand, feel his heat and strength and steadiness.

"So when did you untangle all these emotions?"

"When I saw you covered with blood, lying on

that exam table. The thought that I'd lost you kicked me right in the gut."

The admission lit a bright, warm radiance in *her* gut. Cleo basked in the glow until he tacked on a spoiler.

"Then you bounced up, brushed off the fact you'd gone into a potentially dangerous situation without coordination or backup, and I…"

"Yeah, yeah. I know. You got all angry and huffy again."

She wasn't interested in the past at the moment, only the brush of Jack's belly hair against her knuckles and his interesting announcement.

"Let's get back to this love business. Are you sure about that?"

"I've been sure for a while now. I just wasn't ready to put a name to it until tonight."

He palmed her face, brushing the hair back from her temples. There was more, she saw. Something he had to force out.

"I come with baggage. You've had a taste of it already."

She knew how much it cost him to issue the soft warning. They were both trained to hold everything in, to admit no weaknesses. With a shaky laugh, she reminded him that she'd accumulated her own set of luggage.

"Ha! You think you've got baggage. You'd just better hope Wanda never talks you into taking her to the mall. You'll emerge five hours later feeling like someone drove a spike right between your eyes. Then there's Mae, who wants into Goose's boxers in the worst way. And Doreen and…"

"Whoa! Back up a minute! That elegant, refined country-club type I met in Dallas is hot for *Goose?*"

"Like you wouldn't believe."

"Jesus H. Christ!"

"That's pretty much been Goose's reaction." Impatient now, she yanked on the khakis. "We need to call him and get him looking for Kate. Then, Special Agent Donovan, *I* would very much like to get into *your* boxers."

Despite her stated impatience, they kept it slow. Slow and dreamy.

Like lovers exploring each other for the first time, they traded stroke for stroke, kiss for kiss. His hands glided over her, cupping her breasts, smoothing her hips, stirring eddies of heat. She gloried in his hardness, his taste, his rigid control.

She wanted to draw out the erotic dance, fully intended to milk every sensual moment. Then she spread her legs, and the impatience she could temper but not completely control took hold. Her thighs locked around his, drawing him in, urging him to fill her.

"Not yet. I want to look at you. I want to enjoy you."

Stretching her arms above her head, she let him look. She was wet and ready when he finally slid into her, hot and eager when his body locked with hers. They found their rhythm, the thrust and lift and grind that soon had Cleo panting and Jack clenching his teeth.

He wanted to stretch this out, dammit. This moment. This hour. The tangled sheets, the sweat-slicked bodies, Cleo's hoarse groan as she arched under him. He wanted it to go on forever. He should have known it would last only until she hooked her heels around his calves and contracted her muscles.

His body went rigid, his blood pumped. Grunting, he sealed the erotic vision of her climax in his memory bank before covering her mouth and following her over the edge.

It was only later, long after Cleo had zoned out, that Jack realized that he hadn't given her a chance to respond to his declaration of love before jumping her bones.

Not that he needed to hear her say the words. Actions spoke louder than words, and Cleo's tonight had pretty well shouted her feelings. She wanted him, even with Kate peering over his shoulder like a persistent ghost. That alone was enough to lift some of the weight Jack had been hauling around with him all these years.

Cleo understood he couldn't completely abandon Kate. She accepted the twisted bonds that still tugged at him, just as she'd accepted her stepmother and this cousin-in-law who was always coming up with off-the-wall gadgetry. Much as she liked to moan and groan about them, she'd kill to protect either one. And God help anyone who messed with her dad.

That was Cleo, he thought. Tough, seemingly indestructible on the outside, with a soft underbelly she rarely let anyone see.

Her real underbelly wasn't so bad, either. He felt a stirring low in his groin, felt the blood began to pool.

Cleo had almost taken off the top half of his head the last time he'd startled her out of sleep. He'd damned well tread more cautiously this time.

Tugging her closer, he nested her backside against his hips. The contact got him instantly hard. It also elicited an irritated mmmph from Cleo. Twitching, she burrowed her rear in tighter.

He went from hard to aching, and caution gave way to need. Retaining just enough presence of mind to pin her arms with one of his to protect himself from severe injury, he slid a knee between hers.

She jerked awake then, grumpy and disoriented. "What time izit?"

"Late," he whispered into her ear. "Go back to sleep."

The sheets rustled. Her bottom butted against his belly. She felt him rigid against her and grumbled a protest.

"Oh, sure. Like I can sleep now."

Cleo expected the world would look different when she woke up. The sun would shine brighter, the birds would chirp more shrilly. After all, it wasn't every night a girl tossed out the rule book and got Jack Donovan as a prize.

When she finally dragged her head off the pillow, there wasn't a chirp to be heard. And she was pretty sure that was rain pinging against the curtained windows.

Jack was beside her, though. Fully dressed and bearing a steaming mug. Her sluggish senses leaped to life.

"Is that coffee?"

"Do you think I would dare wake you without it?"

Scrambling upright, she reached for the mug with greedy hands. The first gulp fired her neurons. The second restored her to a semblance of humanity.

"What time is it?"

A grin lit his eyes. "That's the same thing you asked me last night."

"Did I? I don't remember."

The grin got downright wicked. "No problem…as long as you remember what came afterward."

"Oh, yeah. That part is seared into my brain cells."

She allowed herself a few moments to wallow in the erotic imagery. "Back to my original question. You're all dressed and looking like you have somewhere to go. What time is it and what's happening?"

"Almost eight, and what's happening is that we need to pack up for the drive to Weymouth. We've got a plane to find, remember?"

The erotic images fuzzed and fizzled. In their place came the stark photo of a C-47 spinning into the sea and the insidious, all-too-vivid picture of a canister of deadly toxin buried in silt on the ocean's floor.

Downing another gulp, Cleo handed the mug back to Jack and fought her way out of the sheets. Her sleep shirt was twisted up around her hips, her hair was a nest of tangles, and her skin carried the distinct tang of *eau de sex*, but she was all business now.

"What's the plan?"

"Johanna suggests we pack up and drive down to the coast after breakfast. We'll use the rest of the day to check out our diving gear."

"Diving gear?"

"We've come this far," Jack answered with a shrug. "If we locate the wreck, I want in on the dive. So does Johanna. She's certified for both air and technical diving. Same goes for me. What about you?"

Cleo had done some diving in Mexico, strictly for pleasure. Luckily, her last jaunt to Cancún had included a full day's course on enhanced air diving.

"I'm current on both air and Nitrox."

"We're good to go, then. Move it, woman."

The squall passed and the sun was sparkling off the sea when Jack wheeled the rented Taurus into Weymouth.

Cleo was ahead, riding with Johanna in a low-slung '61 Morgan that had made him go weak at the knees the moment she pulled out of the garage. Jack had kept the wing fenders and shiny maroon finish in his sights all the way down to the coast. It made an easy target as it rolled through the touristy seaside resort popularized by King George III two centuries ago.

The main street was a crescent of historic buildings that fronted a long, curving beach. Hotels and B and Bs sat elbow to elbow with tiny amusement cafés, ice cream shops, restaurants and pubs. Although it was still only May, hearty bathers splashed about in the ocean. More sun worshippers occupied blankets and deck chairs. Others strolled the promenade that separated beach from street.

A narrow, twelve-mile isthmus connected Weymouth and the mainland to the Isle of Portland, barely visible in the distance. Man-made stone quays projected from the isthmus to form a deep protected harbor. Watercraft of all kind crowded the harbor as well as the bay beyond—fishing boats, dive boats, hydrofoils, ferries to France and the Channel Islands. There was even, Jack saw, a three-masted tall ship tied at the dock.

Johanna had arranged rooms at a quaint Victorian villa facing the harbor. The Gray Stone Inn offered off-road parking, a glassed-in conservatory and a snooker room. In keeping with the town's sea-faring roots, it also provided wet storage for sailors and divers.

A brisk wind was whipping Cleo's hair and fluttering the ends of Johanna's silk head scarf when Jack parked the Taurus alongside the Morgan. Lifting her bag from the back seat, the British agent swept the harbor with narrowed eyes. A jerk of her chin directed Cleo and Jack's attention to a boat moored farther down the quay.

"That's the *Argos II*. Mulholland's boat."

Unlike its master, the wooden-hulled craft was sleek and spiffy. Paint glowed, brass gleamed, and the teak trim showed a fresh coat of varnish. It looked to be about forty-five feet long, with the wheelhouse above the main cabin, a covered aft deck and two inflatable dive boats lashed to the canopy above the deck. Antennae bristled from the bridge, suggesting state-of-the-art navigational aids and electronics.

Her home for the next few days, Cleo thought as she hefted her gear bag. Or longer. She just wished she could get more excited about this expedition.

Maybe it was the prospect of going out to sea again so soon after her last, disastrous excursion. Maybe it was the thought of that canister lying in wait.

Or maybe it was the fierce scowl on Mulholland's face when he leaped onto the quay and strode in their direction.

"Uh-oh," she murmured. "The skipper doesn't look happy to see us."

"I expect he's not," Johanna said, tucking a wayward strand of hair into her scarf. "I left a message with his mate earlier, advising him that we'd need tanks and dive gear. McBride seemed to think Mulholland would have some words to say about that."

16

A prickly shiver danced down Johanna's spine as Mulholland stalked toward her. The sensation thoroughly annoyed her. Almost as much as the man himself.

Johanna was no fool. She recognized that her reaction was two parts professional and one part pure hormones. As an agent whose instincts had been honed by years in the field, she couldn't quite bring herself to trust him. As a woman, she couldn't get past those ridiculous shoulders.

She could feel a slow fizz in her veins now, even as she took in the set to his jaw and the spots of red riding high on his stubbled cheeks.

Ignoring Cleo and Jack, he skewered her with a fierce glare. "What's this foolishness about you wanting to dive on the transport if and when we find it?"

"So you received my message about securing additional equipment, did you?"

"I did, and I'll be damned if I'll play dive instructor to bloody amateurs."

"Has anyone asked you to?"

At her cool response, his expression turned dangerous. Any other woman might have had second thoughts at that point. Johanna experienced only another, quite irrational thrill.

"You'll not go down, any of you, unless you convince me you know what you're about."

"Fair enough." Appearing unfazed by the currents swirling around him, Donovan hooked his bag over his shoulder. "We'll dump our gear at the inn, then come aboard the *Argos II.* We can get acquainted with the rest of the team and run an equipment check. If the weather holds, we'll suit up and hit the water."

With a curt nod, the captain did an about-face and headed back down the quay.

"Well, that was fun," Cleo commented.

The fizz was still there, just under Johanna's skin. With a short laugh, she lifted her bag.

"It was, wasn't it?"

Two hours later, Cleo, Jack and Johanna stood on the quay with the two other divers who'd responded to Mulholland's summons. A third was expected by evening.

Billy Hawks, the younger of the two, must have

been fresh out of the military. He looked to be in his late twenties, still sported a buzz cut and addressed both Cleo and Johanna with respectful ma'ams. Jack got a half salute and a crisp "Pleased to meet you, sir."

The elder of the two was a weathered Scot named David Argyle. His burr rolled off his tongue so thick and rich that even Cleo, with her ear for languages, had to listen closely when he offered his thorny palm.

"Mulholland says ya hav'na dived in the UK."

"That's right. I've only dived in Mexico."

"You'll find these waters different, ta be sure. If this aircraft wreck lies where the skipper thinks it might, we'll be muckin' aboot in deep, dark seas."

"Sounds like fun."

Hands on hips, she surveyed the items spread out on the dock. She couldn't imagine how they'd stuff all the tanks, harnesses, class-A regulators, computers, dry suits, wreck reels and lights onto the *Argos II.* Not to mention the surface markers, survival sausages, compasses and personal gear like masks and fins.

"I've two sets of twin tanks for each of you," Mulholland informed them. "They're fitted with dual-outlet isolation manifolds."

"What mix will we be using?" Johanna asked. "Twenty-three percent Nitrox or a 23/25 trimix?"

Argyle and Hawks shot her glances filled with dawning respect. The *Argos II*'s skipper merely grunted.

"Depends on where we find the wreck," he said curtly. "Today, all we'll need is straight air."

His tone narrowed Johanna's eyes, but she didn't take him on in front of the other team members. She was saving her fire for when and if she needed it, Cleo guessed. Having seen Lady Marston in action, she had no doubts as to who would win if she and Mulholland decided to duke it out.

"Let's get this gear aboard."

Forming a bucket brigade, they began passing the equipment to Hawks, who stowed it in racks and under the benches that lined the rear deck, all according to Mulholland's directions. He had most of it stashed when the *Argos II*'s first mate trundled a pushcart down the wharf. A bandy-legged salt with patches of pink showing through his sparse white hair, McBride sang out as he approached with a load of canned goods, bottled water and beer.

"Lend a hand here, lads. We'll have to jump lively if we're to catch the slack."

"Where are we going?" Johanna asked Mulholland as they both reached for the same set of tanks.

Their forearms brushed in a contact that must have given each an electric jolt. They certainly separated fast enough, Cleo noted.

"The *British Inventor*," Mulholland replied. "She's lying at about seventeen meters. I want to see how you three handle yourselves before we head for deeper water tomorrow."

* * *

With a reminder to everyone to turn off their mobile phones so as not to interfere with navigational signals, Mulholland took the *Argos II* out of Portland Harbor. As they cut across the bay beyond, Cleo got a good view of the long, narrow isthmus connecting the mainland to the Isle of Portland.

The island rose out of the sea, all grassy hills and scattered villages. At its southernmost tip was a rocky promontory topped by a red-and-white lighthouse.

"Thar's Portland Bill," Dave Argyle said. "Seven tides meet at th' point, boilin' the seas like a cauldron."

Eyes narrowed, Cleo studied the water foaming at the base of the granite cliff. Goose bumps prickled on her skin as she realized she was looking at the last bit of land seen by many of the crew members aboard ships and aircraft that had gone missing over the centuries. Possibly the last for the crew of the C-47 they were searching for.

Frowning, she tried to penetrate the haze beyond the Bill. If Mulholland's calculations were correct, Bouncing Bertha had gone down southwest of the point, in a vast, empty stretch of sea. He seemed to think they could sweep the area easily enough. Cleo hoped he was right.

Turning her back on the rocky promontory, she settled in for the hour-long trip to the dive site. The surface of the sea was glassy bright and the sun warm, but underwater temperatures were still cold enough to warrant Neoprene dry suits. The divers waited to zip themselves in, not wanting to *un*-zip if nature called during the trip to the wreck.

The *British Inventor* was an oil tanker that had sunk in 1940 after hitting a mine. It was a popular wreck to dive on, according to Mulholland, and usually busy on weekends. They lucked out this time, though. No other boats appeared to have converged on the wreck.

"She's pretty broken up," Mulholland advised. "The bow section was salvaged and converted to a new ship. The ribs and plates lie scattered across the seabed. We'll drop our shot over what remains of the stern. Donovan, you'll pair with Argyle. Billy will buddy with Cleo. I'll go down with Lady Marston."

Johanna noted the pairings with a nod. "We'll be working together for some days, Captain. Shall we dispense with titles?"

"However you fancy it."

The careless reply lit a spark in her eyes, but she gave him a determined smile. "Fine. It's Sean and Johanna, then."

The smile came off when she and Cleo scooped up dry suits and went below. Muttering a few well-chosen expletives, Johanna led the way to the rear cabin, tossed her one-piece suit on a bunk and attacked her blouse buttons. When she caught Cleo's eye, a faint flush rose in her cheeks.

"Sorry. I don't know what it is about that man. He brasses me off without half trying."

"So I've noticed." Cleo tugged her sleeveless shirt over her head and added slyly, "Donovan has the same general effect on me."

Chagrined, the brunette paused with her hands on the zipper of her slacks. "Dear Lord! Is it so obvious?"

"That Mulholland stirs your juices? Probably not to him or the rest of the team. I only picked up on it because he stirs my juices, too. Just enough to make me want to take him down a peg or two," she tacked on at Johanna's startled expression.

"Yes. That's it exactly." A reluctant smile played at her lips. "How odd that such supremely self-confident men as Donovan and Mulholland should rouse our ire so easily, when neither of us would tolerate any other sort. I expect it has to do with the business we're in."

"I expect so."

Cleo let it drop, but she was beginning to suspect Mulholland roused more than Johanna's ire. Divesting herself of jeans and underwear, she shimmied into the one-piece, royal-purple bathing suit she'd picked up at one of the tourist shops in Weymouth. The nylon hugged her curves nicely and the hooded dry suit fit over it like a second skin.

She angled for a better view of herself in the mirror over the built-ins and couldn't resist a smirk. Those grueling workout sessions with Goose were finally paying off. She was down to a trim one-twenty which, given her height, translated into long lines and firm flesh.

Her bubble of satisfaction lasted only until Johanna zipped up her suit. The British agent was almost as tall as Cleo but more generously proportioned at hip and bust. The Neoprene showed off every curve to perfection and made Cleo look as flat as a plate-glass window by comparison.

As a consequence, she was prepared for the reaction when Johanna followed her out on deck.

"Jay-sus!"

That came from bandy-legged Dennis McBride, who just about fell through the wheelhouse window. The rest of the men had similar reactions. Billy's jaw dropped. Argyle's breath whistled through his teeth. Donovan managed not to swallow his tongue, but only because he'd already done just that when Johanna had appeared attired in a body-hugging jumpsuit in Malta a few weeks ago. His glance lingered on Johanna for a few seconds before moving to Cleo. The gleam that came into his eyes when he viewed her long, sleek lines more than made up for his momentary lapse.

Mulholland looked like he'd taken the hardest hit. Cleo bit down on the inside of her lip to keep from grinning as the captain's habitual scowl fell off his face and he assumed the stunned expression of someone who'd just taken a two by four right between the eyes.

Johanna appeared oblivious to her impact on the masculine portion of the crew, but her gray eyes held a satisfied gleam as she dropped onto the bench beside Cleo. Hip to hip, they checked straps, hoses and gauges. Satisfied with their operation, they set about programming the strap-on wrist computers Mulholland had rented.

The computers had become essential items of equipment for divers. They provided critical data regarding nitrogen absorption and oxygen toxicity, and indicated when to switch gases on decompression.

Doreen would love one of these little gizmos, Cleo thought as she set the mix to straight oxygen. Her stepcousin-in-law would probably soup it up, though. Change the circuitry, extend the battery life into infinity, or get it to shoot out invisible microfilaments like those in the small, flat case still hooked to Cleo's key chain.

"We've got just over an hour of slack water to work with," Mulholland advised. "Plan on no more than thirty minutes' bottom time."

"Why such a short stay?" Cleo asked.

"This isn't a recreational dive. I just want assurances that you know what you're about. Are your computers set?"

She whipped her hand up. "Aye, aye, Cap'n, *sir!*"

The spiffy salute raised Mulholland's brow, but her cocky grin won the first glimmer of a smile they'd seen on his face all day.

"We just agreed, no titles. Sean will do."

He wasn't bad when he lost the frown, Cleo decided. Not bad at all. No wonder he kept Johanna swinging between suspicion, irritation and attraction.

Their computers set, the divers prepared to hit the sea.

First, though, they had to drop the shot line. Using precise GPS coordinates and visual landmarks from the shoreline, Mulholland positioned the *Argos II* over the wreck and signaled to Dave Argyle to drop the shot. As the weighted lead sank beneath the surface, Argyle quickly played out the line.

Mulholland obviously knew what he was doing. The line snagged and went taut on the first try. Jack and Argyle used the hydraulic lift fitted onto the back of the boat to get into the water at that point. They would follow the shot down, secure the line and send up a marker.

McBride kept the *Argos II* at idle until the bright red float popped to the surface, then moved the boat in to drop the remaining divers next to it.

"Are you ready, ma'am?"

With a smile and a nod for Billy Hawks, Cleo pulled down her face mask, fitted her mouthpiece and frog-walked onto the lift platform. A few seconds later, the sea closed over her.

Her first thought was that Argyle had been right. Diving the waters off the coast of England was nothing like diving Cancún or Cozumel. The water was colder for one thing, a shock to her system after the warm May sunshine. It was also darker, more emerald than turquoise, but not so murky as to require head or flashlights. Sufficient ambient light filtered through for her to follow the shot.

Even with the shot and Billy Hawks to guide her, it took Cleo a while to spot the scattered remains of the *Inventor*. The pile of broken plates lay in a hollow scoured into the gravel bottom. Shoals of bib darted above the wreck, which was decorated with bright patches of anemones. Cleo swam through the bib, aiming for the color, and caught a flicker of movement to her left.

She turned, thinking it might be Jack or Argyle, and came nose to nose with a friendly conger. Startled, she jerked back and sent up a stream of bubbles. When she caught her breath, she reminded herself that these big, flat-nosed eels feasted mainly on crustaceans, squid and fish. As far as she knew, they didn't routinely make a meal out of divers.

The conger must have been used to two-legged creatures invading his turf. Her abrupt movement didn't send him squiggling off. Instead, he poked alongside Cleo as she trailed Billy in a slow exploration.

Gradually, the remains of the *Inventor* wove a silent, haunting spell. Cleo had never quite appreciated the sport of wreck diving. Her dives in Mexico had been to coral reefs teeming with fish, and once to an underwater cave that glowed in iridescent shades of aqua.

There was something eerie about swimming over the skeletal remains of a ship. Mulholland had indicated the *Inventor* hadn't been designated a war grave, but Cleo couldn't help wondering what had happened to its crew. Had they swum to shore? Been rescued by the Coast Guard personnel stationed at Portland navy base? Huddled under blankets while they watched their ship break up and go under?

Having survived a similar experience such a short time ago, Cleo felt a distinct empathy with that long-ago crew. She also began to understand this spooky feeling would intensify tenfold if and when they located Bouncing Bertha. The *Inventor*'s crew had made it to safety. The transport's had not.

Her attention caught by dark shapes on the far side of the heavily encrusted steel plates, she waved to Jack and Dave Argyle. Jack waved back, pointed to his wrist computer and jerked a thumb upward. Surprised he was already signaling their ascent, she checked her wrist computer. More time had passed than she'd realized. She and Hawks had been down for twenty minutes.

Twisting around, she searched for Johanna and Mulholland. She spotted them some distance away, exploring a section of the rusted, broken-apart bow. Their air bubbles rose in twin streams as they moved in almost perfect synchronization. Either Mulholland was matching his stroke to hers, or Johanna packed some power in those long legs.

With another wave, this one aimed in their direction, Cleo poked around with Billy for another ten minutes.

The curious conger was nowhere in sight when Cleo and Billy swam back to the shot line and started up. Neither were Johanna or Mulholland.

Cleo broke the surface and swam over to the lift platform. Billy followed and hit the switch to raise them to the level of the deck. A flick of the switch sent the platform whirring back down to a few inches below the surface.

Jack had already shucked his tanks and weight belt. Making his way through the scattered equipment, he helped Cleo out of hers. McBride appeared with biscuits and mugs of homemade chowder for everyone. The four divers sprawled comfortably on the wide benches and downed the spicy chowder while they waited for Johanna and Mulholland to surface.

Twenty minutes later, they were still waiting.

17

Cleo leaned on the teak rail, her eyes locked on the red float marking the shot. Jack crowded close to her shoulder, with Billy Hawks and Dave Argyle jammed against her other side.

"How long have they been down?"

Jack checked his wrist computer. "I make it close on forty minutes."

Cleo chewed the inside of her cheek. Mulholland had dictated a bottom time of thirty minutes. He and Johanna were already over it by ten.

"Fifty minutes is the maximum for a no-stop dive on air," Billy put in. "If they stay down any longer, they'll have to decompress on the way up."

"Tha skipper kens what he's aboot."

Argyle obviously intended to reassure them, but both he and Billy turned away from the rail and pulled backup sets of tanks off the rack. Hawks was shimmying into his when the red marker dipped below the surface. It bounced back up, then dipped again.

"Someone's tugging on the line!" Cleo called out. "Is that a signal?"

"Could be," Billy replied. "Or it could be the skipper's just untying the shot."

The gaze of everyone aboard the *Argos II* remained riveted on the float. When the red bubble began to drift on the waves, Billy gave a relieved nod.

"That's it. They were just loosening the line. They'll be up directly."

Johanna broke the surface first. With a wave to the crowd lined up at the rail, she started for the boat. Mulholland popped up a few moments later. Towing the shot line, he, too, swam for the platform.

Given the state of armed neutrality between Johanna and the captain of the *Argos II*, Cleo expected fireworks when the two climbed aboard and were divested of their tanks and regulators. Johanna surprised the heck out of her by dragging her hood back, raking a hand through her hair and laughing in sheer exuberance.

"What a fantastic dive!"

Cleo's gaze swung to Mulholland. He surprised her even more by resting his elbows on the rail and grinning up at his dive partner.

"You scared the piss out of me when you disappeared beneath that plate."

"You came after me quick enough." Eyes sparkling, Johanna spun around. "The wreck must have shifted recently. Possibly during that last storm. We found a section of the hull buried in the gravel that looked as if had been laid yesterday. No rust, no anemones, just bright, clean steel. We also found the ship's bell."

"Did you get pictures?" Hawks asked.

Nodding, Mulholland extracted a compact underwater camera from his belly pouch. "We did. They won't compare with wreck photos shot by the likes of John Liddiard, but they'll give you a glimpse of what we saw."

Hawks shook his head. "This is one of the most popular wrecks in the area. It's been dived hundreds, if not thousands of times. I wouldn't have believed there was an inch of the *Inventor* lying undiscovered all these years."

"Divers aplenty will be convergin' on her now," Argyle predicted. "Once word gets round, you'll not be able to drop a shot for all the divers muckin' aboot."

Johanna merely laughed again. "Let them come! Sean and I can claim first sighting of the ship's bell."

Cleo's brows soared. Mulholland's name rolled off her tongue without the least hesitation now. Evidently the thrill of discovery had breached the barriers and made allies of them. Temporarily, at least. As she helped clean and stash their gear, she wondered how long their truce would last.

* * *

Well into the evening, as it turned out.

Most of the weekend divers had packed up and left Weymouth by the time Cleo, Jack and Johanna joined Mulholland and his crew for dinner. There were still plenty of locals milling about in the pubs and restaurants, though. Fishermen in tall Wellingtons with the folded tops flapping, red-faced farmers, dive crews and charter boat captains all rubbed elbows at the bar of the Sea Cow, a popular drinking and eating establishment facing the quay.

The decibel level inside the pub bordered on deafening. Shouts of laughter and the exchange of good-natured insults men seemed to consider appropriate in all circumstances punctuated the steady clink of glasses and clatter of cutlery. The Devonshire natives rolled their *R*'s in the musical way of the coast, while divers and boat captains from other areas of Great Britain added their distinctive voices to the babble.

The team from the *Argos II* had staked out a table near the window. With them was the third diver Mulholland had recruited for the search for Bouncing Bertha.

As short and squat as a bulldog, Dr. Ernesto Cruz had the heavy jowls to match. Mulholland introduced him as the senior medical rating on one of his Royal Navy dive crews.

"Little bugger jumped ship to attend medical school."

"That's not quite the way I remember it, Chief. You threatened to break every bone in my body if I didn't accept that university scholarship."

Mulholland buried his pride in a friendly whap to the doc's shoulder. "You wouldn't guess it to look at him, but damned if this ugly pug hasn't become one of the world's leading experts on the kinetics of inert gas and marine poisoning."

"Just the man we need for this mission," Jack murmured.

That wasn't exactly what Cleo wanted to hear.

Cruz's greeting for Cleo and Jack was friendly enough, but Johanna clearly reigned as star of the evening. "Sean tells me you made quite a dive on the *Inventor.*"

"We did."

"I had the photos developed," Mulholland announced, fanning out the small stack. Johanna gave a gasp of delight and wedged into the seat beside his to paw through the shots. Ale went down easily as they passed the pictures around.

Their commentary drew the attention of a charter boat captain at the next table. He, in turn, hailed his friends over. More ale was ordered and consumed. Soon Mulholland and Johanna had become the center of a lively crowd.

Cleo didn't escape attention, either. One of the locals stared at her quizzically until he made the connection to the news story about the fire at Kew

Gardens. That produced a demand for details and another round from the bar. She dodged the first and declined the second by turning the conversation back to the Inventor.

By then, her stomach was sending out frantic SOS's. Jack heard one especially loud signal, grinned and caught the waiter's eye.

Over starters of butterfly prawns and homemade fish chowder, Donovan extracted the interesting information that Cruz had just returned from Iraq, where he'd treated Royal Navy divers clearing the deepwater port of Umm Qsar. Having spent a temporary duty stint with the psychophysiological-deception detection unit at Umm Qsar, Donovan was soon swapping war stories with Cruz.

It wasn't until they'd moved on to main courses of grilled scallops and perfect, pan-fried skate that fell off Cleo's fork in moist, succulent flakes that talk circled around to the search they'd launch early the next morning.

Keeping his voice low so as not to be heard by those at the next table, Mulholland suggested a meeting later to review the search parameters and operational guidelines a final time. Since Johanna's suite offered more working space than the rooms the dive team had booked near the quay, they set the meeting at the Gray Stone Inn.

Mulholland arrived at the snug, two-room suite first. Johanna chided herself for the sudden leap in her pulse when she opened the door and saw him. He carried his computer and a roll of sea charts under his arm and looked as untidy as ever with those salt-and-pepper bristles darkening his cheeks and that too-long hair brushing his collar.

A mental image of Barty flashed through her mind. He'd always presented such a neat, precise appearance. Her inexplicable attraction to a man so different from her husband in appearance, temperament and manner made her feel as though she was betraying him. As a consequence, her tone took on more of an edge than she'd intended.

"Will this take long, do you think?"

Sean blinked, then gave himself a swift, mental boot. What was it to him if the laughing, vibrant woman from the Sea Cow had disappeared and the lady of the manor had resumed her place? He had no cause to regret the switch. Or ache to lay a kiss on a certain MI6 operative she wouldn't soon forget.

"Not long. Why?"

"I was merely wondering whether or not I should ring the front desk and have them send up tea or coffee."

"We won't need either. This gathering will be short and to the point, as I still plan to go out with the tide tomorrow. I want you and the others aboard by…"

"By 4:00 a.m. Yes, we know."

Sean's temper began to slide. He'd learned to put

a curb on it during his years in the navy. He'd also learned when to let its weight be felt. He'd crushed more than one cheeky subordinate with a few well-chosen words. Lady Marston hardly qualified as a subordinate, but it was time and past to clear the air.

"I've raised a burr under your skin since the first time we met. I've had time to wonder why. It goes back to the murdered Yank. This Captain Caswell."

"Does it?"

"You suspected I was the one who put a bullet into him, didn't you? That I'd somehow uncovered the reason he was searching for a downed C-47 and decided to go after the prize myself."

"The possibility occurred to me," she admitted without so much as a blink or a blush. "I've also considered the possibility you're still intent on claiming the prize. Several million pounds' worth of gold would augment your military pension quite nicely."

He was speechless, blown flat to the deck. Damned if the woman hadn't just called him a bloody pirate right to his face!

"If that's what you think," he shot back, fire in his veins, "it's a wonder you dived with me this afternoon. Even more of a wonder you want to dive the C-47, if and when we find it. Aren't you afraid I'll arrange an unfortunate accident for you and your mates?"

"No."

"Why not?" He advanced on her, letting his stance

and his tone advertise his anger. "We both know how simple it would be to slice an air hose, make it look as though it had caught on a rusted bit of metal."

He outweighed her by a good eight or ten stone, but she didn't back away. Sean knew she'd been trained to handle blokes twice his size. He'd picked up a few parlor tricks himself over the years, though.

"I said I'd *considered* the possibilities. I wouldn't be worth five bob at my job if I hadn't."

It was her tone that pushed him to the edge. Unruffled, unconcerned. As if she entertained not the slightest doubt she could put him in his place and keep him there.

"I've considered a few possibilities as well," he said heavily.

"Indeed?"

"Indeed."

The mocking retort put spots of color into her cheeks. Her chin came up. Her arms folded. "Do you intend to share them with me, or just play word games?"

"Oh, I'll share them."

He took another step, close enough to loom over her. When she stiffened, he half expected her to bring up a knee or jam the ball of her hand into his nose. He was prepared for both, but not for the sudden, speculative look that came into her eyes.

Only an inch or two separated them. He could see the faint blue veins in her eyelids, the inky spike of her lashes. Her hair swirled about her shoulders, a silky spill that made Sean itch to bury his fists in it. He was entertaining thoughts of doing just that when she tipped her head and pinned him with a clear, direct look.

"Are you attracted to me, Captain Mulholland, or merely attempting to intimidate me? If it's the latter, it won't wash, you know."

Bloody hell! Had she read his mind? Could she sense he'd gone taut as a hawser below his belt?

"And if it's the former?"

"I..." She hesitated for the barest of moments, then knocked him flint for cinders. "I may be open to discussion."

Sean's years in the navy stood him in good stead. Instead of reeling under that broadside, he launched an immediate attack.

"Discussion, hell."

His first thought was that she tasted every bit as fine as she looked. He didn't have time for a second before she slid up her arms and locked them around his neck.

Holy Mary, Mother of God!

Sean barely remembered the wife who'd left him early in his navy days. Nor could he put a name to more than one or two of the women who'd relieved his loneliness at ports all around the globe. He was dead certain none of them had kissed with the same skill as Johanna Marston, though.

Chest hammering, he backed her against the wall. He wasn't worried about a knee to the groin now. His one thought, his only thought, was to feed the fire leaping in his veins.

It had reached full flame when she broke the kiss and drew back, wincing. Instantly contrite, he shoved away from the wall.

"I'm sorry. You've got me so twisted around the anchor, I'm more muscle than brains."

"Your muscles aren't the problem, Captain Mulholland." Laughter crept into her voice. "Quite the opposite, in fact. It's your whiskers."

The red scrape on her chin mortified Sean. He'd never marked a woman in his life. He opened his mouth, stammered out another strangled apology. The thump of footsteps in the hallway was all that saved him from making a complete arse of himself.

"That'll be the rest of the crew." He backed off another step. "I'll let them in, shall I, while you put a cold cloth to that whisker burn."

Her amusement deepened, but she merely nodded and made for the bathroom. When the door closed behind her, Sean felt his knees go to jelly.

What in bloody *hell* had he been thinking? He'd all but assaulted the woman. It was a wonder she hadn't reached for the poker beside the fireplace and put a permanent dent in his skull. Thoroughly disgusted with himself, he answered the rap on the door.

"Hey, Sean."

Cleo breezed by, followed by Donovan. The rest of his troop came right on their heels. They filed in, one after another, looking relaxed after their hearty dinner and ready to get down to it.

"Where's Johanna?" Cleo asked, snagging some grapes from the basket atop the minibar.

"In the bedroom. She'll be out presently. I brought the sea charts of the area we'll be searching." Retrieving the heavy roll, he thumped it on the table tucked in the window alcove. "Give me a hand here, David, and we'll lay out the grid pattern."

Mulholland finished detailing the search area just past 9:00 p.m. Resting his elbows on his knees, he surveyed his team.

"That's it, then. I'm estimating it'll take three days to scan the entire grid. Four, at the most. Questions?"

Argyle scraped a hand over his jaw. "There are wrecks aplenty in those sectors. Some charted, some not."

"We'll use Admiralty records and sonar to identify known wrecks. Those we can't identify or eliminate based on size and shape, we'll dive on."

"What about permits?" Hawks asked.

"Captain Daggett took care of those."

Cleo went right to the heart of their search. "If we find Bouncing Bertha and this canister that may or may not be aboard her, how do we safely retrieve it?"

Mulholland didn't minimize the risks. "*If* we find her, I'll go down wearing chemical-protective clothing, helmet, visor and respiratory protection, with an independent secondary life-support unit. I'll conduct an environmental-risk assessment at various stages during the descent and at the wreck site itself. No one else goes into the water unless and until I give the signal. Are we clear on that?"

He speared each of them with a flat, uncompromising stare. They answered with a round of nods.

"If we recover the cylinder, it goes into a transportable vault. We'll decontaminate our equipment, separate any spoil from the silt and contain that, as well, to prevent environmental contamination. Doc Cruz here will assess us for physiological effects at every phase of the search and recovery. Other questions?"

There were none.

"Well, then, I'd say we're set."

Chairs scraped back and feet hit the floorboards. Under cover of the general breakup, Mulholland rolled his charts and sent Johanna a look that held a question. She responded with an enigmatic smile he was damned if he could interpret. Her words left little doubt, however.

"I'll see you in the morning."

Johanna walked them to the door of her cozy suite, cool and calm as a cucumber.

Her facade cracked the moment the door closed.

She collapsed against the sturdy oak panel, swinging wildly between relief and regret.

What in God's name had she got herself into? She was on a mission, one with potentially dangerous consequences. She was daft to add sexual dalliance to the mix.

More to the point, Mulholland was as different from Barty as chalk from cheese. Under ordinary circumstances, the boat captain would be the last man she'd choose for a lover.

Except circumstances *hadn't* been ordinary since Barty died. Johanna ached to be held, ached for something more than a kiss. She'd sent Mulholland on his way tonight, but she knew she wouldn't do so a second time.

18

Cleo's cell phone chirped out the opening stanza of the "Battle Hymn of the Republic" just as she lifted the fluffy duvet to join Jack. He was waiting for her, hands tucked under his head, an anticipatory gleam in his eyes.

"Hold that pose. I'll be right back."

Scooping up his discarded shirt to cover her nakedness, she padded across the room. A quick glance identified the number on the caller ID.

"Hi, Mae."

"Hello, Cleo. Sorry to be calling so late."

"No problem, it's only a little after ten here. What's up?"

When her part-time office assistant hesitated, Cleo went into instant worry mode.

"Is it Pop? Is he okay?"

"What? Oh, yes, dear. Patrick's fine. I talked to Wanda a little while ago and they were trying to decide where to go for dinner."

Make that *Wanda* was trying to decide, Cleo thought as her knotted stomach muscles relaxed. The sound of a voice blaring through a loudspeaker somewhere behind Mae interrupted her thoughts.

"Where are you?"

"At the airport."

"Where are you off to?"

Not that it was any of Cleo's business. A long-time member of the country club set, Mae had buried one husband, divorced another and recently dumped the well-heeled cardiologist she'd been dating for some time. She didn't need the salary Cleo paid her to manage her office, and was certainly entitled to take off whenever and wherever she wanted to.

Cleo was thinking Phoenix or Palm Springs, two of Mae's favorite golf getaways. She *wasn't* expecting the casual bomb her sixty-something officer manager dropped.

"I'm zipping up to Kansas to meet Goose."

"I thought Goose was in Cincinnati."

"He was, but he got a lead on Jack's ex-wife. He thinks she's in Kansas now."

Cleo darted a look at Jack. He'd caught the reference to Cincinnati and lowered his arms. She shrugged in answer to the silent question he aimed her way.

"Fill me in, Mae. What was the lead?"

"Goose canvassed the bars in and around Cincinnati and got a tip that a woman matching Kate Donovan's description had been putting away the booze a few nights ago at a dive on the outskirts of town. The bartender says she climbed into the cab of a semi with a trucker headed south."

Cleo's fist tightened on the phone. She had a great deal of respect for the men and women who hauled freight across country. She'd used their eyes and road smarts on a previous case to chase down a father who'd disregarded a custody order and kidnapped his son.

She also knew there were killers among them, as among every sector of society. The recent string of grisly truck-stop murders of teenaged prostitutes was fresh in her mind as Mae continued.

"Goose got on the phone, made some calls and tracked down the trucker. He says he dumped Jack's ex at a rest stop just north of Wichita last night. Evidently she's not a happy drunk."

No, she wasn't. Cleo had heard the vituperative phone messages the woman had left on Jack's answering machine during one of her binges.

"Goose is flying into Wichita as we speak. I'm going to hop a flight and meet him at the airport."

Cleo couldn't figure that one out. "He asked you for an assist?"

"No, he asked me to relay this information to you. It's my decision to fly up there. If he finds Kate Donovan and she's in as bad a shape as it sounds, he'll need help getting her squared away."

Goose, aka Dave Petrowski, carried at least two hundred and fifty pounds on his heavily muscled frame. The former Special Forces type bounced Cleo on her butt with annoying frequency during their training sessions. He didn't need help getting *anyone* squared away.

Cleo didn't say so, though. Mae was every bit as tough as Goose in her refined way. She also had her sights set on the tattooed biker some fifteen years her junior.

Petrowski was dead meat.

"I've forwarded the office phones to Doreen," Mae said briskly. "She'll handle business calls until I return. You've received several from possible international clients, by the way. They said they'd seen you on the BBC. Did you do a television interview?"

"Yes, I did, although I can't believe that spot would bring in any clients."

"Well, they seemed interested. I gave them your cell phone number. I have to go, dear. They're announcing my flight."

"Call me with an update as soon as you have something. Whatever the time."

"I will."

Chewing on the inside of her lip, Cleo flipped the phone shut. "That was Mae. She said Goose has a lead on Kate."

It was almost as if someone had flicked a switch. His muscles tensed. His face got still and wary.

Cleo didn't try to wrap it up in pretty paper. "A trucker picked up a drunk matching Kate's description at a dive outside Cincinnati. Goose tracked him down by phone, confirmed it was Kate."

"And?"

"And the trucker claims she got obnoxious so he dumped her at a rest stop north of Wichita last night. Goose is on a plane to Kansas now."

Jack nodded, one quick jerk of his chin. He was an OSI agent. He knew what could happen to a woman tossed out at a roadside rest stop.

"Mae promised she or Goose would call with an update from Wichita."

Jack nodded again as Cleo crossed the room. Flicking off the bedside lamp, she shed the shirt and slid in beside him. His arm curled around her, drawing her into his side, but the sizzle had gone out of the night.

"They'll pick up Kate's trail," Cleo promised with more conviction than she felt. "I'm guessing we'll hear from them before we board the *Argos II* tomorrow."

When Jack didn't answer, she propped herself up on his chest. "What are you thinking?"

He pulled in a long, deep breath. She rode the rise, felt the drop as he let it out again.

She guessed he was weighing a missing ex-wife against the search for a missing plane and possible toxic powder. Guilt against duty. Past regrets against present responsibilities.

Cleo didn't ask where she fit in that equation. Jack had warned her he came with baggage. She had to accept that.

"I don't know what I'm thinking," he said at last. "Let's get some sleep. We have to be up again in a few hours. I'll figure it out then."

She settled back down beside him, her head nestled on his shoulder. They lay in silence, listening to the wind off the bay gusting against the windowpanes. Cleo fell asleep to the sound of the wind, with Jack lying stiff beside her.

The "Battle Hymn of the Republic" jerked her awake again. She thrust up with both palms, blinking furiously. She was fighting her way into consciousness when an impatient grunt sounded just above her ear and a heavy weight pressed her into the mattress again.

"Donovan."

He'd reached across her for the phone, almost smothering Cleo under his weight. She bucked, making him shift enough for her to wiggle out from underneath. By the time she'd flopped onto her back, Jack had evidently heard all he needed to.

"Right. I'll tell her. And Goose…"

He stopped, glanced at Cleo. She couldn't see his expression. His face was little more than a pale blur in the darkness. His relief came through like a light-house beacon stabbing through the night, though.

"Thanks."

The cell phone snapped shut. Jack sank back onto the mattress. "Goose tracked Kate to a motel in Wichita. She'd used her credit card to book a room."

"What's he doing with her?"

"He's taking her to the ER."

"Good Lord! Is she that bad?"

"Yes," he answered, his voice tight. "She's that bad. She's got the DTs."

Like every law enforcement agent, Cleo had learned how to handle drunks. She'd also learned that the DTs—short for delirium tremens—often involved extreme confusion, agitation and hallucinations. The shakes usually started within twenty-four to seventy-two hours after a chronic alcoholic either stopped or limited his intake. Extreme cases could be deadly.

Jack hooked an elbow over his face. Cleo guessed he was seeing other ERs, hearing the beep of heart monitors, watching IVs drip. When his arm came down, his voice was low and rough.

"Goose said he'd stay with her. Mae's there, too. I owe them for this, Cleo."

"Yeah, well, the debt may not be as huge as you think. Mae intends to collect her payment from Goose."

As she'd intended, that pulled him from his dark

memories. He gave a disbelieving snort and gathered her against him once more. "That's not going to happen." He waited a couple of beats. "Is it?"

"My money's on Mae."

Snuggling against his warmth, she drifted off to sleep again with the strong, steady beat of his heart in her ear.

The wake-up call came ten minutes later. That's what it felt like to Cleo, anyway.

Muttering curses against sadistic boat captains in general and Mulholland in particular, she tried to burrow into the mattress.

Jack was merciless. Manhandling her out of bed, he propelled her into the bathroom by promising hot coffee.

He proved as good as his word. The pot in the room was gurgling happily when Cleo emerged. As a result, she felt close to human when she and Jack met Johanna in the downstairs lounge.

By contrast, the British agent seemed imbued with a subdued energy that Cleo considered obscene given the hour. "Good morning. I listened to the weather reports whilst I was dressing. They predict early morning showers, blue skies later today."

Jack nodded in approval. Cleo merely grunted. Shouldering their gear, they trooped out into the predawn darkness.

Despite the early hour, Weymouth was coming

alive. The tantalizing scents of yeast and sugar wafted from the bakeries and sweet shops. Trucks rattled over cobbles slick with morning mist. Fishermen squatted on the decks of the boats tied to the quay, working their nets.

The rest of Mulholland's team had beat them to the boat. They were already hard at work checking and restowing equipment under the bright rear deck lights. Billy Hawks reached out a hand to help Johanna and Cleo aboard. Dave Argyle and squat, pug-faced Dr. Cruz scooted over to make room for them and Jack in the rear deck well. Bandy-legged Dennis McBride, bless him, passed around mugs of steaming coffee.

Cleo had her mug halfway to her lips when the captain of the *Argos II* appeared. He must be a morning person, she thought. Like Johanna. They both seemed to have their inner fuses sparking. There was something else, though, something Cleo couldn't put a finger on until Mulholland passed through a swath of light and greeted her with a nod.

"Good morning."

"Mornin', skipper." She cocked her head, studying him in the deck lights. "You're looking bonny this morning. I almost didn't recognize you without all those bristles."

To her surprise, a tide of color rushed into Mulholland's clean-shaven cheeks. He scraped a palm across his jaw and shrugged. "My face mask fits better this way."

When he turned aside, Cleo saw his gaze lock with Johanna's. She saw, as well, the smile that tugged at the British agent's mouth.

"Well, well, well," Cleo murmured when Johanna plopped down beside her on one of the rear deck benches. "That must have been some session you and the skipper had before the rest of us arrived last night. Or did he hang around for a while after we left?"

Johanna gave her one of those cool "I'm sure I don't know what you're talking about" kind of smiles.

"Okay, okay! It's none of my business. I have to say, though, I like his new look."

Pursing her lips, the brunette glanced toward Mulholland. When she brought her gaze back to Cleo, a feline smile glinted in her eyes.

"So do I."

The *Argos II* pulled away from the quay a short time later and passed through the warning lights marking the entrance to the harbor. The bay beyond was calm and smooth, a blanket of rippling black against a sky just beginning to show streaks of dawn.

As Weymouth's lights faded in the distance, sizzling scents emanating from the galley lured everyone but Mulholland below. The team members squeezed elbow to elbow at the narrow table as McBride dished up bangers and mash. Cleo downed three of the fat sausages and a healthy portion of potatoes, along with another mug of coffee. Johanna did the same, then volunteered to carry a plate up to Mulholland. She didn't glance at Cleo as she pushed away from the table.

When she took Mulholland's place at the wheel so he could fork down his breakfast, the bright glow from the navigational screens formed a greenish halo around them. Cleo sent the duo a speculative glance or two, but kept her thoughts to herself. Whatever Johanna had going with the captain was her business, as long as it didn't affect their mission.

That last thought brought Cleo up short. Who was she to impose restrictions? She and Jack had certainly mixed business with pleasure on this case. Several times, as a matter of fact. Their personal relationship hadn't affected their ability to focus on the mission.

It could, though. Cleo would be a fool to deny the possibility. There was solid rationale behind the military's restriction against assigning family members to the same base or ship in a combat zone. The stated reason was to avoid the loss of an entire family, as happened when the five Sullivan brothers went down on the same ship during World War Two. But there was also the unwritten concern that fear for the safety of a sibling or spouse during an attack could distract a soldier from his or her own duties.

God knew she'd charge in with guns blazing if Jack came under fire. She wouldn't stop to think, wouldn't calculate the odds. He'd do the same for her.

Her gaze shifted to the man seated across the table from her. The squint lines at the corners of his eyes were deeper this morning, and his shoulders had a little more slope to them than usual. He hadn't gotten much sleep, Cleo guessed, an hour or two at most. Worries about Kate had no doubt kept him awake.

A wall of emotion slammed into Cleo, so powerful she had to grit her teeth. She hadn't realized until that moment how much a part of her Donovan had become. She'd bulldozed her way into his past, forced him to share the dark, painful memories. That past, she knew with absolute certainty, would now shape her future.

And *no one*, Kate Donovan included, had better give him any more grief!

She had to tell him so. Now.

"Could I talk to you a moment, Jack? Up on deck?"

He followed her out of the galley and up the short flight of stairs to the rear deck. A tug on his sleeve took him behind the bulkhead, out of view of those below.

"I love you," she said fiercely.

"What?"

Okay, that hadn't come out quite the way she'd intended. Drawing in a deep breath, Cleo tried again.

"I love you, Donovan. It just hit me how much down there in the galley."

That came out a little better. Not quite as pugnacious.

"Thanks for telling me. I'd pretty well figured it out, but it's nice to hear the words."

"Okay. Good. Fine."

She expected him to do the man thing at that point and sweep her into a fierce embrace. When he didn't, she grabbed his shirtfront, yanked him down a few inches and ground her lips into his.

"Jesus, Cleo! You want to tell me what brought this on?"

"Nothing in particular. I just thought you should know how I felt."

His tawny brows drew together as he tried to read her eyes. "Why now? Why here?"

She swept a glance across the deck to the streaks of gold spearing through the dark clouds. A new day was being born right before their eyes.

"Look at that sky. Can you think of a better time or place?"

"No, I can't."

Folding his arms around her, he rested his chin on the top of her head. Together they watched the sea turn to gold.

A half hour later, the magic had disappeared and Cleo was hanging over the side of the boat.

19

_"I_t's the sea currents." A sympathetic Billy Hawks passed Cleo some dry crackers. "Two strong tidal currents meet here to form the Portland Race."

She squinted through the early morning mist at the roiling seas ahead and groaned. They were rounding the southernmost tip of the Isle of Portland. The red-and-white-striped lighthouse at the tip of the rocky Bill was barely visible.

She'd already lost her bangers and mash. She was now fighting to hold on to her stomach lining. All that saved Cleo from total humiliation was the fact that Doc Cruz apparently felt as miserable as she did. He sported a green tint to his olive skin and kept an arm draped over the opposite rail. Both of them had stuck Dramamine patches behind their ears. Too late, as it turned out.

Donovan, on the other hand, rode the swells like an old salt. He was hunkered down on Cleo's other side, armed with bottled water and more crackers for the time when she could tolerate either.

Nothing like telling a man you love him one minute, she thought with a grimace, then almost puking all over him the next.

"The Race is the reason this area became such a graveyard for ships and boats," Billy said. "There are more wrecks to be found here than in any other stretch of the Channel."

Cleo really didn't need to be reminded of that. Not with the deck pitching beneath her feet and waves crashing against the hull.

"We'll be out of it soon," Hawks promised. "The seas will calm some then."

"How much is 'some'?"

A grin split his boyish face, making him appear even younger. "Some."

When he left Cleo and Jack at the rail, she groaned again. "And we're doing this why?"

"Because a World War II-era transport that went down somewhere in these waters is our best lead— our only real lead at the moment—to a murdered air force tanker pilot." Jack passed her the plastic bottle. "You remember him, don't you? Captain Doug Caswell."

"Right," she muttered. "Minnesota Fats. Bouncing Bertha. Gold reserves. Round Pegs."

The *Argos II* leveled off enough for her to glug down several swallows. The water swished around in her stomach but remained relatively horizontal. After a few moments, she felt confident enough to munch on a cracker.

Billy Hawks's prediction proved true. Once they were past the treacherous Portland Race the seas calmed—some—and the sun gradually burned off the mist. By the time the *Argos II* approached the designated search area, the sea sparkled and land was only a faint purple smudge.

Water bottle in hand, a somewhat rejuvenated Cleo joined Mulholland in the wheelhouse. Sophisticated navigational aids blipped and beeped on an array of screens. Chatter from other boats crackled through radio speakers. Weather updates flashed across a digital display. Pinned to the bulkhead was the Admiralty chart Mulholland had used last night when briefing them on the search grid.

The grid had seemed gigantic to Cleo then. It now loomed even larger. Her eyes went to a set of coordinates colored a bright magenta. They marked the site of a wreck, she knew, but couldn't remember what the designation stood for.

"What's the M2 again?"

"A British submarine lost with all hands in 1925."

She lifted her bottle toward another wreck site

near the upper corner of their search grid. "And this one, the Black Hawk?"

"She was a Liberty ship, torpedoed in 1944. The coordinates fix the location of her aft section. The forward section was towed into shallow water and salvaged before being sunk, but the stern broke away and sank there, in deep water."

He went on to identify other known wreck sites, including two World War II-era aircraft. One was a Messerschmitt shot down while attacking a convoy, the other a B-17 Flying Fortress ditched after taking hits during a bombing raid. Cleo left the galley with the feeling that the waters beneath the *Argos II* constituted one big scrap heap.

That feeling intensified once they reached the search area. At that point, Mulholland put the boat on idle and deployed the side scanning radar. Doreen would love all this gadgetry, Cleo thought as she watched him ready a slender, torpedo-like tow fish.

"How is this different from regular ships' sonar?"

"The sonar aboard most vessels sends an acoustic pulse straight down. The sound bounces off the ocean floor—or any object lying on it—and returns a signal indicating depth. You can only see the small slice of the sea directly below you."

He skimmed a palm along the tow.

"This sweetheart projects an acoustic beam down *and* ninety degrees to either side. When the sound waves hit an object, they bounce back to the sonar head. The head in turn sends the signals topside to a display monitor. The result is a three-dimensional picture that really takes the biscuit."

At Cleo's blank look, he grinned. "Takes the cake, I think you Yanks say."

She nodded, as impressed by that flashing grin as by the information Mulholland had imparted. Once you got past his prickly exterior, the man had definite possibilities.

Cleo saw the side scan's incredibly vivid imagery firsthand some hours later. They'd traversed one length of the grid and were headed back down the second leg when the sonar picked up the remains of a cargo ship that had gone down in a storm during the sixties.

"There," Mulholland said, pointing out the dark shadow clearly visible against the cobalt-blue seabed, "you can see the cargo holds and smokestack. That's the bridge house forward of the stacks."

Remembering the last cargo ship she'd boarded, Cleo shuddered. She didn't want to think of the *Pitsenbarger* lying broken and abandoned on the ocean floor. A chill crawled along her skin and stayed there while Mulholland and crew hunched over the sonar screen, studying the remains of a once-proud vessel.

They covered almost a third of the search area before heading for home. The wind picked up and the seas got choppy again as they rounded the Bill.

Cleo's stomach was rolling when she stepped onto the quay, but she managed to keep down the thick, crusty sandwiches McBride had supplied for lunch. The mere thought of a heaping platter of fried fish, though, left her feeling queasy. She bowed out of another gathering at the Sea Cow, opting instead to have Jack bring her back a take-out order of their tuna-noodle bake.

Once back in their room, she turned her cell phone on to check for calls. There were two, she saw. One from Goose, another from a number containing a country code she didn't recognize. She rang Goose back first and caught him outside the Wichita hospital, sneaking a smoke.

"It's been a bitch of a twenty-four hours," he admitted, his voice rough with weariness. "The hallucinations have stopped, though, and the ER docs think she's through the worst of it. They're going to release her sometime today. What do you want me to do with her?"

Cleo had been chewing over that question all day. Jack said Kate had no relatives or close friends, and it sounded as if she was still too fragile to dump on a bus and ship back to Cincinnati. Odds were she'd fall right back into the pit Goose and Mae had just dragged her out of. Cleo was darned if she knew what to do with the woman, though.

"I'll talk to Donovan and get back to you on that."

Goose grunted and offered an out. "Mae has a suggestion. She says we could take her back to Dallas and bed her down at Doreen's place until she's back on her feet. Evidently Doreen has a spare bedroom."

"Yes, she does. Her roommate walked a few months ago, but…"

"Mae told me Doreen's mother suffered severe bouts of depression for years before she died. Doreen got her through the worst of them."

"I didn't know that."

Come to think of it, Cleo didn't know very much at all about Doreen's past beyond the fact that she was related to Wistful Wanda and once worked for a high-tech electronics firm. Now she got off on Bart Simpson and worked for North Security and Investigations. More or less.

"Mae called Doreen a while ago to tell her about the situation," Goose continued. "She's game, if that's what Kate wants."

"Kate can't just diddly-bop down to Dallas. She has a job in Cincinnati."

"Not anymore. She got canned. She told us that's what sent her into this latest tailspin."

Oh, hell.

"Jack says she's been ordered to attend court-ordered counseling. If she misses another session, they'll issue an arrest warrant."

"Maybe Donovan can finesse that."

"Maybe."

"She's in bad shape, Cleo. She needs someone to keep an eye on her. Tell Donovan my vote is to go with Mae's suggestion." An admiring note crept into her trainer's gravelly bass. "That woman's got some head on her shoulders. You should have seen how she handled Kate. You'd swear they were long-lost sisters."

"Sisters?"

Jack's ex was probably in her late thirties. Mae took great pride in her sixty-plus years. Either Goose was more tired than Cleo thought or he was seeing the silver-haired office manager with new eyes.

"Yeah," he replied, "the two of them just sort of clicked. We'll stand by until we hear back from you."

"Roger."

Cleo hung up, her mind whirling with all the reasons why letting Goose and Mae transport Kate down to Dallas wasn't a good idea. Unfortunately, she couldn't come up with a feasible alternative.

Mouth pursed, she checked the second call. It had come through at two-twenty this afternoon. She still couldn't place the country code. Northern Europe, maybe. She'd have to check that with the hotel operator.

After verifying the caller hadn't left a message, she hit the send button and let the phone at the other end ring six or seven times. When no answering machine clicked on, Cleo shrugged. If the caller wanted to get in touch with her, he or she could try again.

She flipped the phone shut and headed for the bathroom to shower the salt spray from her face and hair.

20

*T*he assassin sat alone in the high-backed pew, listening while the muted rings of his mobile phone echoed through the side chapel of the great cathedral. His hooded gaze never left the instrument in his hand. He recognized the number displayed on the screen. He'd punched it into the keypad of this small, sleek instrument earlier this afternoon.

The ringing stopped.

The echoes died.

The signal was locked.

Releasing a long breath, he rested his head against the ornately carved pew. He'd taken a risk, placing that call earlier today. A dangerous risk. But he'd needed his prey to return it so he could complete the exchange.

Technology made the hunt so much less complicated these days. Most mobile phones now came with location-tracking chips that linked them into the Global Position-

*ing System. The phone didn't even have to be on for some-
one with GPS access to track its location. Or lock on its
signal.*

*His call this afternoon had pinpointed the location of se-
curity consultant Cleopatra North. At that time she'd been
approximately twelve miles off the coast of England.
Searching, he knew, for a plane that went into the Channel more than sixty years ago.*

*A bone-deep weariness spread through him. He hated
what had to come, loathed the necessity that forced him to
employ his lethal skills yet again. But he couldn't allow her
to find that plane. He couldn't allow anyone to.*

*The creak of ancient cathedral doors swinging on
equally ancient iron hinges brought his head up.*

"Grandpapa?"

*Footsteps sounded on the stone floor of the nave. A lilt-
ing voice called out to him.*

*"Are you ready to go? It's so very cold in here. Grand-
mama wouldn't want you to catch a chill."*

"No, lilla gumman, she wouldn't."

*His gaze lifted to the stained-glass window above the
side altar. A pain undiminished by time pierced his heart.
The woman whose death was commemorated by that window had been his salvation. His life. He'd once killed to protect her. Now he killed to protect what was hers.*

*Touching his fingers to his lips, he blew her a kiss and
tucked the mobile phone into his breast pocket. He'd use it
a final time. Tomorrow.*

Departing the side chapel, he walked the long, echoing

nave of the cathedral. His granddaughter waited for him beside the stone baptismal font. She'd been christened at that font fifteen years ago. Or was it sixteen? He found it hard to believe. She would always be his lilla gumman, *his little lady.*

She slipped her hand in his, her grip gentle in deference to his increasingly fragile bones. "Don't forget you promised to come watch me scull tomorrow."

"I'll have to watch you another day. I have to fly to Paris on business tomorrow."

And then to London. From there, he'd drive to the Devon coast. Covering his tracks came as naturally to him as breathing.

His granddaughter's pretty face fell. "Paris again? Weren't you just there last week?"

"Yes."

"Can't you delay this trip?"

"No, I cannot."

"Then take me with you. We can shop for Mama's birthday present and buy an ice at Berthillon's."

She was his bright, shining star. He rarely denied her smallest whim, but this was unthinkable.

"I'll be gone several days. You can't miss that much school."

"School is boring. I'd rather be with you." She released his hand and skipped backward down the steps of the cathedral. "Please, Grandpapa. Please. We always have such fun together."

A bleakness settled around his heart, as dank and chill

*as the drizzle misting the city many called the Venice of
the North.*

"Not this time."

21

Jack paced the cozy sitting room. The mellow mood engendered by two foaming mugs of beer, a platter of fish and chips, and the prospect of getting Cleo naked had evaporated. He speared a glance at the woman sitting cross-legged on the bed, polishing off the cheesy tuna-noodle bake he'd carried back from the Sea Cow.

"I don't like dragging you, your family *or* your employees into Kate's problems."

"Seems to me we're already in."

"Then it's time I got you out. Carting Kate down to Dallas isn't a smart move."

Shrugging, she downed the last bite of casserole. "It wasn't my idea, but I admit I don't have a better one. Do you?"

No, Jack didn't, and that was what ripped him.

He'd reached Kate's attorney and got him working at that end to preempt an arrest warrant. He'd
also talked to her boss, but couldn't convince the
woman to rehire a substitute teacher she described
as unreliable at best. As a former spouse, Jack had no
authority to shuffle Kate off to another rehab center.

That left three choices, none of them palatable. He
could tell Goose to put Kate on a plane back to
Cincinnati and let her fend for herself. He could
abandon the hunt for Bouncing Bertha and Captain
Doug Caswell's killer, fly home and try once again
to help Kate piece her life back together.

Or he could allow a set of near-strangers to as-
sume responsibility for the woman he'd once vowed
to love, honor and protect. Neither love nor honor
had figured into the equation for a long time, but
that didn't negate the third factor.

"It's not fair to ask Doreen to take on someone
with Kate's history of drinking and depression. She
doesn't know what she's getting into."

"Mae says she does."

"I don't like it," Jack repeated.

"Look, I'm not real thrilled about it, either. Your ex
better have her act together by the time we get home
or I might just have a few things to say to her. Primarily about what she's doing to you."

"Dumping on Kate when she's down won't help
her get back up."

Maybe not, but a no-holds-barred heart-to-heart

with Jack's ex would sure make Cleo feel better. Shoving her plastic fork into the carton, she tossed both into the wastebasket.

"It's your call, Jack. You've traveled down this road before. I can stay in England and work the Caswell case until you get Kate squared away. If this search for Bouncing Bertha doesn't open any new leads, we'll have to fall back and regroup, anyway."

Then again, there was always the possibility the search for Bouncing Bertha might bust the case wide open. Someone had retrieved a Colt .45 from Grenadier Sergeant Gordon's watery grave. If and when they found that grave, they might also find evidence leading them to the person or persons who'd violated it.

She didn't remind Donovan of that, though. He knew the ins and outs of this case as well as she did. Better, considering how he'd fed her only those pieces of information she needed to know.

Nor would Cleo in any way, shape or form suggest that his decision represented a choice between her and his ex. She wasn't prone to depression or dependent on alcohol. She didn't need Jack the way Kate needed him.

She needed him in a different way, she admitted silently, one she was just coming to grips with. But this wasn't the time to say so.

"You really think Doreen can handle her?"

"Ha! We're talking about the techno-whiz who invented the moon-spinner. Kate gives her grief, she'll wrap her in an invisible straitjacket Godzilla couldn't bust out of."

The tight line to Jack's mouth slowly relaxed. The tension and frustration so evident in his face gave way to a reluctant grin.

"That might not be such a bad idea."

"Good." She held up her phone. "You want to talk to Goose or shall I? He's standing by."

"I'll do it."

His short conversation with Goose put the creases back in his face and popped out the cords in his neck. Expecting just that, Cleo was ready when he ended the call and tossed her phone on the table beside the bed.

"You're looking tense, Donovan." She flexed her hands, bending them back. "We need to release your *sen*. You want to go for the full treatment this time?"

"What does that involve?" he asked, wary.

"Hands, elbows and feet. Mine, not yours." Her knuckles cracked in a series of small pops. "First we work your pressure points, then we stretch the muscles. You'll be floating when I finish with you. Groaning, but floating."

"I've got a better idea. How about we work *your* pressure points?"

She pretended to consider the offer. "Well…"

"We'll use hands and elbows and feet," he promised, working the buttons on his shirt. "Mine, not yours. All you have to do is float. And groan."

"I think I can manage that."

His shirt hit the floor. The cotton T-shirt followed. At the sight of his taut abs and precisely defined pecs, Cleo's *sen* took off running.

His glutes weren't bad, either, she decided with a gulp as he kicked off his jeans and shorts. Not bad at all.

As promised, he used his hands and feet, but kept his elbows tucked to his side. Her nipples ached when he finished with them. Her calves tingled from the friction of his soles rubbing against her skin.

When he shimmied down her belly and lifted her legs over his shoulders, she floated. High and wide and wild. Riding sensation after sensation until the ragged moan she couldn't hold back any longer ripped from her throat.

Out in the hallway, Johanna froze. She had one hand raised to rap on the door to Cleo and Jack's room, held a fax in the other.

She barely caught the muffled cry coming from inside the room. If Gray Stone Inn wasn't so old, with a slice of light showing below almost every door, she might not have heard the muted sound at all.

The agent in her went into instant action-response mode. The woman in her reacted almost as quickly. That was no cry for help. That was Cleo in the throes of a shattering climax.

Her fist clenched, crushing the fax. Envy stabbed into her belly. Envy and raw need.

God! It had been so long since she'd given herself up to mindless, erotic pleasure. So long since she'd straddled a man's hips, nipped his shoulder, tasted the tang of salt on his skin.

Johanna stared blindly at the door for another moment. Then she spun on her heel, strode down the stairs and went out into the night.

She tried the *Argos II* first. Mulholland had indicated he was going back to the boat after dinner to take another look at the sonar scans they'd done that day.

Her pulse skittered and picked up speed. The captain's cabin aboard the *Argos II* was compact, but the bunk was long and wide enough to accommodate a man of Mulholland's size. It would make tight quarters for two, though. *Very* tight.

Shockingly vivid images were flickering through her head as she approached the quay. The dark, locked-down boat pulled her up short.

Fists balled, she glared at the wooden-hulled boat. Should she consider this a sign? Return to the Gray Stone Inn? Douse the fires in her blood with a cold shower?

No bloody way.

She retraced her steps to the street, turned right instead of left and pushed through the front door of the King George Hotel. A flash of her credentials elicited Mulholland's room number from the night clerk. She was in the lift, riding it to the next floor, when it occurred to her she'd forgotten to inquire whether Mulholland had taken a single or a double.

No matter. If he was bunking with one of his mates, she'd invent some excuse to coax him back to the boat.

She was spared the necessity. When Mulholland answered her knock, a glance inside his room showed it to be a single.

"Lady Mar…" He made a midcourse correction, his eyes narrowed on her face. "Johanna. What is it?"

If she'd harbored any doubts about her intended course of action, his acres of bare chest resolved them. She could hardly attack the man here in the hall, though. The crumpled paper in her pocket gave her the perfect excuse to gain entry.

"I received a fax from HQ a while ago. I thought you might want to know about it."

"Yes, of course. Come in."

He moved aside. She darted a glance at the rumpled bedcovers, drew in a swift breath and turned to face him.

"Cleo and Jack requested a screen of the security tapes at the Public Records Office. MI6 stepped in to expedite the review."

A polite way of saying MI6 had brought the tapes to the Digital Imaging Lab and picked them apart frame by frame.

"Unfortunately, the security cameras made time-sequenced sweeps so there are gaps in the coverage. It's also unfortunate that the tapes are only saved for thirty days, but they did capture several persons entering the room that houses the World War II archives. HQ has identified all of them except this man."

Smoothing the crumpled fax, she passed it to Mulholland. The digitally enhanced image showed a rear view of a male in a tweed jacket with suede patches at the elbows. The jacket collar stood up and a flat-billed cap in a houndstooth check covered the man's hair, but the wizards at the DI Lab had zoomed in enough to pick up a few silvery strands between cap and collar.

"Everyone accessing the paper archives must sign in. We've matched the names and signatures to the other people on the security tapes. The name this man gave doesn't pop up in any databases."

Mulholland slanted her a swift look. "You think this was the bloke who planted the incendiary device?"

"Possibly. Or he might simply be a World War II buff attempting to research old records. HQ is still trying to work an ID."

"From the back of his head?"

Brushing up against his arm, Johanna pointed to an embroidered insignia faintly visible amid the houndstooth checks of the cap band.

"Do you see this crest? It's the trademark of the Swedish hatmakers, Anders."

"I can't say as I've ever heard of that brand of cap."

"Nor have I. But HQ says it's an old and quite venerable firm that sells only to posh stores. They also design individual caps for a select list of clients. One, I've been informed, is the crown prince of Sweden. Another is the Australian who starred in that dreadful remake of *Tom Jones* last year. We're contacting the firm in Stockholm on the off chance they can identify this particular client."

Frowning, Mulholland folded the fax and handed it back to her. "What about the Yanks? Does Jack have his people working the ID from their end?"

"Actually, I haven't briefed Jack or Cleo about this yet." Johanna tucked the fax in her pocket and lifted her gaze to his. "I went down the hall to their room, but heard a slight sound that suggested they were, ah, otherwise engaged."

"So you came to me."

"So I came to you."

Her words hung on the air. Mulholland raised a palm, scraped it along his chin.

"Johanna, about last night…"

"Yes?"

His hand dropped. Looking both aggrieved and resigned, he muttered a gruff confession. "I didn't sleep ten minutes the whole sodding night."

That was all the impetus she needed. Near swimming in hormones, she laid her palms against his chest.

"Nor did I, if you want to know the truth. May

I...?" She swiped her tongue over suddenly dry lips. "May I suggest a remedy?"

"I'm thinking *I* know how to remedy the situation, Lady Marston."

His hands tunneled into her hair. His mouth came down on hers. The first kiss stoked the fire in her belly. The second ignited his.

With a low growl, he caught her under her knees and swept her up. Two steps took them to the bed. Two minutes saw them naked and straining, mouth against mouth, pelvis to pelvis.

He took his cue from her and wasted little effort on preliminaries. She was panting when he rolled away, in a fever of impatience when he returned from the bathroom tearing at the wrapper of a Johnny with his teeth. She had time for only a short, fervent prayer of thanks that he'd packed one in his kit before he kneed her legs apart. Locking her calves around his, she arched her hips and matched him thrust for thrust.

Johanna woke to the almost forgotten sensations of a heavy arm draped over her waist and the bulge of a man's sex against her bottom cheeks. She lay still for several moments, swamped by memories. Rather to her surprise, they were recent memories, only hours old.

"Are you awake, then?"

The gruff whisper came on a wash of warm breath against her ear. She twisted under the heavy weight, tangling with hairy legs and starched sheets. Mulholland was propped up on one elbow. His face was a pale blur in the darkness, his eyes mere shadows that gave no clue to his mood.

"I'm awake. What time is it?"

"Almost four."

Johanna wished she could see his expression. She tucked the top sheet over her breasts and decided if she was in for a penny, she was in for a pound.

"Well?"

"Well what?"

"Did you get any sleep?"

She saw the gleam of white teeth. The arm hooked over her waist tightened, drawing her into him.

"A few minutes here and there. Do you know you recite Shakespeare in your sleep?"

"Oh, dear!" She gave a little huff of embarrassment. "Barty—my husband—swore I quoted the Bard line for verse, but I never quite believed him. He was always threatening to record me whilst I slept."

Guilt tugged at her with sticky fingers. She shouldn't have mentioned Barty. Not with Mulholland leaning over her naked breasts.

"I'd best get dressed and go back to the inn to gather my gear."

"Not yet." Dipping his head, he dropped a kiss on her shoulder. *"'Being your slave, what should I do but tend upon the hours and times of your desire?'"*

"Was that what I was mumbling? Sonnet 57?"

"No, but I thought that line appropriate to the moment."

Johanna hid her astonishment along with a healthy dose of chagrin. In her line of work, it never paid to stereotype. The most seemingly innocent person could prove the most dangerous. Yet she wouldn't have thought this not-quite-so-scruffy retired Royal Navy diver was the sort to carry Shakespeare's sonnets around in his head.

He'd thrown her off balance from the first moment they'd met. He was still throwing her off. Even now, when she was sure they'd thoroughly satisfied their hunger, she could feel him hardening against her. She found herself wishing she'd made a quick trip to the loo, hoping sleep hadn't soured her breath, wondering if he'd scrape her raw with the fresh set of whiskers he'd sprouted during the night.

She needn't have worried. He proved himself a most considerate lover by rolling her onto her side. With her back to his front, he tended upon the hours and times of her desire *most* satisfactorily!

A sharp rap on the door to his room jerked them both back into consciousness some time later. Cursing, her bed partner reached across her, switched on the light and barked out a brusque command.

"I'm awake. I'll be down shortly. Wait for me in the lounge."

"Sean? I need to talk to you."

Cleo's voice floated through the door panel. She kept it quiet so as not to wake other guests, but loud enough to convey a sense of urgency.

Mulholland twisted around and mouthed a silent command to Johanna to stay put. Pulling on his jersey sweats, he crossed the room and opened the door a few inches. "What is it?"

"Have you heard from Johanna this morning? I tried her room, she's not there. I need to talk to her."

"Is there a problem?"

"No, but the sleepy-eyed receptionist on duty when Jack and I came downstairs said she took a call from Johanna's housekeeper last night. The message was about her brother."

Her brother?

It took Johanna a startled moment to remember she had two. Twin siblings she'd never known about until her mother died last year. One sibling she'd already met. One she would meet for the first time when he flew over for a visit next week.

A sudden coldness gripped her. Alex. This call had to be about Alex, the brother she'd yet to meet. He'd had a relapse, succumbed to the bullet wound that had left him fighting to regain both speech and mobility. The fear she might have lost him before she'd so much as spoken to him sent her springing from the bed. Pulling the sheets around her, she used a hip to nudge Mulholland aside and yanked the door open.

"Which brother?"

Cleo's jaw dropped, but she responded to the urgency in Johanna's demand.

"Marc. Evidently he couldn't reach you on your mobile, so he called your London flat. Your housekeeper in turn called the Gray Stone Inn."

"Why?" Johanna wadded the sheet ends into a tight ball. "Has something happened? Is it Alex?"

"Oh, no! It's nothing like that. Marc just wanted to let you know they're moving up their trip and will arrive tomorrow. Evidently he wants to combine business with pleasure."

Relief crashed through Johanna in great, pounding waves. How odd, how very, very odd, that she should feel such worry for—and a bond with—men who were essentially still strangers. That's what came of sharing a womb, she supposed.

"Thank you for passing the message on. I'll ring Marc when we return to Weymouth this afternoon. It will still be early morning his time."

"Right. See you guys aboard."

When the door closed behind Cleo, Johanna scooped up her clothes. "I'll have to remember to call my housekeeper this afternoon, as well. And tell McDowell to meet them at the airport."

Making mental lists, she headed for the bathroom. Sean watched her depart with a wry grimace.

As quick as that, he thought. One minute they were cuddled together like an old married pair. The next, she was back in her world and he in his.

He was stepping into his trousers when she rushed back into the bedroom. Her dark hair tumbled about her face and her mouth looked well kissed, but she was all brisk business.

"I'll fetch my gear and see you aboard the *Argos II*."

She started for the door, spun back and stretched up on tiptoe to nip his bottom lip.

"*'I am to wait,'*" she quoted in a husky whisper, "*'though waiting so be hell.'*"

She left him standing like a fool, one leg in his trousers. A silly smile tugged at his lips as the lines from Sonnet 58 echoed in his head.

22

Cleo wore a fat grin when she stepped out of the elevator and joined Jack in the deserted lobby of the King George.

Donovan stood beside their gear, looking relaxed and good enough to eat in jeans, a blue T-shirt emblazoned with USAF in big gold letters, and a hooded windbreaker with the new air force insignia stamped on the right breast.

"Did Mulholland know where Johanna is?"

"Ooh, yeah."

She waggled her brows. He cocked his.

"Does that leer mean what I think it does?"

"Ooh, yeah."

His grin came out to match hers. Hooking a hand around her nape, he tugged her in for a quick kiss. "Sounds like the skipper and I both got lucky last night."

"Very lucky."

Her heart did a happy little tap dance against her ribs as she slung her gear bag over her shoulder. She'd left her purse in her room and stuffed necessary items like her wallet and cell phone in the bag. Her key chain with its tiny, superpowered flashlight and Doreen's latest invention weighed down the pocket of her shorts. The keys flapped against the poncho draped over the shorts as she led the way out into the rain-lashed darkness.

She and Donovan had yet to close in on Minnesota Fats's killer. They were in the middle of a hunt for a canister of possibly lethal powder. Jack's ex-wife was probably in Dallas by now, invading Cleo's personal turf. The waves whipped up by the wind and rain would no doubt result in the loss of another breakfast despite the Dramamine patch she'd stuck behind her ear.

But after last night and the kiss Donovan had just laid on her, she had to admit life was good. Very good.

Whistling under her breath, she tugged up the hood on her plastic poncho and strode alongside Jack toward the quay. As it had yesterday morning, Weymouth hummed with a flurry of predawn activity. The driving rain didn't deter a trio of fishermen intent on going out with the tide. A delivery van rattled over the cobbles, huffing out exhaust fumes. The yeasty bouquet of fresh-baked bread tickled Cleo's nose.

She followed the tantalizing aroma to a bakery tucked between a grocer's and a dive shop only a few yards from where the dark, silent *Argos II* was moored. Since they'd beat the rest of the crew to the scene, Cleo decided a little detour was in order.

"Hang on a sec. I want to duck into this bakery and buy some sticky buns to take on board."

"Why don't you give me your bag? I'll take it to the boat and wait for you there."

The inside of the shop constituted a carb addict's Eden. Half the cases still stood empty, but sufficient goodies had made their way onto racks and trays to initiate serious salivation.

A tinkling bell over the door summoned a flour-dusted attendant from the back room. When he filled Cleo's order for a dozen Bath buns, she had him throw in another dozen puff pastries oozing whipped Devon cream. She swiped a finger in the frothy cream and licked it while he wrapped and bagged the items in plastic.

She tucked the plastic sack under the folds of her poncho and exited the shop. Intent on protecting her goodies from the rain, she almost collided with a solitary figure rigged out in rain gear. He caught her arm to keep her from landing on her butt.

"Oops!" Juggling the sack, she righted herself. "Sorry."

Her breezy apology brought her rescuer's head up with a snap. His bright yellow slicker covered most of his face and torso, allowing only the bill of his cap and a high-bridged nose to poke from the hood.

"My fault entirely," he murmured, releasing her arm. "Excuse me, I must go."

The response was polite, the English oddly accented. With an abrupt nod, he sidestepped and continued on his way. The slicker flapped against his trousers as he strode down the darkened street.

When Cleo crossed to the quay, her approach startled a gull from sleep. He took off with a squawk that spooked the others perched around him on rocks and pilings. Raucous cries and flapping wings surrounded Cleo. Ducking, she dug a still-warm bun out of the bag as a peace offering and tore it into sticky chunks. The keen-eyed gulls dive-bombed the morsels she tossed into the sky. They also dive-bombed one another, screeching as they fought for the offerings.

Deciding she needed to get the heck out of gull central, Cleo spun around and retraced her steps. She saw the man from the bakery then, standing beside the open door of a vehicle parked several blocks away. He was watching her, probably wondering if he'd have to come to the aid of the klutzy American again. Cleo waved to signify she'd survived the seagull frenzy.

He didn't return the friendly gesture. Turning his back on her, he slid into the driver's seat and slammed the door. The interior lights cut off. The engine coughed to life. The vehicle left the curb, cut sharply to the right and disappeared down a side street.

Ah, Cleo thought, glimpsing the rental-agency license tag. An out-of-towner. That explained why he didn't roll his *R*'s like the crusty fishermen and jovial farmers in this area.

The rain was coming down in buckets now. Hunching her shoulders, she navigated the slick cobbles and made it to the *Argos II* only half drowned.

The rest of the team had arrived in her absence and were busy loading the refilled tanks and day's supplies onto the boat. Billy Hawks wore a windbreaker and knit cap, both already soaked through. Dave Argyle and Doc Cruz flapped around in plastic ponchos. McBride looked like a Gloucester fisherman in a wide-billed yellow hat that tied under his chin and raincoat fastened with rusted metal clasps.

Mulholland was in the wheelhouse. Cleo could see his beefy silhouette outlined against the glow from the instrument displays. Jack stood at his shoulder, squinting down at one of the screens.

"What's the word?" she asked Hawks as he helped her aboard. "Are we going out in this weather?"

"This front is supposed to pass within a few hours. We should have only a light drizzle by the time we reach the search area."

But getting there wouldn't be a whole lot of fun, Cleo knew. The rain drummed down on the deck cover. Even with the boat still tied to the quay, she had to widen her stance and brace her feet against the rise and fall of the deck. She didn't want to *think* what the ride would be like once they left the protected harbor.

No bangers and mash for her this morning. No cream-filled pastries, either. With real regret, she passed the plastic sack to Billy Hawks.

"I bought some fresh-baked buns to tide you guys over until McBride cooks breakfast."

"That's ace of you."

He opened the sack, sniffed at its contents and plowed a fist into the bag inside. The bun he pulled out now smelled altogether too sweet and cloying to Cleo.

She beat a hasty retreat and went to help Johanna, who was racing along the quay with her gear bag.

The trip out to the search area plunged Cleo into a cold, wet hell. She might as well have left the Dramamine patches back at the Gray Stone Inn.

She didn't dare go below. The confined space only increased her nausea and dizziness. Nor could she climb the short flight of steps to the enclosed wheelhouse. That elevated platform rocked from side to side like a metronome. Her only recourse was to hunch under her plastic poncho on the rear deck and pretend to ignore the waves that foamed and churned for as far as she could see.

"You okay?"

She dragged up her head and glared at a disgustingly healthy-looking Donovan. "Peachy keen."

"For a woman who doesn't take well to the sea, you've sure been venturing out on open water a lot lately." He leaned back against the rail, ignoring the rain and spray that hit the back of his hooded jacket. "First the eastern Med, now the Channel."

"Next time you pull me into a case, make it one involving desert. Or Arctic tundra. Anything but water."

"You need to update your security clearances if that's going to happen," he reminded her, then paused. "*Is* that going to happen?"

"You said it yourself, Donovan. We make a helluva team. No, wait. That was Barnes."

He couldn't have looked more surprised if she'd whacked him in the face with a mackerel.

"The Old Man said that?"

"He did, when he lured me into this mess."

Luring was a slight exaggeration, but Jack didn't need to know she'd jumped at the Caswell murder just to work with him again.

"So what does that mean?" he asked. "Are you thinking about hiring on as a full-time consultant to the OSI?"

"Do you want me to?" she countered.

Like all special agents, Jack had been trained to operate independently in the field. Cleo had gone through the same training. She called Goose for backup when and if she needed it, but she valued her independence and the freedom to take only the cases that intrigued her. Cleo wasn't sure how Jack would take to the notion of working in tandem. She wasn't sure how *she* would take to it. More and more, though, the idea appealed to her.

Evidently it appealed to Jack, too. He answered her question in a way that erased every doubt.

"Yeah, babe," he said with a smile that curled Cleo's toes inside her drenched Oakleys, "I do."

Damn! And she thought her stomach had finished doing loop-de-loops.

"Okay, so who's going to tell the Old Man?"

"That you're prepared to rejoin the ranks of government employees?" Jack hooted in glee. "Let me. *Please,* Cleopatra Aphrodite, let me."

"You call me that one more time, Donovan, and yours will be the first murder I investigate as a full-time government employee."

Laughing, he hooked his elbows on the rail, stretched out his legs and crossed his ankles. Rain pelted through the open space between canopy and deck, but the soaking didn't appear to worry him any more than her threat.

"We'll contact the Old Man as soon as we return to Weymouth. I need to update him on this fax Johanna received."

Cleo hadn't seen the fax yet. She'd been too busy fighting her heaves to go below and it was too wet out here on deck to unfold the paper. Johanna had briefed her, though. Cleo found it extremely interesting that a recent visitor to the war records archives had evidently supplied a false ID.

The pieces were coming together. She could feel it, along with several other unpleasant sensations. At least Donovan's presence provided some distraction from her queasy stomach, which was no doubt his intent.

The small act of kindness added another layer to her feelings concerning Special Agent Jack Donovan. Love figured in there, and a whole lot of lust. A professional's respect for his investigative and leadership skills. Anger at his ex for the guilt she heaped on him.

And now this odd little glow of pleasure that he would hunker down beside her, ignoring wind and rain and churning seas, just to keep her company. She issued a stern order to her stomach to cease and desist, sighed and sank into the circle of his arm.

Although Cleo had harbored severe doubts, Mulholland's faith in the weather forecasters proved justified. The rain gradually let up and the wind subsided. By the time they reached the search area, the sun was trying valiantly to poke through the sullen clouds. Good thing, as the first leg of the grid would take them within four miles of Portland Race and its treacherous currents. Cleo didn't think she could have handled both the rain *and* the Race.

The side-scan torpedo head went over the side. The towline played out. The transducers began to send out signals. Still queasy but determined to re-join the team, Cleo hovered with the others as the sonar once again sent back incredibly vivid images.

Four and a half miles south of Portland Bill they picked up the shadowy outline of a wreck. The shape and scatter pattern confirmed it was the stern section of the Black Hawk.

"I've dived her a couple of times," Mulholland commented, his gaze narrowed on the image. "So have you, Dave. Any idea what that is?"

He froze a section of the scan and traced a finger over a small triangle glowing bright orange against the cobalt-blue of the sea.

Brows knit, the Scot studied the shape. "A piece of the rudder, d'ya think?"

"Whatever it is, it's newly exposed. There's little encrustation to fuzz the signal."

"The storm last week could have shifted the Black Hawk and exposed new sections of her," Johanna put in. "Just as it did the *Inventor*."

Mulholland nodded. "That's what I'm thinking. I'm also thinking that triangle has the approximate size and shape of a wing tip."

The rest of the team jostled for a closer look. Cleo squinted at the small form and searched her memory bank. She was sure Mulholland had told her the Black Hawk was a Liberty Ship. She knew U.S. ship-yards had built thousands of those cargo ships dur-ing the war, some in as little as two months. She didn't think they were large enough to transport aircraft, though.

"Not in their cargo holds," Mulholland confirmed when she posed the question. "But they could ferry planes, tanks, trucks—even railroad locomotives—lashed down on deck."

"What about the Black Hawk? What was she carrying?"

"She was part of a convoy returning from Cherbourg to Cornwall, via the Isle of Wight, in late December 1944. She'd discharged her heavy cargo and cleared her decks at Cherbourg."

"So she wasn't ferrying aircraft."

"No, she wasn't."

A spark jumped through the air, generating little electric currents of excitement. Cleo felt it stirring on her skin as Jack posed the question racing through her mind.

"You think the Black Hawk might have settled atop another wreck? Our wreck?"

"It's possible. The timing is right. Our transport was spotted going down at roughly these coordinates in March of '43. The Black Hawk was torpedoed in December that same year. It's worth checking out, anyway."

The rest of the team agreed. Although the wreck had been explored by a number of divers, Mulholland included, he insisted on making the first descent in full protective gear. *If* they'd beat the astronomical odds and actually found the remains of Bouncing Bertha, the same strong currents that had shifted the massive stern section might also have dislodged a lethal canister.

Once they'd dropped the shot line, Mulholland suited up. His chemical protective bodysuit, helmet, self-contained respiratory unit and secondary life-support unit gave him the look of an astronaut about to take a lunar stroll. Flippers slapping on the deck, he mounted the mechanized platform and gave a thumbs-up. Argyle hit the lower button. Slowly, Mulholland sank into the sea.

Cleo crowded shoulder to shoulder with the others at the rail, her gaze locked on the red buoy marking the shot.

Mulholland had figured the time required to descend to forty-eight meters, factored in additional time for environmental-risk assessments at various stages, and calculated how long he could stay on the bottom to the minute.

Every one of those minutes felt like twenty to Cleo. The *Argos II* rocked on the swells. The sun beat down, slid behind clouds, burned through again. She'd abandoned her poncho when the rain ended, and the sweat pooling at the base of her spine made her wish she'd changed her shorts and tank top for a bathing suit.

The minutes crawled by. No one left the deck. A

massive oil tanker trailed an aquamarine wake a mile or so off the port side. A hydrofoil buzzed by well away to starboard. Silence descended after the hovercraft disappeared, broken only by the slap of the waves against the hull and the muted chatter coming from the ship's radios.

Tension was crawling along every one of Cleo's nerves when—finally!—the red float bobbed.

"He's coming up."

Cleo must have held her breath during most of the long ascent, because it left on a whoosh when Mulholland broke surface. She caught it again when he raised his arm and gave another thumbs-up.

"The water's clean," he announced when they got him aboard and divested him of his helmet. "So is the wreck."

"What about that triangle we spotted? Did you find it?"

"I did." A grin slashed across his face. "No doubt about it. It's a wing tip."

"Holy shit!"

The other divers scrambled for their gear. Mulholland had to wait for his body to breathe nitrogen out of his system before making another descent. Johanna offered to remain topside and buddy down with him, but Cleo suggested she stay instead. She'd pretty much conquered her nausea but didn't mind another fifteen- or twenty-minute wait before sucking on a respirator.

Weighted down with buoyancy packs, powerful searchlights, cameras and backup tanks, the divers hit the water. Jack and Dave Argyle went down the shot line first. Doc Cruz, Billy Hawks and Johanna followed.

"I'd best put a chowder on to simmer," McBride said as they disappeared into the sea. "You'll need thawing out when you come up."

"Thawing out? What's the temperature down at the wreck site?" Cleo asked Mulholland.

"Cold as a witch's tit," he said cheerfully. "You'll want to wear your dry suit."

"Right. I'll go change."

She'd taken only a step when McBride shouted up from the galley. "Hey, Cleo! There's a buzzing sound coming from your gear bag. I think it's your mobile phone."

Buzzing? Her cell phone didn't buzz. It belted out the "Battle Hymn of the Republic." Only when it was switched on, though, and she was sure she'd left it off so as not to interfere with the navigational and sonar signals.

"Sorry 'bout that," she said over her shoulder to Mulholland. "I thought I'd turned it off."

She started forward again, took another step and saw a massive fireball whoosh up from the galley. A half a heartbeat later, the deck erupted under her feet.

23

Slowly, the assassin folded his hand. The sleek little mobile phone in his palm snapped shut.

These modern devices made death so much easier. He could send a signal from a great distance, detonate a bomb with a single electronic pulse. No lying in wait on a dark, snowy night. No wire looped over a head and yanked tight. No blade slashed across a jugular.

No specially weighted bullets fired from a silenced Colt, as when he'd eliminated Caswell.

He'd felt no regret then. None at all. But this one...

This death saddened him. Unbearably.

A pain started in his chest. His lungs squeezed.

Dear God, why did he have to have come face-to-face with her this morning? Why couldn't he forget how much she'd reminded him of his granddaughter? The same friendly smile. The same lively intelligence in her brown eyes.

If he hadn't looked into her face, he wouldn't be questioning the necessity of her death. Wouldn't be standing in a toilet stall at Heathrow, weighing her life against that of his granddaughter's.

Pain lanced through him, relentless, unceasing. He slapped a gloved hand against the stall, gasping for breath. Red spots swam before his eyes. The face of his prey blurred, became that of the child named for his precious Christina.

"Ah, lilla gumman."

He couldn't fail her now. Shuddering, he summoned the strength that had kept him alive against all odds so many years ago. He pushed upright, raised his arm, smashed it down.

The phone shattered against the porcelain toilet. Bits of plastic and electronic circuitry dropped into the bowl.

His breath knifing into him, Fredrik Jarlbörg, Count Valken, yanked on the chain and flushed away the last shreds of his soul.

24

The force of the explosion blew the *Argos II* out of the water. The entire boat was airborne when the forward half disintegrated. The aft deck sheared off, tilted at a ninety-degree angle and crashed down.

Cleo crashed with it.

The blast had knocked her onto her back. Pinned to the deck, she'd flown upward, watched the horizon tilt crazily, had only a heartbeat to brace herself before she rode the wreckage into the sea.

Now the sea was trying to swallow her.

Her lungs burned. Her legs scissored. Her hands clawed at the debris forming an almost impenetrable barrier between her and oxygen.

She'd popped through once, had spotted flames racing for her across oil-slicked waves, and jack-knifed back down. She'd swum as far as she could.

She had to surface again, *now,* or her lungs would burst.

Praying she'd outdistanced the oil slick, she balled her fists and pounded at the debris. A small hole opened, just large enough for her to shoot through. She kicked hard, propelled upward, gulped in air.

Gasping, choking, streaming seawater, she snatched at a floating piece of teak. It was one of the benches from the rear deckwell. Or what was left of the bench.

Hooking her arm over the wood, Cleo flipped her hair out of her eyes and twisted around.

"Dear God!"

Flames rose in a solid wall behind her. Black smoke billowed above the blaze.

Horrified, Cleo stared at the hissing, spitting conflagration. Hysteria bubbled in her throat. This was the second vessel she'd watched burn in less than two months. First the *Pitsenbarger,* now the *Argos II.*

She was never, *ever,* leaving dry land again!

As quickly as the hysteria rose, she gulped it down. This wasn't the time to panic. Mulholland and McBride had been aboard the *Argos II* when she blew. Jack and the others were somewhere beneath her. The shock waves from the blast would have hit them, too. Maybe with stunning force.

Battling a wave of near-paralyzing terror at the thought of Donovan pummeled by a massive percussive blow, she tightened her grip on the bench seat and twisted in the water.

The sight of Mulholland floating facedown on the swells ripped a vicious curse from her throat. Abandoning her refuge, she sliced through the waves.

She was grabbing for his arm when she spotted the jagged piece of metal protruding through his side. Blood poured from the wound, tinting the sea around it a pale pink.

"Sean!"

Dodging the metal spear, she yanked on his arm. It took her three tries to flip him over. She hooked an arm around his throat to keep his head above water and swam him back to the bench. Fighting the sea and his inert weight, she shoved him onto the plank.

She thrashed around, searching for a line to lash him to the teak. Or a life vest! God, where were all those orange vests? A low groan spun her around again.

"Sean! Sean, can you hear me?"

His lids twitched. His body jerked. Cleo had to grab both of his arms to keep him from sliding off the bench.

"Sean, you've got to hold on! I need to look for McBride."

And Jack.

And the others.

Almost suffocating with the fear that the blast had hit the divers, she spit out seawater and tried to drag Mulholland higher up the plank.

"Hold on, Sean. Just hold on."

His fingers curled on the edges of the bench. His eyelids fluttered up. Cleo saw his pupils were dilated, knew he was probably in shock, but she couldn't deal with that now.

Kicking off, she plowed through the debris. McBride had been forward, in the galley. Her mind told her the fireball that had consumed the main cabin of the *Argos II* had consumed its mate as well. Her gut wouldn't let her abandon him without a search.

Battling the swells, she circled the flaming oil slick. Heat seared her skin, smoke and salt ate at her eyes. Halfway around the slick, she spotted the red buoy marking the shot line and cut directly for it.

She was reaching out a hand to tug on the line when a wet-suited diver broke surface. It was Ernesto Cruz, his eyes wild behind his face mask.

The doc tore off his mask, threw a horrified glance at the burning oil slick and dived back under the waves. He surfaced again a moment later, dragging another diver by the arm. Johanna, Cleo saw, her heart slamming against her ribs. Unconscious. Pushed half out of the water by Billy Hawks.

Hawks thrust the woman at Cruz and snatched off his face mask. Blood gushed from his nose but it was his left ear that seemed to be causing him horrific pain. His face twisted in agony, Hawks trod water with one hand and slapped the other against his ear.

The percussive force of the blast must have shattered his eardrum. He was alive, though. So were Cruz and Johanna.

But Jack. Dear God, where was Jack?

Her throat raw from gulping in smoke and sea-water, she shouted at Cruz to get his attention. The doc wrenched his stunned gaze from the flames.

"Cleo, what happened?"

She didn't know, and didn't have time to tell him so.

"Donovan?" she screamed. "Where is he?"

"Last I saw him, he and Dave were about ten meters below us."

They'd gone down the shot first, had to have been deeper when the percussive waves hit. Trying frantically to recall from college physics class whether marine disturbances magnified or decayed with depth, she dove in and rappelled down the shot hand over hand. The pressure on her lungs soon forced her to stop. She searched the hazy depths, screaming Jack's name inside her head, spewing out precious bubbles of air when she saw two dark figures swimming up toward her. Releasing the shot, she somersaulted toward the surface.

Jack and Dave surfaced beside her. Spitting out their mouthpieces, they dragged up their face masks.

"Cleo, what the hell...?"

Donovan broke off. He must have smelled the smoke. Or felt the heat from the flames. Or heard Argyle's anguished "Och, sweet Lord!"

Twisting around, Donovan rode the swells. His stunned glance lingered on the flames for only a second or two before darting to the other divers. Cruz floated with Johanna propped against his shoulder.

Billy Hawks writhed in anguish. Blood washed in pale streaks down his cheeks and chin.

When Jack splashed back to Cleo, the skin over his cheeks had stretched taut and white. She expected him to demand an explanation, pepper her with questions. He had only one.

"Are you okay?"

The hysteria bubbled up again. Hell, no, she wasn't okay! She'd just had a ship blown out from under her. Again.

"I'm okay."

Her hoarse croak didn't convince him. Swimming over, he shoved his mouthpiece at her. She fit her lips over the plastic gratefully. While she sucked in much-needed oxygen, Donovan unsnapped his buoyancy belt and clipped it around her waist.

Cleo could have wept with relief. She hadn't realized how much of her strength she'd used up until she felt the belt lift her.

"What about Mulholland and McBride?"

"Sean's in bad shape," she choked out around the mouthpiece. "I left him clinging to a piece of bench on the other side of the spill. And I couldn't find McBride. He..."

She gulped, seeing again the fireball that had leaped toward her.

"He was down in the galley when the *Argos* went up."

Struggling out of his harness, Jack passed her the tanks and assumed command.

"Dave, see if you can find any life jackets or preservers or anything else that will float among the debris. Doc, you hang on to Johanna and Billy. I'll get Mulholland."

He swam off, fins flipping, arms cutting through the waves in long, sure strokes. Cleo breathed a heartfelt prayer of thanks that they didn't have to battle the churning seas they'd faced earlier this morning and hooked the harness over her arm. Dragging the tanks, which had become a deadweight, she went to assist Dave in his scavenger hunt.

They collected an assortment of floatables. A large piece of the Fiberglas rear deck canopy. A ten-gallon water jug, miraculously still full. A spare shot-line buoy.

Cleo used her free hand to butt the buoy toward Cruz. The doc tried to prop it under Johanna's arm, but she was still too dazed to hang on to it and the damned thing kept popping out.

"It won't hold without a line or a rope," he grunted. "Can you cut the shot line? We'll use that buoy instead."

Cleo threw a glance over her shoulder at the red balloon, sighed and gathered her fast-ebbing strength. When she kicked off, a small weight thumped against her thigh.

Backstroking, she splashed to a halt. Well, hell!

They didn't need the shot line. She still had Doreen's moon-spinner in her shorts pocket.

Her mind racing, she swam back to Cruz, Dave Argyle and their collection of flotsam. She had to sacrifice the tanks then. She couldn't manage the harness *and* the moon-spinner *and* stay afloat.

Tanks and harness sank into the depths. Cleo fumbled the key chain out of her pocket. Her hand shaking with fatigue, she aimed at the ten-gallon water jug.

"Stay clear," she warned Cruz and Argyle.

"What are you doing?"

"Finding out whether I need to give my step-cousin another raise."

"What?"

"Just stay clear."

The line whirred out, snagged the jug and wrapped around the neck. For a heart-stopping moment, Cleo thought the microfilaments had slipped free of the wet plastic. It took her a while to realize the sunlight reflecting off the threads had made the top portion of the container invisible.

"Yes!"

With a burst of renewed energy, she dragged the jug toward the remnant of Fiberglas canopy. Another zap, more invisible threads, and she had the two firmly anchored. She corralled the spare shot-buoy next. Dave Argyle saw what she was doing and swam over with a long length of teak rail.

By the time Jack reappeared, towing Mulholland aboard the bench rail, Cleo, Dave and Doc Cruz had stitched together a raft. Johanna lay atop the floating pieces. The rest of them hung on to any available handhold.

Grunting, Jack shoved the semiconscious Mulholland toward the raft. "Looks like you folks have been busy. Think your ark will hold one more?"

"Sure, no problem."

It took the combined efforts of both Donovan and Dave Argyle to shoulder Mulholland aboard. With two onboard and five clinging to precarious handholds, they scanned the horizon.

Land was a blue smudge in the distance. The oil tanker had disappeared. There wasn't a hydrofoil, fishing boat or pleasure craft in sight.

"Someone on shore will spot the smoke," Cruz predicted. "The Portland Coast Guard station maintains a fifteen-minute readiness state. We'll hear a chopper buzzing over us within thirty."

It was closer to forty minutes, but Cleo didn't have the strength to quibble. Her legs ached from attempting to keep the raft clear of the smoke, her arms felt like lead weights, and salt had invaded every pore.

Dragging her head up, she squinted at the chopper zooming toward them. As it drew nearer, she saw it was a Sikorsky S61N with the distinctive orange-and-white markings of Her Majesty's Coast Guard.

Once overhead, the chopper dropped into a hover. The downdraft from its rotor churned the seas. A loudspeaker blared.

"Ahoy, aboard the raft."

Jack and Cruz responded with frantic waves.

"We're lowering the winch," the speaker boomed. "One of our survival techs will assist you into the basket."

The chopper dropped as low as it could without swamping the makeshift raft. A scuba-equipped rescue tech stepped out of the side hatch and splashed into the sea. The hoist began to whir down.

The chopper ferried the survivors to the Coast Guard station on the Isle of Portland. The medical station the survivors were taken to was small but well equipped.

The station doc working in conjunction with Ernesto Cruz diagnosed Billy Hawks with severe barotrauma. Evidently he'd had sinus problems before, and the added pressure from the blast had ruptured the air spaces in his sinuses. Still in excruciating pain, Billy was airlifted to a hospital to be seen by an ear, nose and throat surgeon.

Johanna, it turned out, had been knocked into Billy by the underwater blast. She'd whacked her head on his tanks and suffered a mild concussion. She was coherent, though, and insisted on walking into the next treatment cubicle to check on Mulholland.

Miraculously, the metal spear had missed any vital organs. The station physician had extracted the object and wanted to airlift him as well, but he jutted out his jaw and flatly refused. He wasn't going anywhere while the search was still on for McBride. While Doc Cruz and the Coast Guard physician stitched him up, Donovan and Dave Argyle went back out with the chopper that had brought them in to assist with the search.

Cleo would have gone, too, except Jack insisted she talk to the inquiry officer detailed to take their initial statements. She and Mulholland had been aboard the *Argos II* when the explosion occurred, Donovan reminded her tersely. They'd seen what happened. The rest of the team hadn't.

That was Donovan. Fill out the damned forms, even with your ears still ringing from the blast.

It was also, Cleo suspected, his way of giving her time to get the wobbles out of her arms and legs. She felt as though she'd run back-to-back Boston marathons. Or had a boat blow up under her.

Her grumbling protest was more show than real. She knew how vital it was to record the impressions of those at the scene of an accident. Time—and worry about responsibility or liability—tended to blur details.

Decked out in borrowed HMCG sweats, she gave her statement to a grave-faced lieutenant, then joined

Johanna and Mulholland in the clinic's five-bed ward. The British agent was also in borrowed sweats and sitting cross-legged on a neatly made bed. Mulholland wore hospital-type pajamas loosely buttoned over his bandaged midsection and stood at the window.

"I should be out there," he said. "Helping with the search for McBride."

Cleo shared a quick look with Johanna. Neither one of them harbored much hope that the wizened mate had survived the explosion. Neither wanted to say so.

Cleo had to get out the worry that had been gnawing at her insides ever since she'd stopped reacting and started thinking. Her throat tight, she stepped over to Mulholland.

"Do you think the signals from that phone call could have sparked the explosion in the galley?"

Johanna lifted a brow. "What phone call?"

Mulholland ignored the second question to address the first. "I've considered the possibility."

"What phone call?" Johanna asked again.

"I turned my cell phone off," Cleo said with quiet desperation. "I know I did."

"McBride said he heard something buzz in your gear bag."

"That's just it. My cell phone doesn't buzz. It serenades."

"I remember you telling me that." His jaw worked. "Just before the *Argos II* went up."

Johanna shoved off the bed. "Will one of you please explain what the bloody hell you're talking about?"

They remained totally absorbed, lost in their own dark thoughts. Exasperated, Johanna stalked across the room and planted herself between them.

"You both said McBride went into the galley to put some chowder on. We assumed the gas cooker must have exploded and ignited the fuel tank. This is the first time either of you has mentioned a phone call."

"I told the inquiry officer about it," Cleo said heavily.

"So did I." Mulholland glanced at each of them in turn. "I also told him that the recovery team should look for evidence of some kind of explosive device."

Johanna sucked in a sharp breath. Cleo merely nodded. She'd run dozens of scenarios through her head—including sabotage.

Now that Mulholland had voiced the possibility aloud, the small, seemingly inconsequential details that had been nagging at her took on a life of their own.

"I bumped into someone coming out of the bakery this morning," she related. "He apologized, I apologized, we went our separate ways. I didn't think anything about it at the time, except for the fact I couldn't place his accent. But then, right before I boarded the boat, I spotted him standing beside his car, watching me. I shrugged that off, too. Now..."

She chewed on the inside of her lip, wondering if

she was just trying to shift her crushing fear she'd forgotten to turn off that damned phone onto someone else.

"Now what?" Mulholland growled.

"Now I'm wondering what an older gentleman was doing driving around Weymouth at 4:00 a.m. in a rental vehicle."

Johanna's head snapped up. "Older gentleman? Was his hair a silvery gray?"

"Probably, although I couldn't see it. He was wearing a rain slicker with a hood that covered his head. And a cap," Cleo added, recalling the inch or so of bill that had poked out from under the hood.

"Dear God!" The blood drained from Johanna's face. "I never showed you the fax."

"The one your HQ sent? No, but you told me all it showed was the back of a man's head." Cleo's stomach lurched. "And his hat. Sunuvabitch!"

As Johanna got her people working the rental car agencies, a cold fury burned in Cleo's gut. At herself, for shrugging off that early morning encounter. At the idea she might have been the instrument to trigger not one, but two explosive devices. At the cold-blooded killer who'd planted them.

The bastard was going down. However long it took, she swore savagely, she'd take him down.

25

Donovan and Dave Argyle returned to the Coast Guard station two hours later. While Argyle conferred with officials in the Rescue Coordination Center, Donovan joined the small group gathered in the five-bed hospital ward.

Salt had crusted on his skin and his hair had dried into short amber spikes under a navy-and-white HMCG cap. His face tight, he delivered a grim report to what remained of the team.

"We didn't spot any sign of McBride. The Coast Guard is switching from search and rescue to a recovery operation."

Mulholland gave a terse nod. He'd witnessed the explosion. Like Cleo, he'd expected the worst. Hearing it said aloud, though, smashed their last hopes against the rocks.

"Dennis was a good mate."

Johanna pushed off the edge of the bed and started for him, as if to offer comfort. The effort drained the little color that was left in her face. With a muttered curse, Mulholland ignored the bandages wrapped around his middle, surged forward and snagged her arm.

"You've tried to do too much, taking notes and making all these calls to headquarters. Sit down, woman, before you fall on your face."

"I just need to rest a moment."

She allowed him to navigate her back to the bed but couldn't let go of the case that had consumed her for days. "Cleo, you'll have to update Jack on the latest developments."

"Will do." She eyed the lines carved into his face by wind and fatigue. "Let's get you some coffee first. You look like you could use it."

In the clinic break room, they found a pot of the sludge that passed for coffee among mariners the world over. Cleo filled a foam cup and shoved it in Donovan's direction. While he downed the contents, she paced the confined space and told him about her near collision with an elderly stranger outside the bakeshop this morning. The flash of startled recognition she thought she'd seen on his face. His faint accent. The bit with the seagulls. The way the stranger had stood silent, watching her. The rental tags on his vehicle. The buzzing McBride said had come from her gear bag.

"Dammit, Jack, I turned my phone off. I'm sure I did."

"Yes, you did. I saw you double check it before you tossed it in your gear bag this morning."

A mountain of guilt rolled off Cleo's shoulders. The possibility her phone might have interfered with navigational or sonar signals and sparked an explosion had been eating at her from the inside out.

She wallowed in relief for all of ten seconds, until Jack downed another slug of the mudlike coffee and heaped the guilt back on again.

"There's new technology out there, though. Transmitters that can send signals strong enough to be received and stored in a phone's memory chip even if it's turned off. All they need is an initial response to lock onto."

She whirled, her eyes widening. "What are you saying?"

"I'm saying someone *could* have dialed your phone previously, locked onto the signal when you answered and made a subsequent call that would be received by your phone whether it was on or off."

She thought back, went stiff as a board. "Dammit all to hell!"

"What?"

"I got a couple of calls yesterday while we were at sea. I didn't see them on the log until after we came in last night. One was from Goose. I didn't recognize the other."

Jack's brows snapped together. "You returned the call?"

"I did. Mae said she'd received several queries after the BBC aired that spot on the explosion at Kew Gardens. I thought it might be a potential client so I hit Redial to see who picked up."

"Who did?"

"No one. Nor did an answering machine kick in."

Abandoning his coffee, Jack shoved back his chair. "Our Cyber Crimes Unit can pluck that number off your servicing satellite link. I need to get to a phone and contact them. Sit tight, I'll be right back."

Sit tight, hell! Cleo dogged on his heels as he charged down the hall to the nursing station. Donovan's secure, clear streaming videophone had gone down with the *Argos II*. Like Cleo and Johanna, he now had to use borrowed equipment.

The corpsman manning the station surrendered his desk without argument. His superiors had already verified Johanna's credentials with MI6 headquarters and issued instructions to provide Lady Marston and her associates full cooperation.

The Coast Guard station operator put Jack's call through at top priority. He reached the head of the Cyber Crimes Unit and explained his request. The CCU was every bit as good—and as fast—as Donovan had promised. They bounced Cleo's cell phone number off a special satellite screen and supplied a list of calls made to her number in the past twenty-four hours.

There were three. The one from Goose. Two from country code 46.

"Sweden's code is 46," Jack informed Cleo. "The city code checks to Stockholm."

That was the accent she'd heard in the early hours of the dawn. A slight elongation of the vowels. Not enough to make her think of Francis McDormand in *Fargo*, but distinctive enough to have made her wonder if English was his native language.

"What about the final digits in the number?" she asked. "Who or what do they trace to?"

"A cell phone purchased two weeks ago." A muscle jumped in Jack's jaw. "Its signal went dead this morning, less than a minute after yours died."

She swore, long and low, dredging up curses she'd learned in a dozen different countries.

"Did CCU run the purchaser information?"

"They did."

"Let me guess. Hat Man used a false ID and stolen credit card to make the purchase."

"Both bounced in the system when CCU ran them," he confirmed.

"Still, we know when he bought it. Do we know where?"

"At a wireless technologies shop in Stockholm."

"Stockholm. Same location as the hatmaker. We're closing in on him, Jack."

"Yeah, we are." A feral satisfaction glittered in his eyes. "CCU got GPS locks on the two calls he made to your phone. The one this morning originated from Heathrow Airport."

"Bastard! He blew us out of the water, then boarded a plane and made his escape. What about yesterday afternoon's call?"

"That one originated from a central location in Stockholm. CCU ran the street address. It checks to Storkyrkan Cathedral in the heart of Old Town."

"A priest?" Cleo grimaced. "Hat Man is a priest?"

"My guess is he picked a public place to make the call so the signal couldn't be traced back to his home or work address. It needs to be checked out, though."

She flicked a glance at her watch. Amazingly, it was still running. Equally amazing after all that had happened, the time was just a little past noon.

"We could jump a flight over today."

"You sure you're up for it?"

"I'm sure. Let's check with Johanna. Her folks might have turned up something more on the cap or the rental car."

MI6 had turned up not only a vehicle rented at the Heathrow Hertz desk yesterday by an elderly gentleman with silver hair. They'd also confirmed that he'd flown in from Paris.

"The clerk on the Hertz desk said our man indicated his flight had been delayed." Johanna was white as a corpse, still obviously hammered by pain but determined to keep things moving at her end. "I had our people run the name on the rental agreement against the passenger lists of all incoming flights. Jean-Paul Rivard arrived from Paris aboard Air France flight 1620. He departed this morning, returning to Paris."

"Except there is no Jean-Paul Rivard," Cleo guessed.

"Correct. There is no Jean-Paul Rivard. Not one who matches this man's age and general description, at any rate. The address on his international driver's license and passport check to a postal box in Stockholm."

"Bingo," Jack said softly.

"Exactly," Johanna echoed. "We've contacted the Swedish Intelligence and Security Directorate to request surveillance of the postal box."

"What about the hatmaker?" Cleo asked. "Anything more from him?"

"The owner indicates half his clientele for that particular brand of cap is past sixty. The wool fabric and flat shape are specifically designed to prevent heat loss among older gentlemen. They're willing to work with us, though. Cleo's description, added to the image we retrieved from the security tape at Kew, might prove adequate for a more positive ID."

"Sounds as though our best lead is Stockholm," Jack said. "Cleo and I think we should zip over there this afternoon."

"I'll accompany you." Johanna pushed to her feet. "We'll need to go back to the Gray Stone Inn first to…"

She broke off, swaying, and threw out a hand to steady herself. Mulholland caught it in his hamlike fist and sat her back down again.

"You're not going anywhere."

"I just...just need a moment."

"You need more than that. Don't be a bloody fool, woman."

Johanna managed a pale ghost of a smile. "This from the man who quoted Shakespearean sonnets to me only this morning?"

"You weren't concussed this morning."

"Just give me a moment," she said again, forcing steel into both her voice and her eyes. "I'm working a case, Sean, one that's become rather more personal to me in the past few hours. I need to arrange a flight and the necessary clearances for Cleo and Jack to carry their weapons aboard. I also," she added sharply when Mulholland started to protest, "intend to be in on the kill. I want you to remain and coordinate efforts here."

She didn't say it, but it was understood the search would continue for McBride *and* for the canister of toxic powder that might be buried under the stern section of the Black Hawk. Mulholland's initial dive had indicated no environmental toxicity in the area of the wreck. Cleo only hoped the percussive blast from the *Argos II* hadn't disturbed the status quo.

Now that she thought about it, the prospect of facing Hat Man held infinitely more appeal than staying here. She could get *him* in her gun sight. It was hard to take aim at a microbe.

"Dave or Ernesto can coordinate the search," Mulholland snapped. "If you go, I go."

"Now who's being the fool?" The color that had leeched out of her cheeks a few moments ago raced back. "You've a hole in your side."

"And you've a dent in your head. If you go," he repeated, "I go."

"Very well, but I give you fair warning. If you open your wound and faint dead away, I'm leaving you right where you fall."

Mulholland's reply would have made even his fellow Royal Navy divers blush.

A Coast Guard launch ferried the four of them from Portland to Weymouth Harbor and deposited them almost at the door of the Gray Stone Inn.

Word had already spread about the accident at sea. The crews of boats that hadn't responded to the search-and-rescue call huddled around radios tuned to the emergency net. Tourists stood shoulder to shoulder at outdoor cafés, watching the drama unfold on television screens.

Heads turned when the cutter tied up at the quay. Recognizing one of their own in Mulholland, dive crews started for the launch. In a town that took its livelihood from the sea, any disaster affected them all.

Cleo and the other three had already discussed the

issue and agreed to leave it to the ensign commanding the launch to answer questions. Well trained in rescue operations, she knew exactly how much information to release—and withhold—regarding ongoing efforts.

Mulholland ran interference for Johanna. Jack did the same for Cleo. The two women took unashamed advantage of the male bulk to cut directly to the Gray Stone Inn.

The inn's landlord stood in a corner of the reception lounge, his gaze glued to television screen. He glanced up when the quartet entered, took one look at their borrowed clothing and salt-encrusted hair, and came rushing over.

"So it was the *Argos II*, then! I feared as much. Are you all right?"

"We're okay."

"Thank God! What happened? The news reports said there was an explosion."

"There was," Johanna replied. "We've yet to determine the cause. We'll need our bill."

If the landlord thought it odd that they were booking out of Weymouth with the rescue operation in full swing, he didn't say so.

"I'll have it ready for you when you come down, Lady Marston."

Johanna and Sean detoured to her room, Jack and Cleo to theirs. A quick shower and change put Donovan in gray slacks, a yellow Oxford shirt and his lightweight summer sport coat. While he went down the hall to provide Mulholland with a clean shirt, Cleo took her turn in the shower, then jumped into her spare pair of jeans, a silky short-sleeved turtleneck in black and the flax-colored jacket she'd worn on the flight over.

Her Oakleys were still squishy, so she traded them for stacked sandals. The Glock went into the purse she'd left in the room this morning. Thank God she'd also left her passport. The key ring with Doreen's miraculous microfilaments joined the Glock. Her wallet, however, was at the bottom of the English Channel, along with her ID, credit cards and cash.

"I hope Johanna can get me through security," she muttered to Donovan as they gathered their few remaining possessions and crammed them into one of the inn's plastic laundry bags. "Except for my passport, I'm currently ID-less."

He gave her a tight smile. "If Johanna can't get you through, I will. You're working for the United States government, remember?"

"Oh. Right."

The smile had started Cleo's nerves snapping. More than a little feral, it told her Donovan was in full hunt mode. Like her, he wanted blood.

Johanna used the trip from Weymouth to Heathrow to initiate a flurry of calls on a borrowed cell phone. She and Mulholland drove up in the Mor-

gan. The Americans followed in the Taurus. Hero-
ically, Cleo refrained from commenting on the dif-
ferences between the performance and appearance of
the two vehicles, but she vowed silently she'd do the
renting if—when—she and Jack worked another gig.

Once they arrived at Heathrow, a young man who
peered at them through round glasses that made
him look like a stubble-bearded Harry Potter came
up to them.

"I have the credentials you requested for you and
Petty Officer Mulholland, Lady Marston."

"Thank you, Brewster." She slipped the flat leather
case into her bag without looking at it. Sean flipped
his open, frowned at the photo taken from his Royal
Navy records and snapped the case shut.

"Ms. North and Special Agent Donovan have their
passports, but she lost her identification cards."

"So I was informed. I've requested an iris scan to get
her through airport security. If you'll step this way…"

He escorted them to a small office equipped with
an assortment of video screens and cameras.

"Ms. North, if you'll just step in front of the camera, place your chin on the rest and look straight at
the red light."

Cleo did as instructed. One click of the shutter
was all it took to translate the more than two hundred
independent characteristics of her right iris into digital code. The camera operator used a keyboard to tag

the code with her name, address and passport information, then hit Save.

"That's it, then."

"That's it? I don't need to carry a printout or something with me?"

"All you need do is show your passport again at the gate and look into the camera. The system will ID you. Won't take but a blink."

Once back on the concourse, the efficient Brewster supplied tickets all around and the necessary clearances for Johanna, Jack and Cleo to carry their weapons aboard. At Johanna's direction, he'd also coordinated with the Swedish Intelligence and Security Directorate.

"SISD was quite intrigued to learn you're requesting assistance on a case with possible connections to World War II activities," he commented.

"Yes, I imagine so."

"One of their agents will meet you at Arlanda Airport."

Their small team was becoming an army, Cleo thought. That was fine with her—as long as no one got in her way when she came face-to-face with Hat Man.

26

"The Portland Coast Guard Rescue Coordination Center has now confirmed the vessel was the Argos II, out of Dover."

The modulated tones of the BBC announcer filled the study.

"The RCC has also confirmed at least one member of the crew was below deck at the time of the explosion and is presumed dead. No name has been released at this point. Further updates will follow as they are received."

Infinitely weary, Fredrik reached out a shaking hand and switched the radio station. The newscast gave way to the finely sculpted piano trills from Wilhelm Peterson-Berger's great masterpiece, Flowers from Frösö Island.

The notes flowed over Fredrik but failed to give him the peace they usually did. He was beyond peace. Beyond joy. Pain still squeezed at his chest. Not as severe as when it had doubled him over at Heathrow, but steady and relentless. It wasn't his heart that would kill him, though, but his own failings.

He'd waited too long to trigger the device he'd slipped into the carton of supplies going aboard the Argos II. He'd intended to give the crew time to get well out to sea and give himself time to be well away from Weymouth. He'd thought the weather would keep everyone aboard below decks, had planned for the explosion to consume them all.

But some had survived.

He eased back in the tapestry-covered chair, hoping the American, Cleo North, was among the survivors. First Kew. Now this. She'd proved far tougher to destroy than any of his previous targets. He'd never pitted himself against such a worthy adversary.

If she had survived, she'd come after him. She'd make the connection to the signal he'd sent to her phone. Sooner, he would guess, rather than later. If she hadn't been seriously injured, if she had to drag herself aboard a plane or a ferry, she'd come after him.

The ache in his chest a constant now, he turned his gaze to the window. Formal gardens stretched in neat undulations from the rear piazza to the fjord. Pebbled walkways led to a three-tiered fountain and intersected the boxwood hedges framing Christina's beloved rosebushes. The bare stalks were just beginning to show new green.

He could count his life in hours now. He had to spend those hours with Christina and her roses. Hands shaking, he pushed out of his chair.

27

Mulholland downed a double shot of whiskey during the short flight to Stockholm's Arlanda Airport to dull his pain. Cleo craved a beer, but she didn't have the excuse of a hole in her side. Besides which, she didn't dare risk alcohol on an empty stomach. She hadn't eaten since the cheesy tuna-noodle bake last night, and had come damned close to losing even that this morning.

Thankfully, Johanna convinced the steward to supply them with crusty turkey sandwiches and tea. Cleo consumed two stuffed baguettes and a full pot of tea during the fifty-minute flight.

As promised, an agent from the Swedish Intelligence and Security Division was waiting when they landed. Big, reddish-blond and as bushy-bearded as a Viking, he flashed his credentials.

"Lady Marston? I'm Carl Ericsson."

His accented English sounded much like Hat Man's, Cleo noted immediately, but the emphasis seemed to come on different syllables.

"I've been instructed to escort you and your party and provide any assistance you might require."

"Thank you."

When Johanna made the introductions, the Viking gave Jack a nod and Cleo a curious glance. Sean raised his shaggy brows.

No surprise there. Mulholland's loaned trousers fit fairly well, but his shoulders strained the seams of Jack's shirt and threatened to pop the buttons. Then there was the wide bandage wrapped around his midsection, clearly visible through the cotton.

"If you'll come with me, I have a car waiting."

The car whisked them over a series of canals and interconnected islands into a modern business district characterized by concrete and glass. To avoid the logjam of traffic into the Old City, Ericsson had one of the department's water taxis waiting at the police wharf.

Cleo had visited Stockholm years ago with her dad. She remembered it as a city of space and light, situated on fourteen or fifteen different islands separated by canals and fjords and connected by beautiful bridges. She also remembered palace guards in spiffy blue uniforms, jackboots and Prussian-style headgear topped with spikes. The spikes were gone, she saw as their water taxi cruised past the magnificent royal residence. The Kevlar-helmeted guards now held submachine guns at the ready. A sign of the times.

Ericsson directed the water taxi to a landing just beyond the palace. He helped the ladies out and gave Cleo's stacked heels a dubious glance.

"The streets in the heart of Gamla Stan—our old city—are closed to vehicular traffic. You might have difficulty navigating the cobbles in those shoes."

His warning proved prophetic. Cleo made it less than a block before she gave up the struggle. A quick dive into a tourist shop produced a pair of the only footgear available. Tossing her sandals into a trash can, she clopped along in orange flip-flops topped with bright purple dahlias the size of basketballs.

Their first stop was the cathedral dominating the small island of Gamla Stan. According to Ericsson, Storkyrkan Cathedral had been constructed in the thirteenth century, reconstructed after fires in the fifteenth and seventeenth centuries, and served as the site of all royal coronations, weddings and funerals. The present structure included a soaring vaulted nave, numerous side altars and stained-glass windows that showered glittering jewels of light throughout the interior.

Tourists jammed the aisles, snapping shot after shot of the magnificent wall paintings, the baroque pipe organ and the statue of St. George and the

Dragon, reportedly the oldest wooden statue in northern Europe. A few worshippers ignored the throngs and sat alone in high-backed pews.

Ericsson had greased the skids and arranged an interview with the archbishop's chief of staff. That gentleman confirmed that no priest or member of his staff fit the description of the elderly man Cleo had spoken to in the dark hours before dawn. Nor could he match the description to a specific parishioner.

"Our cathedral serves several thousand of our faith," he said apologetically. "Many are elderly."

"And drawn from some of the oldest houses in Sweden," the SISD agent added in an undertone as they were escorted from the archbishop's office. "My superiors have asked me to keep them advised of our progress in our investigation."

Cleo shook her head, amazed all over again at the twists and turns this case had taken. The hunt for the killer of an air force tanker pilot had so far involved the Cambria mafia, a World War II-era transport lost over the English Channel, a fortune in gold bullion and a canister of itching powder with the lethal potential of anthrax. If the investigation led to Sweden's King Carl Gustaf, she might just have to renegotiate her consulting fee with General Barnes.

"Shall we visit the mobile phone store next?" the Viking suggested. "It's just a few blocks away, off Västerlänggatan, the main shopping street in Gamla Stan."

Forewarned, Cleo wasn't surprised to find the narrow street teeming with tourists. Digital cameras clicked away, recording for folks back home colorful details of the eight-hundred-year-old structures facing one another across the cobbles. Massive wooden doors, ornate stone facades and fanciful statues adorned the tall structures that had once served as both residences and places of business for the merchants who traded the goods brought back by generations of seafaring Swedes.

The scents of chocolate and cinnamon wafted from sidewalk cafés crowded into postage-stamp-size spaces. Crystal sparkled in shop windows, throwing off rainbows of color. Sculpture and artwork filled second- and third-story studios. Restaurants tucked into wine cellars and rear courtyards wooed customers with displayed menus offering every possible delight.

The electronics shop they were looking for was in a rose-colored merchant's house sporting a stone lion above the door. The shop windows displayed an array of products that supported Sweden's claim to being a leader in wireless technologies.

The inside was a techie's wet dream. Doreen would've had an orgasm on the spot, Cleo thought as she looked around. While the store manager finished with the customer at the counter, she examined an array of phones incorporating the latest 3G bandwidth technology.

"Look at this." She directed Jack's attention to a

sleek, wafer-thin unit that was all screen. "This little jobber offers improved e-mail with attachments, Web browsing, video conferencing, news services and real-time clips from the Swedish Song Contest."

Ericsson smiled at the reference. "The song contest is one of our biggest national events. With more than ninety-six percent of our population owning mobile phones, you'll find many use it as a portable link to the festival."

Good grief! Ninety-six percent of all Swedes owned mobile phones? Tagging the customer who purchased a unit at this shop two months ago might prove more difficult than she'd anticipated.

The store manager confirmed Cleo's fears. He produced the sales receipt readily enough, but informed them the part-time employee who'd made the sale had been fired several weeks ago. The clerk provided the names and address of the university student's parents, but held out little hope he would remember the sale or the customer. The reason behind his firing was his unfortunate tendency to smoke pot on duty. The kid had barely remembered his own name when the store manager caught him with a joint behind the shop.

Jack had already determined the name and address listed on the receipt and service contract were false, as was the credit card used to pay for both. Ericsson slipped the paper documents into an evidence bag, though, on the off chance SISD's lab could raise usable prints.

"That pretty much narrows us down to our hat-maker," Cleo said when they exited the shop.

"I contacted the head of the firm when I received your communiqué," Ericsson informed them. "He promised to personally screen his client list and compose a list of names of those who might match the individual we're looking for."

"From what I understand, that might be a long list."

The computer printout ran to several pages.

The present owner and manager of Anders and Sons was the sixth generation by that name to sit behind the baroque desk in his heavily paneled office. It soon became apparent he knew the business.

"Thirteen to sixteen percent of the body's blood volume is circulating through the brain at any one time. It's critical for that blood to maintain the proper temperature for the brain to function, particularly in cold climates such as we experience in Sweden. To prevent loss of body heat through the top of the head, we weave the checked wool used in this style of cap especially tightly. As a consequence, it's extremely popular with older customers."

"Popular *and* pricey," Jack observed, raising a brow at the item cost included on the printout.

Cleo made a mental note to buy him one for Christmas. He'd look sporty in that flat-billed tweed. Just as quickly, she scratched the item off her shopping list. If the wearer of one of these caps had triggered the explosion that killed Dennis McBride, Donovan wouldn't want to wear a reminder.

"When one's hair thins," the manager replied with a polite smile, "one appreciates added protection no matter what the cost."

Oops. Good thing she'd scratched the cap. Jack wouldn't appreciate the suggestion his hair—or anything else above his waist—was thinning.

"I recognize a number of names on this list," Ericsson commented, skimming through the printout. "Some are quite famous."

The other three crowded behind him to look over his shoulder. To Cleo's intense relief, she didn't see King Carl Gustaf included on the list.

"If they're as well known as you indicate, SISD ought to be able to pull up newspaper or magazine photos on them."

"SISD can do better than that," Ericsson replied, whipping out his cell phone. It was one of those ultra-high-tech jobs, similar to the ones Cleo had drooled over in the electronics store. Phone in hand, he gave Anders a polite smile that carried the weight of the Swedish government behind it.

"Is there somewhere we could work privately? Here perhaps, or another office?"

The hatmaker to princes and movie stars appeared somewhat startled at being asked to vacate his office, but acceded with a regal nod.

"Please, remain here. I'll see you're not disturbed."

Ericsson's thumb was flying over the keypad before the door closed behind Anders. Hooking into the Web, he called up the Swedish-language version of Google.

"Sit here beside me, Ms. North, so you can see the pictures as they come up on screen."

The first was a world-famous stage actor who'd retired in the early seventies. A drooping mustache covered the bottom half of his face. The top half looked nothing like the man outside the bakeshop.

"Nope, that's not him."

A retired admiral and former commander of the Swedish navy followed the actor.

"No."

The governor of a northern province popped up next.

"No."

Ericsson's thumb scrambled over the keys. Several of the names returned no hits. Those he marked for follow-up.

They finished the first page, started on the next. Cleo's narrowed, laserlike gaze scanned the faces that came up on the two-inch screen.

A Nobel Prize winner.

A horse breeder with a champion stud.

A shipping magnate.

"No," Cleo muttered. "No. No. *Wait!*"

Her screech sent Ericsson's thumb skittering over the keypad.

"Go back to that last one!"

He brought back the picture of a count who'd garnered fame in the horticultural world for the rose he'd propagated and named after his wife.

Cleo hunched closer to the screen, studying the hooded hawk's eyes and beak of a nose. "That's him."

"Count Valken cannot be the man you saw." Ericsson was emphatic.

"Why not?" Johanna demanded. Like Jack and Sean, she was hanging over the man's shoulder.

"His family is one of the oldest in Sweden. His son is a highly respected cardiologist and patron of the arts. His daughter represents Skåne County West in our Riksdag. Rumor has it she will announce her candidacy for prime minister next month."

"We're interested in the man, not his family," Jack pointed out evenly. "What's his background?"

"Money and public service run in the count's blood." Ericsson fiddled with the keypad, adjusting levels of brightness. "He himself served in the Riksdag before the war. There's some talk the count profited immensely by laundering gold looted by Germany during the war, but… Well, Sweden remained neutral during that conflict, as you recall. Both sides desperately needed the ore from our iron mines and were willing to respect our neutrality if we supplied it."

He shifted his shoulders, obviously addressing a subject of some sensitivity, but Cleo hadn't heard much beyond the mention of gold.

Damn! She'd never realized wars were fought as fiercely on financial battlegrounds as on the killing fields.

"What's more," Ericsson continued, "it came out after the war that the count sent his fleet of ships across the Baltic in the dark of night to assist in the evacuation of Danish Jews rounded up for transportation to concentration camps. More than eight thousand escaped in that boatlift. Many owe their lives to Fredrik Julbörg, Count Valken."

"Julbörg!" Cleo's head jerked up. Her glance whipped to Johanna. "I'll lay you odds *that's* what your Mr. Potts was trying to say! Julbörg, not Jarlsberg."

"You know, I believe you may be right."

The excitement leaping in the Englishwoman's face belied her typically British understatement.

Johanna flicked a glance at the antique pendulum clock on the far wall. It was almost five, but this was the Baltic. Late May meant long days and nights of shimmering white light.

"Do you have Count Valken's address?" she asked her Swedish counterpart.

"Yes, of course. His castle is situated on a private island only a few kilometers from Stockholm center."

"Let's go."

A fairy-tale palace in rose-colored brick and ornately carved stone, Castle Grejle boasted turrets sheathed in weathered copper, manicured lawns spilling down to the water's edge, and a private boat dock more heavily protected than Fort Knox.

Ericsson held his shield up to a security camera's eye and spoke into a speaker mounted on the iron gate guarding the dock. After a brief exchange in Swedish, he pocketed his credentials and waited.

"There was an attempted kidnapping some years ago," he explained. "Two men succeeded in getting the count's granddaughter into their boat before he, ah, intervened and saved the state the cost of a lengthy and very expensive trial."

Jack's eyes narrowed. "How old would you say this count is?"

"Eighty-six or seven."

"And he took out two kidnappers?"

"One with a boat hook, the other with his bare hands."

Very slowly, very calmly, Jack turned his back to the security camera. Reaching under his coat flap, he retrieved his Sig from his underarm holster and released the magazine. Satisfied that it carried a full clip, he snapped the magazine back into place.

Cleo and Johanna took similar precautions. Ericsson reluctantly followed suit. Mulholland settled for wrapping his fist around the wooden pole used by their taxi driver to push off snags and sand bars.

"Remember," Ericsson said sharply, "the count is a Swedish national. You—none of you—exercise jurisdiction over him."

"This is your show," Jack agreed with a nod.

Cleo wasn't fooled. She sensed his suppressed violence, felt it racing through her as well. The hunters had picked up the spoor.

A good five minutes passed before a voice came through the speaker.

"Count Valken is at home," Ericsson translated. "He's agreed to meet with us."

The red beam spearing the water taxi blinked. The iron gate swung open. The SISD craft putt-putted through the opening and nudged the stone steps of the dock.

Ericsson exited first, then turned to assist Johanna and Cleo. As they followed him along a pebbled walk, the hairs on the back of her neck lifted. She was close. So close. She felt it in every pore. Hiking the strap of her shoulder bag higher on her shoulder, she unzipped the pouch and rested her hand within easy reach of her Glock.

A butler in striped trousers and a tailored jacket met them at the steps to the residence and engaged Ericsson in a brief exchange.

"The count is in the rose garden at the side of the house," the SISD agent translated. "He requests we join him there."

Their footsteps crunched on the pebbles as they followed the butler along a curving carriage drive toward a vine-covered arch. Cleo heard the sounds of spilling water before she saw the three-tiered fountain at the center of a garden outlined with boxwood hedges. The top tier consisted of a young girl laughing over her shoulder as she trailed water from her ewer to the ducklings scattered around the second tier.

Cleo had never seen such delicate artistry in iron. She half expected to hear the girl's laughter floating across the garden. The butler turned to politely allow the women to proceed him through the arch and smiled when he noted the direction of Cleo's gaze.

"This statue is of Christina," he said in heavily accented English. "Granddaughter to the count."

"She's beautiful."

"Yes, and so much like her grandmama. This way, please."

He led them past beds planted with splashes of brilliant color. Although it was late May, spring had obviously just arrived in the Baltic. Tulips in shades of pink and velvety purple tipped their faces to the afternoon sun. Winter-hardy fuchsias dripped with blood-red blossoms.

A terraced rose garden was laid out with geometric precision around the fountain. The roses were just emerging from their winter dormancy. Their still-black stalks showed the first tender green of spring.

Cleo wasn't interested in the rosebushes, however, but in the individual sitting on a wheeled garden caddy among them. She thought at first she'd tagged the wrong person. This frail, stoop-shouldered old man in a canvas work jacket couldn't be the same one who'd gripped her arm with surprising strength outside the bakery this morning.

His back was to them. He must have heard their approach on the terrace below the one where he worked, but continued to turn the earth with a trowel until the butler stopped and announced them.

"Special Agent Ericsson and his party are here to see you, sir."

With slow, measured movements, the count shoved his trowel into the dirt and swiveled on the low seat. The terracing put his eyes at the same level as his visitors'. The moment he looked into Cleo's, she knew they'd found their killer.

28

"So." The count rested his gnarled hands on his knees. His gaze held Cleo's. "You have come."

"Did you think I wouldn't?"

A sigh feathered through his thin, bloodless lips. "No, Ms. North, I have been expecting you."

Cleo sucked in a breath. She hadn't thought it would be this easy. None of them had. She saw Jack's hand inch toward his jacket flap, heard Sean's muttered curse. Johanna remained still and watchful as a hawk beside a suddenly stiff Ericsson.

He was calculating the repercussions, Cleo guessed swiftly. Wondering just how much political heat he'd take when this bust went down.

The count surveyed each of them, slowly, deliberately, and issued a soft order to his butler.

"Leave us, Henrich."

"Yes, sir."

His measured tread sounded on the pebbled walk. No one spoke, no one shifted their intent gaze, until the bubbling fountain drowned the soft footfalls.

Johanna broke the silence. "Count Valken, were you in Weymouth, on the coast of England, early this morning?"

"Yes, Lady Marston, I was."

The quiet response acted like a cattle prod on the SISD agent and jerked him into action. "Wait! Wait, please. Don't ask the count any further questions until I advise him of his rights under the law."

He reverted to his native tongue, firing out the phrases burned into the brain of every law enforcement officer. Valken sat unmoving through the recitation, hands on his knees.

"Yes," he said when Ericsson finished, deliberately switching back to English. "I understand these rights."

Johanna picked up where she'd left off. "Did you plant an explosive device aboard the *Argos II?*"

"Yes."

"Bloody, sodding bastard."

Sean surged forward, the boat pole swinging. Jack dodged the pole and blocked the skipper with his body. Cleo couldn't hear what Donovan hissed in Mulholland's ear, but he got his attention. Fury suffusing his face, Mulholland jerked the pole down.

The count didn't so much as blink during the brief,

violent exchange. His hooded gaze stayed on Johanna as she asked the question screaming inside Cleo's head.

"Why?"

"I couldn't allow you to find the transport you're searching for. I couldn't allow anyone to find it."

Jack jumped on that. "I'm Special Agent Jack Donovan, United States Air Force Office of Special Investigations. I'm investigating the murder of a Captain Douglas Caswell."

"Ah, yes. Captain Caswell." The count showed emotion for the first time. His lip curling, he dismissed the tanker pilot with a sneer. "Such a venal, greedy man. He deserved to die."

"Did you shoot him?"

"Yes."

This whole scene was fast taking on an unreal quality. Cleo had worked her share of murder investigations. One particularly gruesome case had haunted her for years, until she'd finally nailed the killer in Santa Fe some months back.

She couldn't ever remember standing in a sunlit garden, though, with a fountain bubbling joyously behind her while a suspect calmly admitted his guilt.

Standard procedure at this point would be to cuff him, haul him to SISD headquarters and record his statement. Years of hard-learned experience, though, said to keep the bastard talking and give him as much rope as he wanted to hang himself.

Johanna grabbed the lead again. The weight of

her government was on her back, Cleo knew, and a small metal cylinder foremost in her mind.

"Why couldn't you allow Captain Caswell or anyone else to find Bouncing Bertha?"

"No one could know what she carried," he said, a haunted look coming into his clouded eyes. "And didn't carry."

The possibilities went off like rockets inside Cleo's head. The gold! He'd recovered the gold. Or the canister.

Or both.

"How could you…?" Johanna stopped, forced the sharp edge from her voice, started again. "How could you know what was or wasn't aboard the Dakota unless you'd found the wreck. Or…"

Johanna stopped again, her breath hitching. The truth seemed to smack her in the face at the same moment it hit Cleo.

"Or he was aboard the plane himself when it went down," she gasped.

His age. His almost indiscernible accent. The Colt .45 he used to kill Caswell. His skill with incendiary devices. They all fit.

"You're Grenadier Sergeant Clive Gordon." The scenario flashed through Cleo's mind like a DVD set on fast-forward. "You survived the crash, were rescued at sea, continued your mission."

The enormity of the lie this man had lived for more than sixty years staggered Cleo. Carl Ericsson looked as if he wanted to ask what the hell she was talking about, but he kept his mouth clamped shut. Jack and Mulholland, too, remained silent as Johanna completed the litany.

"You hunted down your target. Eliminated him. Stepped into his life."

The man's gaze rested on her face for long seconds. For a wild moment, Cleo wondered if he was seeing in Johanna the person he'd once been. The highly skilled SOE agent. The assassin dispatched by a desperate government to bring down the enemies of his country.

"You have most of it right," he said after another long moment, his words almost lost in the music from the fountain. "Except for the transport. I never boarded that Dakota. Potts sent me a message, asking me to contact him. I had trouble getting a line and the Dakota left without me."

Johanna reared back, clearly stunned by the implications. Jack and Mulholland looked almost as grim. If this man *had* been carrying a canister of potentially lethal powder, it wasn't aboard Bouncing Bertha.

So where the hell was it?

The question thundered in Cleo's head as the count...grenadier sergeant...Hat Man resumed his incredible tale.

"Flight operations put me on another aircraft hours later. Just before we left, we heard they'd lost contact with the Dakota."

There was bitter irony buried in there somewhere. Maybe someday they'd all appreciate it. Not today, though. Not with divers searching for Dennis McBride's body.

"I continued my mission. I hunted down Count Valken. I disposed of him and stepped into his life."

"Jädrar!"

Ericsson spit the phrase out. Cleo didn't have a clue what it meant, but she bet it wasn't friendly.

Its recipient took it without a word but lifted a shaking hand. The movement galvanized the five people on the lower tier.

Jack's Sig snicked out of its holster. Mulholland swung the boat pole in a swift arc. Johanna and Ericsson whipped out their weapons and dropped into a shooter's stance. Cleo had her .38 out of her purse and cocked before her silver-haired target froze with his hand in midair.

"I'm sorry. My chest... I..."

"Are you in pain?" Johanna asked, holding her stance.

"No! No, it's just a shortness of breath. I must finish this here, in Christina's rose garden."

He dropped his hand to his lap. Sweat beaded his upper lip. His words came faster now, on short, quick puffs.

"Christina—my wife—barely knew the man she was to marry. She'd met him only a few times. It was an arranged bethrothal, you see, a blending of his wealth and her family's connections. I took his place, wooing her as I thought he would. I never intended to marry her. Or to love her."

He'd lost his first wife in the Blitz, Cleo remembered. And his son. Johanna had admitted the tragic losses had made him the perfect candidate for Operation Round Peg. Cleo had pitied him then. She didn't now.

"What about your country, you bloody traitor?" Johanna asked. "You'd been sent on a wartime mission to infiltrate enemy ranks."

His back straightened. His nostrils flared. He looked every inch the aristocrat he'd become.

"I accomplished my mission. I sent Potts detailed information on Nazi gold transactions. I eliminated more than two dozen Swedes who used a flag of neutrality to collaborate with the Germans." Ignoring Ericsson's growl, he tilted his chin to a proud angle. "I disposed of Germans, too. More than I can remember. I sent a fleet of boats to help the Danish Jews escape. I did what I was sent to do and more, and for that I considered my continued impersonation justified."

"So you killed to maintain it." Scorn dripped from Johanna's voice. "Captain Caswell. Dennis McBride. You would have killed us all to retain your title and your wealth."

"No! I did that for my children. My granddaughter." Johanna made a visible effort to rein in her fury.

She, too, had been sent on a mission. "What about the equipment you carried with you?"

"The Colt? I have it still, as you're well aware. The rest I buried long ago."

"Where?"

His head turned. The harsh lines of his face softened. "There," he whispered. "Under the Rose Christina."

Cleo flicked a glance at the bare stalks. So, evidently, did Johanna. Jack never took his eyes off the old man, which is why his Sig spit out a loud retort only a half second after the assassin's hand came up.

Valken must have had the Colt tucked under his canvas work shirt. He held it grasped in a white-knuckled fist, looked down at the blood spurting from his upper arm and understood. They wanted him to stand trial. Answer for his sins.

Deliberately, he raised his arm another few inches. The barrel pointed to his temple.

"Don't do it," Jack warned, pumping another round into the chamber.

"One of us must."

Donovan spit out a curse. None of the others moved. Their target stretched his lips in a smile.

"I've only one bullet left. It's the last of the specials issued to SOE operatives. Appropriate, is it not?"

His gaze drifted to the rosebush. The Colt bucked. He toppled backward into fresh-turned dirt.

29

SISD dispatched a crime-scene Unit to bag and tag evidence, a meat wagon to do the same for the count, and a Hazardous Materials Disposal Team to recover the items buried under the Rose Christina. The Hazmat crew dug up a rotting canvas satchel, the crumbling remains of a rubber gas mask, a wireless transmitter and a codebook.

And, finally, a small, sinister container.

The hazardous materials folks treated the canister with the respect it warranted. Using digitally controlled mechanical arms, an operator in full chemical-protective gear lifted the cylinder from the soil, wrapped it with a silicon sealer and deposited it into another airtight container. That, in turn, was sealed inside a transport box.

Only then did the crowd observing from a safe distance let out a collective sigh.

It was close to 10:00 p.m. before SISD finished taking statements from everyone concerned, almost midnight when Ericsson delivered the Americans and the Brits to the airport. They caught the last flight to London and took Johanna up on her offer to spend the rest of the night at her flat.

"Or longer," she murmured to Mulholland as they buckled in.

He rested his head against the seat back, weariness and pain evident in the tight lines of his face. "Do you really want me there, Johanna? In your world?"

She searched for a way to communicate the contradictory feelings he'd stirred in her from their first meeting, and found only one. "'If thou wilt leave me,'" she quoted softly, "'do not leave me last.'"

His mouth relaxed into a smile. "Eight-nine?"

"Ninety."

She settled in beside him, amazed at the surprises life served up. She'd never imagined she'd find such delight in a man like Mulholland. Or such pleasure.

Once airborne, Johanna used her government connections to put a call through to the Coast Guard Rescue Coordination Center. Her request for an update returned grim news.

"I'm sorry, Sean. RCC says their divers recovered what they think may be some human remains." Her hand slid over his. "They were too charred to issue an official identification, but Ernesto Cruz says to tell you he had no doubt. He also said to tell you he's checked on Billy Hawks. He'll be all right."

Nodding, Mulholland turned his hand palm up. His fingers wove into hers. They remained that way for most of the flight and the rehash of Grenadier Sergeant Clive Gordon's long, twisting journey.

It wasn't until they'd reclaimed their vehicles at Heathrow and driven up to London that Johanna discovered she already had a house full of visitors. Still on U.S. time, her guests had sent the servants to bed and were enjoying a late-night cocktail in the study.

With a trill of delight Johanna recognized the dark-haired male sprawled in an easy chair, cradling a crystal tumbler and a healthy measure of Glenlivet.

"Marc!"

He looked around, and a crooked smile spread across his face. "No, I'm Alex. And you can only be Johanna."

"You're…you're Alex?" Exasperated with herself, she shook her head. "How stupid of me. I knew you and Marc were identical twins, but I hadn't expected you to look so…so…"

"So identical?" Marc supplied with a grin, rising from a deep-backed settee. A tall, slender blonde rose with him. Crossing the room, Diane Walker Sloan gave her new sister-in-law a kiss on the cheek.

"Don't feel bad, Johanna. I've known Marc for twenty years, Alex for almost as long, and still get a jolt every time I see them side by side."

"Good gracious! That's hardly reassuring, coming from Marc's wife." Johanna's glance darted from one male to the other and back again. "Will it take me that long to distinguish one of you from the other?"

"Only time will tell." Marc, too, gave her a kiss, before turning to greet Cleo. "Hello, Brown Eyes. You look good. Whipped, but good."

"Thanks, I think."

Jack got a handshake, Mulholland an assessing look as Johanna hurried to make the introductions.

"Marc, this is Sean Mulholland. We've been working together for the past few days."

She thought that was as good a way as any to describe their assorted activities.

"Sean, this is my brother Marc and his bride, Diane. And this…"

She turned to the man struggling out of his chair, took a hasty step to help him and caught Marc's quick headshake.

"This is my brother Alexander," she finished as the second twin steadied himself with a cane.

He limped across the room, dragging his right foot. The fierce concentration on his face suggested he was mentally scripting every muscle movement, but the fact that he could walk at all astonished Johanna. Just a few short months ago he'd been slumped over a desk, oozing blood from a bullet hole in his temple.

Biting her lip, she watched his slow, painful

progress across the room. When he stood before her, he held out his left hand. His right he kept wrapped around the head of his cane.

"We meet at last, Johanna."

"So we do."

She grasped his hand, struck by the shadows in his eyes. And no wonder, when someone close to him had betrayed him and the country he'd served for so many years, and shot him into the bargain.

"I'm so sorry I wasn't here when you arrived. We were in Stockholm and have only just returned."

"Stockholm? I thought Marc said you were somewhere on the coast of England."

"Yes, we were, but… Well, it's rather a long story and not one we need to go into tonight. Shall we join you for a drink and talk instead about your plans whilst you're in England? I so hope you'll be able to spend some time with me at my country house."

He pivoted unsteadily on his cane. Johanna bit her lip again and slipped her arm through Sean's. It was a reflexive move—as much to keep from reaching out to assist Alex as to pull Mulholland into the family circle.

He didn't think he belonged there. She could see the withdrawal in his face. He certainly made it plain enough in his polite protest.

"I'm not fit for polite company. If you'll point me to a shower, a spare bed and an aspirin, I'll leave you to talk with your brothers."

"You're hurting," she said, instantly contrite for having kept him on his feet so long. "Excuse me," she said to the others. "I'll escort Sean upstairs and return shortly."

"We should all go up," Marc countered, sliding a hand under his wife's elbow. "I don't know what this business was you had in Stockholm, but if it involved Cleo, I suspect there were bullets fired or shoulder-held missiles launched."

Cleo cocked her head. "Excuse me?"

"I was with you on your last two adventures, Brown Eyes. I speak from experience." A grin slashed across his face. "Tell me, am I right?"

"Okay," she huffed, "you're right. There were some fireworks."

"I thought so. I'm looking forward to hearing the details tomorrow."

"You'll have to get them from Johanna," Jack countered. "Cleo and I are driving up to Mildenhall early in the morning to close out a murder investigation. We'll be flying home from there."

That was the first Cleo had heard of the quick turnaround, but she understood the urgency behind it. They'd wrapped up one problem. Now they needed to get back to Dallas and wrap up the one waiting for them there.

Ignoring her protests, Jack rolled her out of bed just after 6:00 a.m. She showered and dressed, grumbling the whole time about so-called morning people, then gulped down coffee, juice and two of the sweet buns Johanna's housekeeper set out for them.

The house was hushed and silent when they let themselves out. The streets weren't. Cleo and Jack tangled with the inevitable London traffic but managed to escape relatively unscathed.

Their meeting with the commander of the OSI detachment at Mildenhall was short and sweet. Jack dictated his statement, Cleo dictated hers, and flame-haired Major Paul Morrison closed his case.

It was still oh-dark-thirty back in the States, too early to call in an update to General Barnes, thank God. Cleo wasn't up to seeing his bushy brows and piercing stare coming at her from Major Morrison's videophone. Jack left word at the ops center that he and Cleo were heading for home and would update the general after they arrived. He also left Cleo's office number as a contact point.

Morrison escorted them to the Taurus and saw them off with grateful handshakes. "I owe you both for this one. I'm sure glad it wasn't me out on that dive boat when it blew. I can't swim worth a damn. I never venture into water deeper than my ankles."

"I'm adopting that as my new modus operandi," Cleo muttered to Jack as they drove off. "No wading into or sailing on water more than two inches deep. It's showers or two-inch sitz baths for me from here on out."

"No problem. I've seen the shower at your place. We'll both fit."

That gave her something to think about during the long flight back to the States. That, and her imminent meeting with Jack's ex. Although Cleo knew it took two to make or break a marriage, she was prepared to dislike Kate Donovan intensely for what she'd put Jack through.

30

"Hey, kiddo. Welcome home."

The sight of her dad with his feet propped up and a beer in hand instantly erased Cleo's gritty fatigue from twelve solid hours of travel.

"Hiya, Pop."

Tossing her keys on the kitchen counter, she led Jack into the living room of her north Dallas condo and discovered her father wasn't her only visitor. Goose occupied the sturdiest chair in the room. Doreen lay in her usual sprawl on the leather sofa.

Both Patrick North and Goose got to their feet to engage Donovan in the male ritual of hand pumping. Doreen waved a languid hand.

"Hi, cuz. Hey, Jack. How was London?"

Jack answered for them both. "Busy. Interesting. Exciting."

"Yeah, I can see that," Goose commented, using his six-six vantage point to project a glance down at Cleo's head. "What's with the bald patch?"

Grimacing, she fingered the bare spot. It was just beginning to sprout fuzzy hairs and itched liked the dickens under the bandage. She could handle the itching. She wasn't sure she could handle the fact that the sprouts were coming in white.

"That was a little present from a second-rate bookie."

"Hmm." Goose shifted his glance to Jack's navy-and-white ball cap. "And that? HMCG stands for Her Majesty's Coast Guard, right?"

"Right."

"You and Cleo require Coast Guard assistance while you were in England?"

"As a matter of fact, we did."

"Oh, Lord!" Patrick aimed a wry glance at his daughter. "You didn't blow up another ship, did you?"

"Hey! This one wasn't my fault."

A loud snicker emanated from the still-prone Doreen. "That's what you said about the last one."

Cleo might have come back with a sharp retort if mention of the disaster at sea hadn't reminded her of the moon-spinner. "You know those light-re-fracting microfilaments you forced me to take on this trip?"

"Uh-oh. You aren't going to tell me you wrapped yourself in the threads and couldn't get out, are you?"

"No, I used them to lash debris together for a raft. I owe you, cuz."

"Well, whaddya know!"

Doreen's gleeful whinny had everyone else in the room grimacing. Gritting her teeth against the assault, Cleo waited until the cackles had subsided to ask Goose what he was doing at her condo.

"I'm waiting on Mae. She's supposed to be here any moment." A tinge of red crept into his cheeks. "She's got me signed up for golf lessons at the country club."

Cleo didn't hoot, but the effort almost strangled her. "Well, I guess that explains the absence of your usual yards of clanking chain."

She wasn't sure how the leather vest would go over with the country club set, though.

"What about you, Pop?"

"I'm waiting on Wanda and Kate."

"Wanda *and* Kate?" She shot Jack a quick look. "Where are they?"

"Shopping."

Duh! Where else would her stepmom be? But with Kate Donovan?

"They've been gone for almost four hours," Patrick said. "Should be back soon."

Soon, Cleo had learned, was a relative term when Waffling Wanda hit the mall.

"Why don't I get a beer for Jack and me, then you three can fill us in on how Kate is doing?"

Doreen levitated to an upright position to make room for them on the sofa. Somewhat to Cleo's surprise, she reported that Kate had made a model roommate.

"She cooks, she cleans, she watches *The Simpsons* with me. She even found my solder sucker."

"Oookay."

Doreen cackled. "It's a tool for desoldering a joint to correct a mistake or replace an electronic component."

"What about her physical condition?" Elbows on knees, Jack rolled his beer back and forth between his palms. Dewdrops splatted unheeded to the carpet. "You said she got through the worst of the DTs, but the hallucinations, disorientation and hyperactivity can recur for weeks after total withdrawal from alcohol."

He said it quietly, without particular emphasis, but there was no doubt he spoke from experience.

"The doc in Kansas gave her a prescription for Valium," Goose told him, "with instructions to gradually reduce the dosage."

"Kate's been on and off Valium for years."

"He also recommended increased doses of vitamins, particularly thiamine. The regimen seems to be working this time."

Jack didn't comment, and Cleo managed to swallow the "so far" that almost slipped out.

"I think spending these past few days with Wanda

has helped, too," Patrick put in. "Kate has a real flair
for decorating. She helped Wanda find exactly the
light fixtures she was looking for."

Thank you, Lord!

"Kate said she always wanted to go into interior
design," Patrick added. "She should have. She's really good."

"Interior design?" Jack blinked in surprise. "Her
goal was always to be a teacher. It took her years to
get her degree and teaching certificate because the air
force moved me so often and not all of her credits
would transfer, but she kept at it."

"Maybe because teaching was the kind of career
she could take with her on those moves," Patrick
guessed. "A business like interior decorating would
be a different story. She'd have to rebuild a client
base after every move, shell out for advertising, find
new sources for materials."

Jack nodded, but the fact that his wife had harbored dreams she'd never shared with him clearly
didn't go down well.

Cleo sat next to him on the sofa, shoulder to
shoulder, hip to hip. She could feel his muscles
tighten, almost see the guilt pile on in thick layers.
She knew him. He was taking the blame for this
one, too.

Before she could find a way to cut through all
those layers the front door opened and her stepmother walked in, followed by Jack's ex-wife.

Cleo formed two swift impressions. One, Kate looked like an escapee from a concentration camp. Two, Wanda had bought out half of Dallas.

Patrick North rose and greeted his wife with a joy that reminded his daughter there was no accounting for taste. Or for love. Dropping a kiss on Wanda's peppermint-pink lips, he relieved her of a half-dozen shopping bags.

"Looks like you had a successful expedition."

"We did!" Petite, perky and permed to within an inch of her life, Wanda beamed up at her husband. "Kate discovered the most amazing store. It's a sort of Home Depot for women. They carry light fixtures, fabrics, appliances, Christmas ornaments, even designer sinks and toilet stools."

Arms outstretched, Patrick tipped the bags from side to side like a scale. "Feels like you've got a couple sinks in here."

"No sinks, but I did buy new pulls for the kitchen cabinets. Three sets, in fact. I couldn't decide between them. Kate said I might as well bring all three home and see how they... Oh! Hello, Cleo."

Wanda's Barbie-doll vivaciousness sputtered and died. Eyes wide, she threw an apprehensive look around the room. She'd had firsthand experience of her stepdaughter's unfortunate propensity for attracting renegade arms dealers and murderers. Spotting no strangers or drawn weapons, she relaxed.

"I didn't know you were home. When did you and Jack get in?"

"Just a little while ago." Crossing to the woman standing stiff and silent by the door, Cleo held out her hand. "Hi, Kate. I'm Cleo, Patrick's daughter."

She figured that was the safest introduction. She didn't know what, if anything, Jack had told his ex about his personal life since their divorce.

"I'm glad to meet you, Cleo." Kate's hand was small and birdlike. The rest of her wasn't much bigger. "I've heard a lot about you."

"Uh-oh. Don't believe any of it except what Pop told you. He knows he has to say nice things about me or I'll tell Wanda a few things he'd prefer she never hear."

Kate made the appropriate response, but it was clear her whole being was riveted on her former husband. Cleo stepped aside as he approached and dropped a kiss on the woman's cheek.

"Hello, Kate."

"Hello, Jack."

"You okay?"

She swallowed and forced a shaky smile. "I've been better."

"Yeah, I hear this was a bad one." He was silent for several beats. "You want to talk about it?"

Kate hesitated, her glance going past him to the others in the room. Patrick and Wanda took a sudden interest in the shopping bags. Goose swept his beer glass up and headed for the kitchen. Doreen went horizontal.

Much as it pained Cleo to offer Jack up on the altar of guilt and regret, she knew she couldn't bulldoze her way into this one.

"How about I put on some coffee? Jack, you and Kate can go out on the patio and get caught up. I'll bring the coffee when it's ready."

She couldn't tell from his neutral expression whether he wanted or dreaded a private tête-à-tête with his ex, but he took Cleo up on her suggestion. The sliding glass doors shut behind him and Kate and left a small silence.

It was broken by a series of shrill yips outside the front door.

"Uh-oh. Baby alert. Better get those shopping bags up on the counter, Pop."

Patrick scrambled to comply. He barely had the sacks out of danger before the front door opened and Mae's miniature schnauzer barreled in, delirious with joy at seeing her favorite people—or any people. Unfortunately, joy in Baby equated to squirts of puppy pee on shoes, chairs, tables and laps.

"Baby! Down!"

Exasperated, Mae tried to corral her exuberant pet. Goose had more success. One swipe of his giant paw caught the schnauzer in mid-spring. Far from being offended, Baby squirmed with delight, got in several wet slurps and dribbled down Goose's arm.

To Cleo's amazement, Goose didn't pulverize the schnauzer. Instead, he tucked the wiggling animal inside his leather vest and kept it there while Mae fished a knit shirt out of the bag she'd carried in with her.

"This is an extra-extra large. I hope it fits."

Cleo's jaw dropped. Goose in a polo shirt was tough enough to imagine. Goose in a *lavender* polo shirt boggled the mind.

"You'd better get changed. We meet with the golf pro in half an hour."

Goose dutifully retreated to the bedroom with puppy and polo. Mae folded the bag into neat squares, smiling at Cleo.

"I know, I know. It's a silly rule. But men have to wear collared shirts at the country club. When did you get home, dear?"

"We just got here."

"We? Did Jack come back with you?"

"He's out on the patio. With Kate."

"Ah. I see."

Cleo wished *she* did. The pleated silk shades inside the double-glass sliding doors were designed to block the hot Texas sun. When lowered, however, they also blocked all view of the patio.

"I was just about to make a pot of coffee. Do you have time for a cup?"

"A quick one." Mae trailed her into the kitchen, curious about the case that had taken her to London. "Did you and Jack wrap up that murder investigation?"

"Yes, we did."

"I'll have to update the account and send a final statement of expenses to...to whom?"

"Brigadier General Sam Barnes," Cleo said with some glee.

"Oh! General Barnes called a few hours ago. Didn't you see the message?"

"I haven't checked my office yet."

"He wanted to speak to you or Jack as soon as you got in. It sounded urgent."

He'd probably heard about the *Argos II.* No way Cleo was taking this one.

"I'll get the coffee going and take the phone out to Jack."

She fiddled with the filter and grounds while Mae filled the pot. When the coffeemaker started to burp, she had to ask.

"How the heck did you get Goose to agree to golf lessons?"

"It was a trade. He does golf with me, I do Sturgis with him."

"Sturgis? You mean that motorcycle rally up in North Dakota?"

"South Dakota, dear."

Cleo's mind did the boggling thing again. She tried to picture Mae kicked back on Goose's Hogg, feet propped on the handlebars, swapping road stories with ten or fifteen thousand beer-swilling, bandana'd bikers.

"Okay, this is none of my business, but have you and Goose…uh…you know."

"You're right, dear, it's none of your business. But no, we haven't. Yet." A smug little smile played at Mae's mouth. "Goose is in for a surprise when it happens, though. I picked up a new workout CD a few weeks ago. Exercises for Sensual Seniors. It's put out by the same company that produces Viagra. I'm so tight now, Goose is going to think he's plowing into a twenty-year-old."

Oh, God! That was more than Cleo wanted to know.

"I'd better take this coffee out to Jack and Kate."

"And the phone," Mae reminded her. "Jack needs to call General Barnes."

Tucking the counter phone under her arm, Cleo snatched two mugs from the cupboard, grabbed the pot and headed for the patio.

Donovan stood with shoulders stiff, hands shoved in his pockets. Kate sat hunched in one of the loungers. Tears swam in her eyes, but she blinked them back at Cleo's appearance.

"Sorry to interrupt. The coffee was ready. And you need to call the Old Man, Jack. He left a message with Mae earlier. She says it's urgent."

When Jack made no move to take the phone, Cleo dumped it and her other burdens on the patio table. She would have left them again, but Kate gave a long, shuddering sigh and rose.

"Go ahead and make the call, Jack. We've said all we need to say."

"Kate..."

"I'm okay. I *will* be okay," she corrected. "I'm going to get myself together this time. I swear I am."

"Your lawyer will have to petition for a change of venue for your court-mandated counseling if you're going to stay in Dallas."

"I know."

A shriek jumped into Cleo's throat. She ground her teeth together to hold it while Kate hesitated. She looked as though she wanted to say more but couldn't find the right words. Finally she murmured something about helping Wanda and went back into the house.

"She's...?" Gulping, Cleo forced air into her lungs. "She's going to stay in Dallas?"

"She's thinking about it. Wanda took her by the Dallas Trade Mart and Textile Institute. Evidently they offer a two-year program in interior design."

There was a short pause, barely enough time for Cleo to devise an exquisitely painful torture for Wicked Wanda.

"Are you all right with that?"

"With your ex living a few blocks away and becoming my stepmom's shopping bud? Sure."

"I can send her back to Cincinnati, Cleo. She'll go if I tell her this won't work."

"I'm not the one who will make it work or not

work. I'm only here between cases. You need to talk to Doreen and Mae and Pop. And Wanda."

"I will."

Unsure whether to believe her, Jack curled a knuckle under her chin and tipped her face to his. His eyes didn't look as bruised as Kate's had, but the old regrets were there. Along with a new resolve.

"I told her about us."

"Good. Now she knows I'll blind, disfigure or otherwise maim her if she tries to sink her claws into you again."

Or hurt him.

God, she'd better not hurt him!

"There's no chance of that." His thumb traced her lower lip. "Your claws are too firmly embedded, Cleopatra Aphrodite."

"We need to come to an understanding," Cleo huffed. "You do *not* speak my middle name aloud again. Ever! In return, I do *not* render you unable to father children."

"We probably need to talk about that."

"What? Rendering you?"

"Children." His thumb made another pass. "Like how many and when."

"Don't you think there are a few other details we should iron out first?"

"Like what?"

"Like where we'll live and—"

She broke off, flashing an annoyed glance at the phone. The caller ID displayed a 240 area code.

"It's for you," she told Donovan hastily. "General Barnes."

"Let it ring."

"Jack, he's called twice now."

"Let it ring. I have more important business to attend to at the moment."

His arms went around her. Cleo nestled against his chest, her heart tripping when his lips curved in the Jack Donovan Special. His expression held no regrets now. No shadows. Just the crooked grin that curled her toes.

"Much more important business."

A quiet Amish community...a terrifying threat

KAREN HARPER

One morning Leah Kurtz wakes her infant daughter and immediately knows something is wrong. Very wrong. She is convinced that her baby has been switched with another child. When no one believes her, Leah turns to an unlikely ally—an outsider—despite the fact that her Amish community frowns on its members seeking help in the outside world. Leah is only concerned with the truth. But sometimes, finding the truth may have deadly consequences.

"The book is strongest in its loving depiction of Amish life, its creation of a dark mood and its development of the central romance."

—*Publishers Weekly* on *Dark Road Home*

DARK ANGEL

Available the first week of June 2005, wherever paperbacks are sold!

MIRA®

Merline Lovelace

32164 THE FIRST MISTAKE	___ $6.99 U.S.	___ $8.50 CAN.
32172 THE MIDDLE SIN	___ $6.99 U.S.	___ $8.50 CAN.

(limited quantities available)

TOTAL AMOUNT	$ _____
POSTAGE & HANDLING	$ _____
($1.00 FOR 1 BOOK, 50¢ for each additional)	
APPLICABLE TAXES*	$ _____
TOTAL PAYABLE	$ _____

(check or money order—please do not send cash)

To order, complete this form and send it, along with a check or money order for the total above, payable to MIRA Books, to: **In the U.S.:** 3010 Walden Avenue, P.O. Box 9077, Buffalo, NY 14269-9077; **In Canada:** P.O. Box 636, Fort Erie, Ontario, L2A 5X3.

Name: _____
Address: _____ City: _____
State/Prov.: _____ Zip/Postal Code: _____
Account Number (if applicable): _____

075 CSAS

*New York residents remit applicable sales taxes.
*Canadian residents remit applicable GST and provincial taxes.

MIRA®

www.MIRABooks.com

MML0605BL